THE SHA
SEEMED T
FROM LE

. . . and for just a moment Sinunu couldn't tell what they were doing. Then it hit her. They were checking all the doors, making sure they were locked. Then suddenly the shadows stiffened, going completely still. Sinunu heard Truxa mutter a quiet chant, then give a soft clap, setting off a spell. For the first time she had a good idea just what they were up against. If Sandman was right, these were vampires.

The closest was a human male. He stood almost two meters, and his upper torso was covered in spiked studs that had surely been implanted, making him look like some vampiric porcupine. Sinunu watched as two twenty-centimeter razors snicked from his forearms. He smiled, showing his fangs.

Just behind him, tiny by comparison, was a vampire woman. A mishmash of scars lined her face, making her lips form a lopsided V shape where the bottom lip had been crudely sewn back together.

Unlike the first vampire, she seemed completely unmodified until she held up her small hands and ten-centimeter scalpels slid from beneath her fingers.

"It's time to play," said the woman, and suddenly they were moving. Fast.

SHADOWRUN

THE TERMINUS EXPERIMENT

Jonathan E. Bond
and Jak Koke

A ROC BOOK

ROC
Published by the Penguin Group
Penguin Putman Inc., 375 Hudson Street,
New York, New York 10014, U.S.A.
Penguin Books Ltd, 27 Wrights Lane,
London W8 5TZ, England
Penguin Books Australia Ltd,
Ringwood, Victoria, Australia
Penguin Books Canada Ltd, 10 Alcon Avenue,
Toronto, Ontario, Canada M4V 3B2
Penguin Books (N.Z.) Ltd, 182-190 Wairau Road,
Auckland 10, New Zealand

Penguin Books Ltd, Registered Offices:
Harmondsworth, Middlesex, England

First published by Roc, an imprint of Dutton NAL,
a member of Penguin Putnam Inc.

First Printing, January, 1999
10 9 8 7 6 5 4 3 2 1

Series Editor: Donna Ippolito
Cover: Michael Evans

Printed in the United States of America.

For Jacqueline

who inspired with
patience, strength and beauty.

ACKNOWLEDGMENTS

Jonathan and Jak would like to thank Brian "Hell's Tour Guide" Proett for dogging Jonathan when he wanted to play instead of write, Seana for keeping Jak sane when long hours kept him at the keyboard, Cyndi Blackshear for being understanding when Jonathan forgot to pay the rent because he was too busy writing, Mark Teppo for his insightful comments, and all the folks at the Rooster and Silver Dollar for putting up with Jonathan's foul moods when the book ran late.

Much appreciation goes to Donna Ippolito and Mike Mulvihill for pointing out where we were being stupid without making us feel like idiots, and to the team at Roc Books—Jennifer Heddle and Laura Anne Gilman—for their professional work bringing the novel into print. Finally, special thanks goes to Mike Stackpole for letting us play with one of his characters, as well as taking time out of his busy schedule to talk to Jonathan, a writer he didn't even know.

NORTH

CIRCA 2060

AMERICA

CIRCA 2060

Prologue

Doctor Raul Pakow blinked twice into the scanning-tunneling microscope. He was exhausted, but couldn't even rub his eyes because of the damn biohazard suit he was wearing.

He sat back and activated the heads-up display on the faceplate of the suit. 11:58:59. Almost midnight here in Seattle. Three a.m. in New York. Two months already he'd been in Seattle, but his body still seemed back on East Coast time. Back in New York, where Shiva would be sleeping soft and warm in their bed right now, where he'd left behind everything he'd ever been and ever loved . . .

From where he sat Pakow had a clear view through the Plexiglas into the private lab of the man who'd brought him here from New York. He was surprised not to see Doctor Wake also hard at work in there, where he'd been just minutes before. Pakow closed his eyes wearily, thinking how it was only Plexiglas separating them but that it could just as easily have been a gulf of a thousand years.

Pakow's lab had the sterile feel of every clean room he'd ever been in, but Wake's work area was an almost frightening mixture of science and the arcane. To himself, Pakow had silently begun calling it the mad scientist's laboratory.

Science had been turned upside down by the return of magic some fifty years ago, and Wake's lab was no exception. Medical equipment rested side by side with fetishes and magical implements that Pakow couldn't even begin to comprehend. Long golden rods and books with ram's heads on the covers. Parchment scrolls and strange diagrams covered with indecipherable symbols in faded ink. The entire floor of Wake's lab was coal black, throwing into sharp relief the blood-red pentagram that stretched almost ten meters in diameter, completely encompassing the carefully arranged implements he had gathered for his use.

Pakow gave himself a mental shake, knowing he couldn't sit here dreaming all night. It was time to run his final check. He tapped a key on the terminal beside him to record the hour and date—00:00:00/12-08-2058—then turned back to his microscope.

Picking up the datacord set into the microscope's base, he ran it through the small, clean port in the helmet of the biohazard suit, easing the cord through the tight, sterilizing passage. Pakow had been fitted with three datajacks into his right temple. One for the Matrix, one for off-line memory, and the third to jack into the virtual-reality equipment used in most labs. As the datacord clicked softly into the third port, his vision blurred for an instant, seeming to condense down to a pinpoint and then expand at lightning speed, exploding into lurid purples and yellows.

To Pakow, the infinitesimal virus he'd been studying was suddenly five meters high. He turned and stepped into the heart of the rocket-shaped image, double-checking the projected outcome of the new RNA sequence. He had predicted that even though the virus would be similar to the original, the injected transposon cocktail would suppress the expression of certain detrimental genes.

Inside the core of the virus, Pakow reached out a chrome-gilt hand to touch the spongy mass at the center. He loaded the new RNA sequence, which took the form of a large, neon-green hypodermic needle filled with glowing amber fluid.

Using his free hand, Pakow separated the proteins of the virus and stabbed upward with the needle, releasing the fluid.

A stream of amber coursed outward, greedily attaching itself to the viral protein matter and insinuating flecks of golden material at different places along the RNA strand.

Within seconds it was finished, and Pakow stepped out of the virus to observe the effects of what he'd done.

Outwardly, the virus stayed stable, one of the concerns Doctor Wake had expressed early on, but its shape began to shift subtly. Where it had started out looking like a hexagonal rocket, the new sequence bulged slightly at the head, taking on an almost circular form.

As soon as the virus had mutated completely, Pakow pulled his view back until the image was tiny again. He turned to his left and lifted one hand, causing a small digital display to form in mid-air. Entering the combination he wanted, Pakow overlaid the display of the virus with a simulated projection of a human already infected with the original strain.

Placing the newly formed virus into the subject's bloodstream, Pakow was able to track its amber-colored progress.

As predicted, the new virus assimilated the older version and supplanted it completely. The effects of the modified strain altered the subject exactly as planned. Many of the deleterious effects of the original were modified or eradicated completely.

Pakow smiled to himself. *Send a killer to kill a killer, or something like that.*

Reaching once again for the digital display, he sped up the time lapse, and watched as the final modifications to the new virus did their work. Within the first year, nothing new showed. By the beginning of the second year, however, the new virus began to deteriorate. Slowly at first, then much more rapidly, eventually killing the host.

Satisfied, Pakow jacked out.

"Well?" The voice came from directly behind Pakow, making him jump in his chair.

Turning, Pakow found Oslo Wake looking over his shoulder.

Even in the biohazard suit, Wake was a thin man, and possibly the tallest human Pakow had ever encountered. Well over two meters tall, he was a skeleton wrapped in the florescent orange suit that clung to his frame.

Through the clear helmet, Wake's face was gaunt to the point of emaciation, cheeks hollowed and sharp, his forehead stretched parchment-tight over an angular brow. His blue eyes were sunk into the sockets of his skull like some childhood nightmare, his head covered in a snow-white mass of hair that tangled and spiked off his scalp like some live thing trying to fight its way free.

"Provided the other aspects of the procedure go as you've suggested, I feel very confident in this Beta strain," Pakow said. "You realize, of course, that without extensive testing, I can't promise anything. With a virus of this nature, there's always the chance I may have overlooked something. What I can tell you is that the virus will remain stable, will negate any previous infection, and will deteriorate within two years, killing the host."

Wake rocked back on his heels, smiling. "My dear, Doctor Pakow, you have more than justified my faith in you. Once again, I apologize for the conditions under which you've been forced to work. And despite it all, you have outperformed even my highest expectations." A small tic in Wake's right cheek made his face jump in a second-long, lopsided grin.

Something in the other man's voice raised the hackles on Pakow's neck. Looking at Wake now, it was hard to believe this was the same man who'd approached him just two months ago at the conference where Pakow had been giving a paper on viral mutations in specific metahuman genotypes. The lecture had been poorly attended, and Pakow had come to the conclusion halfway through that maybe a total of two people in the whole room had any idea what he was talking about.

After the lecture Wake had come up to him, speaking in that soft voice about a new direction for his research—something totally out of the mainstream—and a chance to push the parameters of lab work farther and faster than would be possible under any laboratory conditions Pakow had ever heard of, here or anywhere else.

And so far, all those promises had come true. Wake had lived up to his reputation as a genius of the first caliber, proposing methods and directions that would never have even occurred to Pakow. He himself had managed to identify certain problems in Wake's research, but he couldn't help wondering if Wake might have let those flaws remain on purpose, just so Pakow could feel like he was contributing.

Still, it had been Pakow who'd made the final breakthrough on the Beta strain, or the "mystery virus." At first the virus had been resistant to every form of mutagen, but he'd finally cracked it. That was about the time he'd first noticed the changes in Wake. The mood swings and the secretive tendencies, and now the facial tic.

Despite Pakow's fears about Wake, he couldn't help a flush of pride at his praise, as well as a healthy dose of curiosity. "Is it my imagination, or have I actually passed some sort of test in your mind, Dr. Wake?"

Wake's smile faded, and for just a moment, Pakow thought he'd pushed too far. Then, Wake nodded gently, and spoke in that soft voice of his. "You've worked very diligently without complaint, and have proven yourself invaluable to this project, Dr. Pakow. I think the time has come for you to be given the whole picture. Follow me."

Pakow rose and trailed after Wake without another word being spoken. Skirting the workbench that held the scanning-tunneling microscope, the two moved to the decontamination chamber at the far end of the lab. As they stepped into the small room, a spray of white mist showered over them. They gave the mist a moment to clear, then changed out of their biosuits and continued out into the corridor. The relative dimness of the white-tiled hall was gloomy to Pakow after so many hours under the bright glare of the florescents illuminating the clean room.

Wake had still not uttered another word, but Pakow continued following him to the elevators. Wake pressed his palm to the DNA scanner, saying, "Wake, Oslo." There was a small beep from the scanner as it confirmed, then Wake said, "Level eight."

A small shiver of anticipation ran through Pakow as he watched the elevator numbers, which ran in descending order. They counted down from the first floor, which was above-ground, to the tenth, at the lowest level.

When Pakow had first arrived at this small compound out in the middle of Hell's Kitchen, a wasteland just on the outskirts of the Seattle sprawl, it seemed that he and Wake were the building's sole occupants, though there was room enough to house a small army. And even though he'd been given the complete run of the top four floors, he was restricted from visiting the bottom six. That hadn't really bothered him. He knew all about life in a research facility. Even with his high security clearance at Universal Omnitech, many areas had remained off limits to him. Still, he couldn't help wondering about those bottom six floors.

The prospect that he was actually going to see what went on down there gave him chills.

The elevator reached level eight and stopped. The door, however, didn't open. Pakow looked over at Wake. "Is there a problem?"

Wake had a strange look on his face. "There are things in this world that no human being should have to know."

Involuntarily, Pakow took a step back. "Excuse me?"

Wake turned to him, tic jumping, and smiled softly. "I've had my reasons for keeping you in the dark about certain aspects of my research, but the gravest of them is that no person should have to know how close metahumanity is to extinction."

Pakow was about to speak, when Wake raised his hand. "You are on the brink of learning something that will forever change how you view the world, Dr. Pakow, and if I didn't need your help, I would never subject you to this knowledge.

I've reached the extent of my skill in metagenetics. That's why I drafted you."

Fear pushed its way down Pakow's spine. "I don't understand."

Wake nodded. "I know. Have you ever heard of an organization calling itself Ordo Maximus?"

Pakow thought a moment. "I think so. Aren't they a bunch of rich British snobs with nothing better to do than play cricket or polo and flirt with magic?" He shrugged. "What have they got to do with any of this?"

"Everything. The fact that you think of them in those terms shows that their propaganda has been very successful. They are masters of misdirection, and they would like nothing better than for the entire world to believe the way you do. However, the truth is something far more sinister."

Pakow laughed, though he didn't know why. "You must be kidding."

Wake smiled strangely. "Unfortunately, I'm not."

Pakow stared at the other man for a moment. "All right," he said. "I'll bite."

Wake's chuckle was a soft, almost frightened thing. "Appropriate choice of words, my friend. How would you feel if I told you that Ordo Maximus, those cricket-watching, polo-playing snobs, was actually a front for something very evil, something like a secret society of vampires?"

Pakow wanted to laugh again, because the idea was absurd, but the sound stuck in his throat. "You say 'something like,' but what you really mean is that Ordo Maximus actually *is* a bunch of vampires?"

Wake nodded.

"And just how do you know this?"

Wake laughed again. "Because they're the ones funding this project."

With that, Wake tapped a pad next to the elevator door, which immediately hissed open. "Welcome, Doctor Pakow, to the Terminus Experiment."

The first thing Pakow noticed was the drop in temperature. The air from the room beyond was chill and damp. The next thing he noticed was the graveyard silence.

Peering around the door, he saw a cavernous room, stretching back into blackness, the ceiling shrouded in shadow.

"After you," said Wake.

Pakow took a cautious step forward onto the bare cement flooring, and the room instantly flared into light. Brown acoustic tiling on the walls diffused the harsh light somewhat, but Pakow barely noticed.

To his left, a bank of plexiglass windows sloped upward to the ceiling, and a garish blue light filtered from somewhere below.

"This way," said Wake, directing him to the windows. "I have plans to make this room a bit more comfortable, seeing as we'll be spending a lot of time down here, but that will take a few weeks. Still, the facility is up and running."

Wake stepped up to the plexiglass barrier overlooking a room roughly thirty meters in diameter. Like Wake's lab upstairs, this one also had a pentagram carved into the flooring. Only the colors were different. Instead of black on red, this was green on white. Directly in the center, where the star formed a hexagon, rested a massive tank with plexiglass sides. The tank was filled with a glowing blue fluid, and it was from here the garish light originated. Pakow could make out the form of a naked man floating lightly in the fluid. The face was covered with a breathing mask, and wires attached at various places to his bare flesh.

"What is this place?" Pakow's voice was a whisper, though it sounded loud in the quiet room.

"This, my good Doctor Pakow, is the culmination of all the work you have done in the last month."

Pakow turned slowly to find Wake's emaciated features looking at him thoughtfully. "You know," said Wake, "it's kind of ironic. When the people funding this project decided to give it the name Terminus, they were thinking of a terminus line, the line that separates day from night. Of course, terminus also means the end of something."

Pakow looked down at the tank, at the man floating there. "I don't understand. What's going on here? Who is that man, and what are you doing to him?"

Wake laughed. "What's going on here is the biggest double-cross ever pulled off in the name of metahumanity. As far as that 'man' down there is concerned, his name is Marco D'imato, and he is a vampire. He was infected with the HMHVV virus about six or seven years ago, and he's been leading a double life ever since. And with regard to what *I'm* doing to him, the answer is nothing. However, what *we're* about to do to him is something that goes beyond anything this world has ever seen."

Wake's words hit Pakow like a bullet train. "You can't be serious. You're not going to—"

Wake smiled. "Oh, but I am. When you came on board, I promised that you would see applications of your research faster than you ever dreamed possible. Well, here it is—instant gratification."

Pakow put up a hand. "You can't. That virus is totally untested. It would take months of work to make sure I had all the bugs out."

Wake shrugged. "Then think of this as the first phase of testing. The process has already begun. Look."

Pakow turned back to the window, and looked at the man in the fluid. It was hard to tell from this distance, but he looked strong, virile, his pale skin ghosting through the fluid. As Pakow watched, a familiar trail of amber began to cloud the blue and turn it green.

Pakow couldn't tear his eyes away from what was happening, even though Wake had started talking again. "The solution in the tank is actually a fairly simple DMSO-based liquid with a few other things thrown into the mix. Things not of a strictly scientific nature."

What was going on before his eyes was the antithesis of

everything Raul Pakow believed in. Products were to be tested first, extensively. Still, he felt a small thrill run through him. Every other product whose development he'd been part of had been beaten to death before it could ever be actually tested on people. And by the time that happened, all the thrill had gone out of it. Right here, right now, Pakow's skill and knowledge were being put on the line, the ultimate high-wire act without a net.

Filled with apprehension and anticipation, he watched as the tank turned fully green. For the longest moment, nothing happened, then Pakow's worst nightmares came to life.

The figure in the tank convulsed, in an undulating, rippling movement that no normal human should have been able to accomplish. Even through the green of the liquid, Pakow could tell that the man's skin was darkening, as if he were being slowly roasted alive.

"What's happening to him?"

Wake sounded almost disconnected as he answered. "The pigmentation of his skin is changing. That's to be expected. After all, the virus you tailor-made for him is designed to allow a vampire to survive in the sunlight. One of the basest defenses against ultraviolet burns is darker skin."

Suddenly, the form convulsed again, and this time it didn't stop. The thrashing seemed to roll through the body at such a fast rate that for a moment, Pakow couldn't believe what he was seeing.

"Well," said Wake lightly, "that certainly wasn't part of the game plan."

The form in the tank twisted, its spine shrinking and corkscrewing until the man's right hip bone jutted forward at a ninety-degree angle.

As the shuddering stopped, Pakow finally managed to tear his eyes away from the utterly deformed thing that had been a perfectly formed man just moments before. "I told you," he said. "I told you it needed further testing, that it wasn't ready."

Wake smiled, and put two skeletal hands on Pakow's shoulders. "Relax, Doctor. Nobody is blaming you for anything."

Pakow felt a rage building in his gut. "Blaming me? Are you out of your mind? We've just killed a man!"

Wake shook his head softly. "No, my friend. We haven't killed anyone. Mr. D'imato is still very much alive. The anger you feel right now is completely misdirected." Turning Pakow's head back to the tank, back to the blackened, twisted form floating there, Wake said, "That thing down there is a vampire. I know that's hard for you to understand at this moment, but you've got to trust me, because I can prove it to you. Even if were true that Mr. D'imato had died, we'd merely have rid the world of one more bloodsucking leech."

Pakow turned back and looked Wake in the eye. The man was completely serious, and the tic in his cheek had become much more pronounced.

"What have I gotten myself into?" Pakow said, the words coming like a kind of moan.

Wake laughed, and drew Pakow away from the window, back toward the elevator. "What you're involved in is a plan to save the world. Come back upstairs, Dr. Pakow, and I'll explain everything to you."

1

Vampires are stronger and faster than metahumans, and driven to kill by a combination of hunger and homicidal rage. Yet, most exist as solitary monsters or small bands of outcasts. Be warned, my friends. One faction of vampires, hiding behind an innocent facade, is even now working to release all vampires from their dark hiding places and let them walk free as masters of metahumanity. This group extends its web of treachery and deceit through many nations and countless organizations, but its roots lie in England's Ordo Maximus.

—Martin de Vries, *Shadows at Noon,* posted to Shadowland BBS, 24 May 2057

I don't know if you'll get this, but I have nowhere else to turn. Some people say you're not even real, yet you may be the only person in the world who can help. I've read the Shadows at Noon *posting from back in '57. That's why I'm trying to contact you. There's something going on here in Seattle, something you should know about . . .*

—Dr. Raul Pakow, message posted to "Stalker," Shadowland BBS, 02 May 2060

Hot July sweat, cool bay breezes, and the sounds of far-off laughter. Twilight, a dangerous time, second only to the wee hours. A time when joy girls are made to swallow industrial solvents, when gogangers beat the homeless to death for sport.

With the coming of night, the humid smell of the Seattle

sprawl grew overpowering, and down by the dockside the sick essence took on a dangerous feel. In the deepening gloom, the scent of industrial garbage was like the rot of an open, malignant tumor, the sour brine odor . . . gangrenous.

Shadows congealed in the alleyways, feeding off, growing from the stench. It was always this way, because something gets loose in those fleeting moments between day and night. Something travels on the foul breeze. Like nerve gas on the wind.

The dim alley faded to darkness. Even the bright bulbs from the loading docks—the ones designed to burn during the long night hours—were black. Smashed into thousands of twinkling crystals that reflected the aching red skyline.

Hookers and homeless had been avoiding this stretch of alleyway ever since the first hint of night. Mostly it was instinct, that, and a knowledge of the twilight rules. They knew Death was on the wind and the best way to avoid meeting it prematurely was to stay out of the way.

Tonight, Death's angels rested in the alcove of a warehouse's loading dock. Two forms, their shadows bloated by the sharp angles of automatic weaponry.

The younger man wore no shirt, only dark trousers, combat boots, a black headband to hold back his long blond hair, and a single diamond stud in his left ear. He sat with legs folded, his bare back to the cool concrete wall beside the heavy corrugated doorway. Not a muscle moving, his breathing deep, steadied with the aid of his magic. He had been seated in exactly the same position for almost two hours.

The older man moved about from time to time, rough camos hissing quietly with each step of his cybernetic limbs as he paced in the dark silence. His artificial joints were stiffer than the younger man's natural ones. His required stretching every once in a while, but he didn't complain. The time was near, and everything was ready.

Ready and waiting.

These men's existence had become a process of patient immobility, then quick action, then stillness again. They had become masters of the waiting game. Head-trick kings. They used various mental exercises to make the time pass quickly while still remaining alert.

Because it was patience that assured no mistakes were made, and these men could afford no slips when the time came to move. To strike. Not tonight.

If ever they needed all their hunting skill, it was now. If they moved a millisecond too slowly, or made the slightest misstep, they would instantly change from hunter into the hunted. Soon the moment of quick action would begin, and the bright curve of headlights told them their waiting was almost at an end.

Two slices of lacquered midnight, the lead Ford Americar and the trailing Rolls Royce Phaeton, slid down the deserted alleyway. Both cars boasted powerful engines that rumbled quietly, the sound bouncing off the tall brick canyons on either side. Headlights cut crazily as first the Ford, and then the Rolls Royce, swerved to avoid the piles of refuse filling the narrow passageway.

The Americar was occupied by three humans and one ork, all in dark suits and mirrored sunglasses, despite the dim lighting. The Phaeton's driver was a powerfully built man, also in dark suit and glasses. He held the wheel with one hand, the hand made of articulated chrome.

Sitting next to him was Derek D'imato, a man of thirty-five, or he had been once. Before the treatment. Now he was something else entirely. Something a whole drekload more powerful than any human could hope to be. More powerful, more intelligent. More fragging everything.

In air-conditioned comfort, Derek looked for the sign—a quick flash of headlights in the dark of the alley. He was angry, hot, despite the cool air blowing from the Phaeton's vents.

Derek was on time, and he hoped Burney Costello would be, too. Burney had a reputation for being punctual only when it suited his purposes. Derek hoped it suited Burney's purposes tonight. Anything to finish this bit of business and get back home.

Derek would never have agreed to meet here. This was not a place for a man who wielded power. Even less a place for a man who wielded the power of a god among men. But *Derek* hadn't made the arrangements, hadn't been part of the planning.

Shock tactics. Surprise deployments. Aggressive maneuvering. All these things were part of the plan, a plan made by a soldier. Derek's father, Marco D'imato.

It sounded like so much bulldrek to Derek, who had begun to wonder if maybe his father *was* starting to lose it. He'd heard the men talking when they thought no one could hear. Heard them saying that his father seemed to be going around the bend. Derek had understood why it seemed that way to them, and had dismissed their muttering dissent. There was too much they didn't know.

Now, he wondered if they were right. This plan, his father's plan, was forcing him to run an errand that should have fallen to a messenger, not the son of Marco D'imato—owner and CEO of Fratellanza, Inc.

Marco had been uncharacteristically patient when assigning Derek the job, and Derek had been quick to grasp his father's logic. If Burney Costello was to give up the beach-front property willingly, he would have to be convinced of Marco's determination. Nothing would convince him more than Derek showing up for the meet. For the heir apparent to the family empire to put in a personal appearance . . . well, it would help Burney realize that Fratellanza, Inc. was serious.

There was also the fact that Burney would surely give in to Derek, where he might not yield to a mere messenger.

Marco had insisted that the switch be a surprise, and at the time Derek had agreed. Now, however, trolling down the dirty alleyway, looking for headlight flashes from a car he couldn't see, he was having second thoughts.

It wasn't that he was afraid. That was laughable. No, it was that this errand was interfering with his nightly routine, and that made Derek feel anxious, a hungry knot tightening in his chest. He hadn't fed, and didn't like going this long without quenching his thirst. Derek looked at the man sitting next to him, deftly maneuvering the car, and had to put a damper on his desire to simply take the man, here and now.

They passed the loading dock of a warehouse, and were almost to the end of the alley, when a sick feeling began to burn in the pit of Derek's stomach.

They eased past a shadowy alcove, the glint of a corrugated metal door flashing briefly in the headlights.

Did they hide *the fragging car?*

Then he saw them. Out of his side window, dark splotches casting giant shadows in the afterglow of his headlights. Like demons in the night, something out of a cheap horror trid. He saw the muzzles of the guns, and the horror trid became a full-fledged nightmare.

Derek moved, with a swiftness that no metahuman could hope to match without spending hundreds of thousands of nuyen, but it was too late. The lead car exploded in a ball of flame, and the night was lit up by automatic gunfire, the sound like rumbling thunder in the narrow alley.

The Phaeton, suddenly without direction, rolled further down the alley until it gently bumped into the burning wreckage of the lead car. And all the while the barrage continued until there was no glass left intact, until great, gaping holes formed in the driver's side. Big enough that the two angels of Death could see most of the effects of their work.

On cue, the flying bullets ceased.

With practiced speed, the two men dragged the eviscerated passenger from the Phaeton over the decapitated body of the driver, whose mangled head dropped to the pebbled pavement. Lifting the body of their target, still miraculously intact, the two men quickly sealed it in an airtight bag that the younger man had flipped out onto the ground littered with broken glass. When the bag was secure and all the air evacuated from it, each grabbed an end and moved swiftly up the alley, past the burning wreck, to the minivan parked at the corner.

The night was empty once more, empty except for hot sweat, cool breezes. The sounds of far-off laughter.

And the smell of new blood and gunpowder.

"He's sparking. Should be coming round soon." Short Eyes' voice drifted through the hollows of the warehouse.

Martin de Vries stood as still as stone and tried to block out the cacophony of sensations. The warehouse smelled of old tires and oil, a residue from its days as storage for an auto shop. Over the hum of the portable generator that provided power to the place, he could hear the sounds of ships' engines out on Union Bay, the sounds of people moving about on the street, even the murmuring of men speaking to each other down on the docks.

The night air of the warehouse was cool against his skin, tingling with salt from the sea and pollutants from the factories in Ballard. Reaching into the pocket of his vest, he pulled out a small jade statue. Carved in the likeness of a four-armed demoness, the statue seemed to glow in the dim light, as if the small stone creature had swallowed something of incredible power.

One more time into the breach for you and I, thought de Vries, as he felt the calm strength of the statue pour into him, *though this isn't how you and I like to do things, is it? No fight, no struggle, simply putting evil out of its misery. Takes all the pleasure out of it.*

"Is everything in place?" De Vries glanced at Short Eyes as he once again pocketed the statue.

Short Eyes grunted, running her long fingernails though

her hoop-length hair, pushing it back to slot a datacord into one of her five datajacks.

De Vries knew that she was now getting a fully recreated view of the entire room as she brought the four trid cameras on-line. That was part of Short Eyes' talent. To most, four simultaneous points of view would be disorienting, maybe even nauseating. But de Vries knew that Short Eyes welcomed the view.

De Vries glanced briefly at the trideo screen next to one of the cameras as Short Eyes used her headware to meld the composite into a comprehensible image. In the screen, de Vries saw a close-up of his own face. Pale skin gleamed like polished marble against the black of his hair, and his hazel eyes narrowed over an aquiline nose.

"Stay chilly," Short Eyes said. "Everything's rock."

As de Vries watched himself on the screen, a small grin spread across his full, slightly bluish lips. The tips of his delicately curved incisors showed twin crescents of stark white against the skin of those lips. "Excellent, my dear. The priest?"

"Give me the go, and I'll slot," she said.

"In a moment," de Vries said. "First I must tend to our guest. He is already awake, although he's trying to hide that fact."

Derek D'imato was strapped to a metal chair in the center of a ritual circle, his face reposed in what appeared to be sleep. Severely chopped black hair framed strong masculine features, a straight prominent nose, and a wide, sensuous mouth. Long lashes fell almost to his aristocratic cheek bones. Close scrutiny, however, revealed make-up. In fact, it was caked on, though artfully done, and where Derek's sweat had run down his face, tracks of darkness invaded the healthy-looking tan.

Despite appearances, de Vries knew Derek was faking. No matter how much he tried to maintain the illusion of stupor, the drug would have worn off more than two minutes ago.

The man's thousand-nuyen suit was ripped to shreds in places and showed stains all down the front, though there were no wounds visible on him. The stains didn't look like blood. De Vries knew blood, knew all of its stages, all of its secrets. These dark stains were too black, too shiny, to be what the uninfected would call blood.

"Derek, you may stop pretending now. I've done this far too many times to misjudge the sedative you were given."

Derek didn't open his eyes, but simply said, "Old man, you have no idea how deep in drek you've decided to go wading. When I get out of this, I'm going to rip you apart piece by piece and suck the marrow from your bones."

De Vries noticed there was something definitely wrong with Derek's mouth, but he couldn't place it. It was just wrong, that was all.

Short Eyes gasped, a clearly audible hiss of breath through her human teeth.

De Vries just laughed. "I have no doubt you would try, my young friend, though it's my guess you're the one with no idea how deep your troubles are running."

Derek opened his eyes with a snap, and the deep blue screamed into de Vries' mind like pallid, vile lasers. Though this young man and he shared a common bond of sorts, de Vries felt a momentary shock at the sheer hatred and barely hinged insanity in those eyes.

"Do you have any idea who I am?" Derek's voice was almost a screech.

De Vries smiled. "Of course. You're Derek D'imato, son of Marco D'imato, principal owner of a private security corporation named Fratellanza, Inc. I also know *what* you are. If I didn't, you wouldn't be here right now."

A look of stunned incredulity crossed Derek's rugged features. "Who in the hell are you?"

"My name is Martin de Vries."

Sudden, unearthly silence. Derek had gone completely still.

When he spoke, his tone was soft, cautious. "Bulldrek. De-Vries is a myth."

De Vries was surprised to hear Short Eyes answer. "Shut your hole, *simpey*."

De Vries shot a glance at Short Eyes as he pulled a pack of Platinum Selects from the pocket of his duster. Lighting one, he inhaled deeply and let the smoke jet out in twin plumes from his nostrils. "My dear, it is time to set things in motion. Why don't you load up our special surprise for our guest?"

De Vries smiled as Short Eyes reached to the chipjack interface set into the back of her skull, just below her scalp. Instantly, her mannerisms changed as she became Priest, the BTL personality chip she'd obtained just for today. Her facial expression went from confronting to solemn; she straightened her back and brought her feet together, bowing her head in de Vries' direction. She looked like a different person altogether.

Short Eyes' voice came deep and accented. "Priest here."

De Vries looked back at the greasy face of Derek D'imato, whose confusion was obvious. "You are wondering about Priest, yes?" He took another drag on his Select. "Actually, you have my sincerest apologies at not being able to obtain a bona fide member of the holy cloth. You see, I know of your family's background in Catholicism, and seeing as I'll be sending a trid of this evening's activities to your father, I thought it would console him to know that his son had something of a proper send-off."

Derek shook his head. "You're crazy."

De Vries looked down at his cigarette, noticed it was burning low, and pulled another from the pack. Lighting the second with the glowing butt of the first, he said, "You don't think your father will appreciate my sense of humor?"

Derek said nothing.

"Prepare for last rites," de Vries said. He took a deep drag off the fresh Select while tossing the butt of the old one to the floor and crushing it with the heel of his boot.

"What the frag are you talking about?" Derek's carefully

cautious facade went ragged at the seams, then unraveled. "I don't believe any of this. You're just a vampire with delusions of grandeur."

"No," de Vries said. "I am a living dichotomy." He gave a harsh laugh. "A vampire who hunts vampires."

Priest walked up to the edge of the ritual circle. "You are the devil's work, Mr. D'imato," she said in deep, solemn tones. "Martin has salvaged his soul by forfeiting the taking of blood from innocents. God has made him an agent of His vengeance."

Derek's face twisted with rage, his eye flicking to de Vries. "You're insane, old man. Just because you despise what you are doesn't make you the agent of God."

"You're wrong," said Priest. "That's exactly what it makes him. And as his witness and priest of the Holy Catholic and Apostolic Church, I pronounce sentence on you, Derek D'imato. Witnessed and recorded."

De Vries smiled. "She has a way with words, don't you think?"

"I declare you an abomination in the eyes of the righteous," said Priest.

"Shut up! Shut up! Shut up!" Foam-flecked spittle flew from Derek's mouth, and his incisors tore a small, bloodless wound in his lower lip. "How can you do this? We're the same."

De Vries felt his anger surge. "We are nothing alike, you and I."

Derek's torn lip healed up almost immediately. "Whatever you say, vampire. But you and I are not that different."

De Vries ignored him and turned to face Short Eyes. He gestured with one fine-boned hand. "Priest, it is time."

Priest walked across the room and picked up a ceramic basin filled with water, a silver spoon, and a large sponge. She carried them back to the edge of the circle. "I am ready."

De Vries silently acknowledged her, then gathered his

power around him. When he was ready, he drew himself up and stepped close to Derek.

"Don't come near me." Derek's voice was calm again, the edge of insanity turned to something far more cunning.

"You were raised Catholic, weren't you, Derek? I should think you would appreciate all the trouble I've gone through for you. For you and your father, who has forgotten his faith."

Derek just grunted, his unreal blue eyes tracking de Vries.

De Vries took the towel from Priest and wet it in the basin's water. "Are you ready for your final baptism?" He wrung the excess water from the sponge.

"After all," de Vries continued, "you were baptized as a child, and seeing as you have just recently been born a child of darkness, I thought baptism was a fitting way to prepare you for what I have in store." De Vries chuckled as he moved the sponge close to Derek's face, watching carefully as the man's neck muscles bulged, trying to move away.

Abruptly, Derek's head lunged violently forward and he tried to sink his fangs into de Vries' wrist.

De Vries spoke a word, and the air around Derek's head seemed to crackle with magical electricity. Derek's fangs stopped a mere centimeter from contact with de Vries' skin.

"You like that?" asked de Vries. "I learned it from a young woman in New Orleans about a year ago. You feel the pressure on your throat? You move too much, and you lose your head. You know what happens to a vampire who loses his head?"

With a soft chuckle, de Vries wiped at Derek's immobile face, and with each touch of the sponge, the caked make-up disappeared. Underneath, Derek D'imato's skin was black. Not the black of someone with African blood, no, the intense sun of that continent had never touched something so dark. As the make-up was patiently washed away, the darkness became so absolute that Derek's features began to meld with each other. Even in the camera's floods, the black flesh absorbed the light and gave nothing back.

When de Vries was done, Derek had become a faceless nightmare, with only the tiny crescents of his teeth and the violent white and blue of his eyes to testify that this was a face, and not some black pit.

De Vries dropped the brown-smudged sponge, and took the small silver spoon from the bowl. With two swift, precise motions, he used the lip of the spoon to pluck the blue discs from Derek's eyes. Then he dropped the spoon back into the bowl

Derek didn't blink, and now his eyes were simply white, with two small pinholes of night at their center.

"Holy mother of God," whispered Priest.

De Vries stepped back. "What did I tell you? If his kind is allowed to spread its infection, metahumanity is doomed."

Priest shook her head as if to clear it after too much strong drink. "Are you ready, then?"

De Vries laid a hand on Priest's shoulder, and looked at Derek. "You are familiar with the sacrament of extreme unction? As a good Catholic boy, you should be."

Derek glared at them both.

Beside him, Priest chuckled. "You know, last rites? I even know it in Latin."

De Vries grinned at Derek, who still couldn't move. "You see, I have taken pains to make this as formal as possible. Your father should appreciate that." He made a small passing motion with his hand, and Derek's nothing face continued its truncated arc, his teeth snapping shut on the air where de Vries' hand had been when Derek had begun his attack.

"You'll pay for this, de Vries!" he screamed. "My father will make you and this chiphead priest suffer beyond anything you've ever imagined."

Priest began to chant as de Vries lit incense along the edges of the circle. *"Per istam Sanctum unctionem et suam piissimam misericordiam, indulgeat tibi Dominus quidquid deliquisti . . ."*

Priest finished anointing Derek, though instead of actually

touching him, she simply sprinkled water at him from outside the circle.

There was one final touch de Vries wanted to make. He turned to face one of the cameras, looking straight into it. "Marco D'imato," he said. "I have taken your son, and he is no more to you. Soon, you will be visited in the dark of night, and I will set you on the road to follow him."

It was time.

Derek screamed as de Vries turned back to him. And there was little wonder why. Short Eyes had taken the Priest chip, and was back to her normal self. She had also pulled a small surgical pump from out of her bag and was holding it out to de Vries. This wasn't how de Vries preferred to work, but if the information he'd received was correct, for him to ingest Derek's blood would have devastating consequences. So new methods had to be found. Stepping up to Derek, he spoke the word he'd learned in New Orleans last summer, and Derek's head snapped into stillness once again.

De Vries attached the surgical pump to the side of the chair and fastened the drain tubing to the side of Derek's neck. The surgical pump had been modified so that it would clamp independently onto Derek's head, and the hose would drain the blood from his jugular. At the same time, the silver needle on the pump would stop Derek's natural regeneration from closing the wound. Clamping the needle into the skin of Derek's neck, causing it to puncture the jugular, de Vries started the small motor at the base of the pump.

A tiny whirring noise filled the warehouse as the suction pump began to siphon Derek's black blood from his neck, down the tubing, and into the large bucket Short Eyes had placed on the floor at de Vries' feet.

Like petrol from a car, thought de Vries with a sad smile. With a wave of his hand, he released Derek's head from the barrier.

Derek screamed, a loud piercing wail that shattered one of the windowpanes, high in the warehouse.

2

Hey, Stem, I need a favor—off the record. I thought you OC guys might be able to get me something on a small security corp named Fratellanza, Inc. here in town. I hear the name means "brotherhood" and that these guys popped up out of nowhere about seven years ago. The scan I got says they're a little family-owned organization, which is growing fast. Some of my snoops say they're Mafia, and considering what happened today, it seems plausible. The son of Fratellanza's owner died in a very peculiar way a few weeks back, and we've been holding the body pending certain tests. Then, today I found out that the stiff had been released to the family and that my captain had closed the case. I don't want to get in his face on this, but the whole thing's got me wondering. Think you could do a little leg-work on your end? I'll owe you one.

—Inter-departmental email, Lone Star Security Services Inc., Mike Powell, Department of Homicide, to Stem Carlson, Department of Organized Crime, 03 August 2060. Transmission intercept by Fratellanza deckers. Scan word: Fratellanza, 05 August 2060

Rachel Harlan stood naked in the cluttered studio, her strawberry-blonde hair cascading down her back and shoulders. She wiped sleep from her eyes, then walked over to

Warren's latest sculpture and threw back the cover cloth. Underneath was a demon, vicious and cruel, straining to break free of its marble prison.

Rachel studied the creature's partially formed wings, outspread and anxious to take flight. The face was unfinished, but she could picture what it would look like when Warren was done sculpting it—a ruined visage, scarred and twisted with a rage so intense it scared her.

Rachel reached out and ran her fingertips over the hewn stone. Anyone watching might have been struck by the sharp contrast of her beauty to its ugliness. Where Rachel's nose was pert and straight, the sculpture's hooked into a hideous beak. Rachel's eyes were wide and blue, her lips full and naturally red. The demon eyes would shine with dark intensity. Its lips would be torn by its jagged line of teeth.

Rachel shuddered. She didn't understand Warren's choice of subjects, but he was the artist, not her. This demon sent a chill like ice running all the way down her spine.

She stepped back from the table—actually a large wooden door propped up on twin metal filing cabinets—and studied the block of marble from a distance.

The damn thing is ugly, she thought, then quickly tossed the cover cloth back over it.

When Warren had selected the marble block from the quarry, Rachel thought he was seeing an angel inside the large chunk of rock. An angel would have been sweet.

But now she knew that he'd been seeing a demon all along. And she didn't know what was more frightening, the demon or Warren's mood while carving it. He'd been distant and sullen all week, and she couldn't figure out why.

She turned from the block and crossed the large, open studio, her bare footsteps echoing on the hardwood floors and bouncing off the high, white stucco ceiling.

She walked to the trid, past the midnight-blue futon couch that was the large room's only furniture, except for easels and worktable. She slipped a chip of Cool Phantom's "Millennium Bygones" into the rack, letting the lead singer's soothing voice pour out of the wall speakers. She swayed to the music as she made her way into the kitchen.

A surprise August drizzle spattered against the window pane, clouding her view of the tire retreading shop across the street. It was cool in the kitchen, and she felt a tightening around her nipples as the chill did its work on her skin.

She poured two cups of fresh-brewed soykaf into the mugs she'd gotten Warren for Christmas that year.

"Babe?" From the bedroom, Warren's voice was an early morning rasp, harsh against the background of soft music and slow rain; still, it made her smile.

"What?"

"You making 'kaf?"

Rachel's smile stretched into a grin as she looked out the kitchen window at the early morning drizzle. "Already made."

She could hear Warren shifting in bed. "You bringing me some?"

She laughed. "Already poured."

"I worship the ground you walk on."

She picked up the mugs, ready to head for the bedroom, then hesitated an instant, looking out at the cold rain. There was something perfect about the moment, and she wanted to let it linger, like the scent of perfume hangs in the air after the passage of a beautiful woman.

But the moment passed, and she sighed as she crossed to the bedroom, holding the steaming mugs in front of her.

The bedroom looked as if a small hurricane had hit it. The walls were crammed with prints of various artists, but the dominant force was Michael Parks. His surreal pictures hung at angles, overlapping the others.

The futon, twin to the one in the studio, was opened into a bed and occupied the center of the room. Sprawled across it was Warren, his long, dark hair spreading against the white pillowcase as he turned to look at her.

Rachel paused, her sense of the sublime triggered. It still amazed her that they were together. He was gorgeous; he was an artist. What had she done to deserve him?

Warren stared back at her with gawking admiration, and Rachel felt self-conscious. She smiled and put the coffee mugs in front of her breasts.

"Oh, that certainly covers up a lot," Warren said, laughing. "I can still see your—"

"You want kaf or breakfast?"

"Kaf first," he said. "Breakfast later." He struggled into a sitting position, revealing his tightly muscled stomach.

Rachel handed him one of the cups. "Black," she said, "with tons of sugar."

Warren blew on the soykaf, making the steam billow out gently. He took a sip, then another, but his eyes never left her body.

His look was devilish and aroused the first stirrings of desire. Her skin tightened again, but this time it wasn't from a chill. "Just 'cause they're hard," she said, "doesn't *necessarily* mean I'm horny." A smile played at the corners of her mouth.

Warren laughed. "And just because I'm looking at the menu doesn't mean I want to order."

Rachel moved fast, grabbing a pillow with her free hand and targeting Warren's face with an expert throw. The pillow hit him in the side of the head.

He grinned and set his soykaf on the floor beside the bed. "Oh course you know . . ."

"Yeah, yeah . . . this means war." She leaned over and set her mug on the lamp stand. Then, with a laugh, she was on him. She swarmed over him, her naked body covering his. She pushed him onto his back, her desire for him suddenly urgent.

They wrestled for a moment, Rachel straining to pin his arms above his head, and finally succeeding. *I'm getting stronger,* she thought. *Those workouts with Flak are helping.*

"I win," she whispered.

Warren's breath was warm on her face. "The battle, maybe." He kissed her on the lips, softly. A brush of skin on skin.

She released his arms and returned the kiss, a little more forcefully, then harder and harder.

Warren's skin was warm against her, and he smelled of sleep. He tossed the blankets off and pulled Rachel onto him so that she straddled his hips.

Rachel brushed her fingernails along the ripples of his stomach, then bent to take his left nipple in her mouth. Her hair tumbled over his chest as she bared her teeth against his nipple and suddenly bit it.

Warren gasped, and grew hard against her.

Rachel looked him in the eye, resting her chin on his chest. "Are you ready to order now, or do you need some more time with the menu?"

He reached down and took her face between his hands. Pulling her toward him, he kissed her fiercely, suddenly out of control.

She plunged her hands into his long hair and kissed him hard, sucking his tongue into her mouth. He tasted of fresh soykaf.

Warren ran his fingers down her back, making her shudder and moan into his mouth.

He pulled back. "Miss, I'm ready to order."

Her voice had grown throaty. "Oh?"

"I think I'll have the special, with orange juice in a tall glass."

She laughed again, and began a smooth rocking motion of her hips. "One special," she said. "Coming up."

She leaned over Warren, her hair cascading down over his

face. She covered his mouth with hers, biting his lip as she pushed her hips down over him.

Warren moaned, holding her tightly, forcing her to take it slow. Prolonging her pleasure.

By the time they were done, their soykaf was no longer steaming. Rachel was covered in sweat, her hair a damp tangle down her back, which quickly chilled in the cool air. Her throat was dry. "Water," she croaked, as she fell off Warren and lay on her side.

Warren laughed and got out of bed, the sheen of sweat on his back making him look like he'd been dipped in oil. He returned a few moments later with two bottles of mineral water, and Rachel chugged half of hers before pulling the bottle from her lips.

Warren lay down beside her, and she ran her fingers through his hair. "Baby, that was so rocket."

He smiled, and gently reached out to tweak her nipple. "You say that as though it hasn't been good every time."

"Well, your mood this past week has been pretty fragging dark."

Warren shot up suddenly and started pulling on his clothes. "Oh, drek!" he said.

"Were are you going now, Storey? You can't just jam and run. I'm not that kind of girl."

Warren threw on some jeans and a sweatshirt. "I completely forgot about something I've gotta do today."

"Forgot?"

"Oh, I've got this damn funeral."

Rachel was suddenly sorry she'd been joking. She stood and hugged him. "Oh, baby." She kissed his neck softly. "I'm sorry."

Warren reached for his black engineer boots and pulled the right one on, without socks. "Don't be. He was a real prick."

"Whose funeral?"

Warren pulled on the other boot. "You remember the telecom call I got from my dad, about a few weeks ago?"

Rachel frowned. "The same guy?"

Warren nodded.

Rachel shook her head. "I don't get it. If he died back then, how come they're just burying him now?"

Warren shrugged. "There was some big investigation, something to do with the way he died. Lone Star wouldn't release the body until now."

Rachel reached out and touched Warren's shoulder. "Do you really have to go?"

He twisted to look Rachel into the eyes. "Rachel, believe me, there's nothing I'd rather do than stay here and make love to you until some time tomorrow morning. And barring that, I was hoping we could catch some breakfast, and then maybe a matinee."

Warren stroked her cheek. "And maybe some time real soon I'll be able to explain why I have to go to a funeral for someone I could give a frag about. But for now, you'll just have to trust me when I say that I wouldn't go if it wasn't important."

"When will you be back?"

Warren shook his head. "Not sure, but it'll be a couple hours, easy. Maybe more. Will you be here?"

She shook her head. "No. I think I'll head over to my place. Get cleaned up to go to work."

Just the thought of the having to go to The Joy Club made her tense. It wasn't too far from Warren's doss, just a few blocks over in yakuza turf downtown, but to her it was another world. She didn't do any horizontal bop, so she didn't make the money some of the other girls did, and she was sick of the whole thing. Rachel shook her head at the thought. There weren't very many opportunities for someone like her, and strip-dancing was still one of the most lucrative. It was only lately that she thought she might have found a better way.

Rachel hadn't told Warren yet, but she wanted to become a shadowrunner. The Joy Club's bartender, a troll named Flak, had a team of his own and he'd been teaching her. Maybe he thought she was just another wannabe, but Rachel didn't care. She was serious. From the scan she'd heard, running the shadows brought better nuyen than flashing your goods to drunk idiots. And according to Flak, every once in a while—not often, but every now and then—you got to do something good. Something that could help somebody.

She'd been practicing with a gun and saving up for a datajack. Recently, she'd helped Corinna, another dancer at the club, hire Flak and his team. Some guy had been abusing Corinna and she wanted to teach him a lesson. Flak had assured her that his team was more than up to the task.

Acting as a fixer for a friend had given Rachel a feeling unlike anything she'd ever felt, especially considering that her means of livelihood was taking off her clothes for the men and women who came into the club. The only thing that might have made it better would have been participating in the run herself. Flak had told her just the other day that she was close to ready, that her progress was excellent.

She looked at the small, old-fashioned clock on the night table. If his timetable were correct, he and his team would be making their run in just a few minutes. Just thinking about it sent a small tremor of anticipation through her. Finally, a way out of the life she was leading.

Warren gave her sad eyes. "I'm sorry, Rach," he said. "If I didn't have to go, believe me, I wouldn't."

Rachel sighed, then nodded. "I know. But you remember this, Warren Storey. You owe me. A full day, no less."

Warren smiled and kissed her. "Promise."

He retrieved his sweatshirt from the floor and pulled it over his head.

Rachel leaned back against the wall and stared at him. "You're going to a funeral dressed like that?"

Warren looked down at his ripped Harvard sweatshirt and ragged jeans tucked into his boots. Then he grinned up at her. "I figure if the little shit is in Hell looking up, I should let him know exactly what I think of him."

Rachel didn't return his smile. "Be careful, Warren. You scare me when you're in this mood."

Warren bent and kissed her, then turned and walked out. He grabbed his black leather jacket and motorcycle helmet on his way out the kitchen door.

3

The racists of the Sixth World tell us that the newly Awakened races are demons, monsters—not human and therefore our enemy. But even as they rouse the ignorant masses against our harmless brothers, the real demonspawn lurk in the shadows, growing stronger on the blood of the living. They are the vampires, the so-called living dead.

—Martin de Vries, *Shadows at Noon* posted to Shadowland BBS, 24 May 2057

Light morning rain spattered against the rusted, pitted metal of the fire escape as Sinunu Sol climbed, her heavy boots making so little noise as to be completely silent against the backdrop of the soft street noise from below. The Capitol Hill district was unusually quiet this morning, with only the occasional car rumbling through the twisting, turning streets of downtown Seattle. That was fine with Sinunu. Considering the whammy she and her team were about to pull, the less people watching, the longer it would take Lone Star to scan to what was going on.

Dressed in skin-tight black synthleather and a dark brown wrap-around duster that contrasted with her albino skin, Sinunu caught a glimpse of herself in a dirty pane of glass as she topped the last landing before the ladder to the roof. Her shock of white hair was slicked back by the rain, and her pink eyes seemed to float in her ghost face. She smiled at her reflection as she moved past.

Sinunu was riding the groove, everything clicking on all twenty-four, and in the slot. It felt just fine. She and the crew hadn't worked for almost a month, and she'd thought she might go crazy for the want of action. So, even though this was mostly a charity gig—with the little dancer squiff only able to cop up enough to pay expenses—it just didn't matter.

She climbed the ladder quickly, feeling the grit of time under her pale hands. Stepping over the dirty brick of the caping wall, her foot touched the rooftop just as the rain started to slacken. Bits of grainy sand skittered under her heavy boots as she moved quickly across the roof.

She reached the large ventilation intake, and opened her duster. Strapped there, in six separate leather holsters, were the pieces of her Barret Model 121 sniper rifle. With precise moves that wasted no energy, Sinunu assembled the rifle in less than twenty seconds, taking the time to double-check the silencer's fitting. Slotting the caseless ammo, she lowered the tripod and quickly carried the weapon over to the edge of the roof top.

From there, she could see the target's front bay window on the second story. Through the window, the man himself was visible, talking to someone out of her line of sight.

Probably that damn ork he's got for a bodyguard, Sinunu thought. *That puffed up razorboy couldn't guard water from getting wet.*

The target, a rich weasel named Carlos Sevase, didn't look too happy, and that made Sinunu smile. Carlos was everything she detested about men. He was small-minded, petty, and came complete with a mean streak that included hurting pretty young girls who didn't do exactly what he wanted.

Sinunu was fairly sure that Carlos had just learned that his latest punching bag had booked, and was nowhere to be found. At least not by him. The crew had moved her out of town last night, after Truxa had done her best to patch the girl up. Corinna was the girl's name, and when Sinunu had seen that bruised face, she'd had to do a full ten-breath count to get her anger under control.

Corinna was going to lay low for a few days, just long enough for Sinunu, Flak, Truxa, and Sandman to convince Carlos that maybe he should learn to play nice.

Sinunu smiled again when she thought about how this was going to go down. Looking across at Carlos, her smile grew into a grin. *Thirty seconds with Flak will have that boy in tears.*

Sinunu forced the grin from her face, and concentrated. She subvocalized into the headset mike of her Philips tacticom. "This is Bird's Eye, got the—"

Suddenly her senses kicked into high gear. The patter of rain had covered the approach and dampened the smell, but she still knew he was there before he even spoke.

"Well, well. What do we have here? I suggest you release your hold on the rifle slowly and roll over onto your back, hands on your head."

Sinunu cursed under her breath and did as she was told.

The man towering over her was elven, a fact that surprised her because the only meta of record Carlos had on the payroll was the ork. This guy was tall, with jet black hair done in dreds down his back. His dark skin glistened in the rain.

He held a Cobra Colt in his thin hands. The weapon's stubby design made it look as if the designers had forgotten to add a barrel.

"Hey, there, pretty boy, you know how to use that gun, or do you just think it makes you look tough?"

The elf grinned. "I know a bit more than you."

He took one more step toward her, and without lowering the weapon, held up his left hand. Talking into a headset almost identical to Sinunu's, he said, "Got one on the roof. I'll finish this and find the rest of the mice for you."

He took one more step and Sinunu moved. Everything

slowed around her as her talent took over. The elf's face froze in that stupid, mean-looking grin as Sinunu cocked her right leg back and rammed it straight through his kneecap, splintering bone.

Suddenly without any balance, the elf tumbled forward, a scream giving away his pain. With ease, Sinunu lifted herself off the rooftop with her left leg and caught him just under the chin with the toe of her right boot.

The elf's head shot back, blood spraying as teeth splintered in his mouth and flew through the air.

He collapsed into a heap at Sinunu's feet. "You don't know squat, you damn amateur. Maybe that'll teach you not to get too close."

Without another look at him, she rolled back over to the sniper rifle, and subvocalized into her tacticom. "Like I was saying, this is Bird's Eye, and I've got the back door covered."

Sandman's voice in her ear sounded like a ghost through the headset. He was in the stepvan parked just down below in the alley, but his transmission via the Matrix always gave his voice an ethereal sound. "Front doors pop. No auto sec devices, and just the three of them in the room. You can party whenever you're ready to put on your boogie shoes. Just give the door a little push."

Then she heard Flak's voice. "You ready with the bang-bang, Trux?"

There was a pause that stretched long enough for Sinunu to realize she'd stopped breathing. *Take it easy. Truxa can handle anything these punks throw.* Even as she thought the words, she had a hard time believing them.

Truxa Fin was the team's elven mage and she was also Sinunu's lover. Sinunu knew she had a problem being overprotective, but there was nothing she could do about how she felt.

After a second more, Truxa's voice, bright and cheerful, sounded over the tacticom. "Sorry about that. Had a problem with the now previous tenant of the apartment. It seems he took exception to my presence, but he's feeling much better about things since he decided to vacate. I'm in the slot and ready to roll."

"Then it's party time."

Through the window, Sinunu watched as Carlos suddenly whipped around toward the front door, and even though she couldn't see it, she knew what had happened. Two hundred kilos of very pissed-off troll had just smashed through his front door.

There was a brief pause, and a body flew through the air, crashing into the wall opposite the bay window. *So much for the ork.*

That's when things started to go south.

"I got heat signatures on the floor above, moving fast, and it don't look like a meeting of the glee club." Sandman's Matrix-distorted voice sounded harried, and Sinunu briefly wondered what had gotten him so agitated. Then, she knew.

The sound of gunfire rolled softly across the street, and she could hear the distinctive screaming roar of Flak's Vindicator as it cranked up to rock and roll.

Carlos was still standing with his back to her, and now she could see Flak, facing away from her, the spinning barrel of the Vindicator spitting fire.

In the same instant she also saw Carlos reach into his suit coat to pull out an Ares Predator.

Without thinking, Sinunu triggered the Barret, and felt the small recoil as the heavy slug shattered the bay window. The round caught Carlos in the back of the neck, almost taking his head off as the force spun him completely around. The sounds of gunfire echoed loudly through the streets now that the window was gone.

Sinunu spoke quickly into the tacticom. "Back door is open."

The wall at the back of the apartment seemed to come apart,

blowing inward, and suddenly, there was Truxa alongside Flak, her tiny hands making complicated motions in the air.

A ball of flame about the size of a small car ripped through the air and flashed out of sight toward the front door, and Sinunu could hear the screams of men who couldn't get out of the way in time.

Flak never let up on his spray of lead as he and Truxa backed to the window, stepping over the body of Carlos.

From far away, the wail of Lone Star sirens could now be heard over the din of the firefight.

Just below her, Sinunu watched as the blue stepvan peeled out of the alley and stopped just under the second-floor picture window.

"Flak, back door. Go!"

In a simple motion, Truxa grabbed the big troll's back and hung on as he turned and leapt from the window, landing with ease on the roof of the stepvan, which buckled slightly under his weight. The van accelerated back out into the street, with Truxa and Flak still on the roof.

Sinunu watched as smoke began billowing out of the window. A couple of men in dark body armor made their way through the smoke and tried to level their weapons at the fleeing vehicle.

Too bad you spent so much on body armor, boys. All the less nuyen going to your grieving widows. With that thought, Sinunu opened fire.

Three rounds, three head shots, three kills, clean and by the book.

Climbing rapidly to her feet, she took the Barret apart quickly, placing each piece back into its individual holster.

Slowing only to pick up the Colt Cobra from where it had fallen, then putting two rounds into the unconscious elf's head, Sinunu exited the roof top.

When she reached the alley, she carefully wiped the Cobra clean and dropped it into a dumpster. Then she tightened her duster around her and headed toward the street, where a gaggle of Lone Star patrol cars had just arrived screaming on the scene.

She figured she might as well watch the show. That, and make sure Carlos was hauled out in a body bag. She'd meet up with the rest of the crew later.

4

Mike, got your request and did a little digging. Unfortunately, there isn't much to tell. Fratellanza, Inc. seems to be legit, despite the fact that they've got contracts with some high-ranking Mafia and Yakuza members. Especially since Butcher Bigio got the nod as the new capo of Seattle. Fratellanza's small, but they got a rep for doing personal security like nobody else. I'll keep my ears open on the son's death, but I think you're probably wasting your time on the Mafia angle.

—Inter-departmental email, Lone Star Security Services Inc., Stem Carlson, Department of Organized Crime, to Mike Powell, Department of Homicide, 03 August 2060. Transmission intercept by Fratellanza deckers. Scan word: Fratellanza, 05 August 2060

The morning rain fell in gentle sweeps, bordering on mist. Tall, opulent gravestones lined the roadway, extending back as far as the eye could see through the drizzle. Dotting the landscape were spires of rock topped with everything from carved angels and lions to robed saints and mitered popes.

The graveyard was a huge, grassy expanse near the University of Washington. Founded in the early eighteen hundreds, it was old enough that even the burial ground's thirty thousand square meters had become crowded.

Stone statues fought, elbow to elbow, with granite markers

for the remaining clear areas. The only free space was deep in the heart of the grounds. There stood the small mausoleum where the city's founding father was buried.

The cost to bury a loved one here was astronomical. But to the people attending the funeral today, money was no object.

Just behind the founding father's mausoleum, a group of the city's wealthy had gathered to bury one of their own. In their tailored suits and designer dresses, with not an income in the group below several hundred thousand nuyen a year, most of them would have found the idea of an annual salary ludicrous. One had money, and it was managed. There was no thought of a wage.

Among the dead man's mourners were a number of the family's business acquaintances, those whom Fratellanza, Inc. counted among its stable of clients.

The corporate brotherhood.

Fratellanza, Inc. had started small, but rather than trying to compete with Lone Star or Knight Errant, its owners had taken a different angle. Instead of trying to offer comprehensive protection for their clients' assets, they'd concentrated strictly on personal security, leaving all other sec duties to the bigger boys. This had allowed them to offer a level of personal service and pampering that the larger, more unwieldy corps didn't even try to match. In this way, Fratellanza had carved a small niche for itself that had become immensely profitable, beyond what the size of the corporation might have indicated.

Many of Fratellanza's best and brightest had also turned out for the funeral. Derek D'imato was the son of CEO Marco D'imato. Showing respect was important to an employee's long-term health and prosperity.

Old men and young, with their wives. All of them appropriately grim-faced, a few even shedding tears. For some, however, the demise of Derek D'imato was a priceless gift in an ugly wrapper. Some of the mourners stood to gain much by this burial. So for many, tears were harder to find, unless they were tears of joy.

Also present were three solo women, each from a distinctly different social circle. The chesty brunette was a high-society girl, used to fast cars and faster men. The two blondes looked enough alike to be sisters, though one was originally from Sweden, where her father had made his money in pharmaceuticals, and the other was from the Confederate American States, heiress to nearly a hundred million nuyen in real estate. Each woman cried, foolishly thinking the same thought. That she had been the only one to lose her lover.

Then there was the D'imato family.

The man in the dark overcoat pushed his older brother's wheelchair to the grave site. Twin wheels left deep grooves in the lush green of the immaculately kept lawn.

The priest began his benediction. The crippled man did not cry, and no one expected him to. This was Marco D'imato—Derek's father and founder of Fratellanza, Inc.

No, Marco D'imato was not the type to shed tears at a death. Though if any of those present had known the reason behind that implacable calm, that steely expression, their horror would have far outweighed their grief.

"The light burns me, brother," Marco said, sitting in his wheelchair, relishing the sprinkle of rain. "And yet I endure it and survive." Through the heavy makeup he wore, the daylight was a glorious scalding on his skin. Everything seemed so bright that it took all his willpower to remember why he was here. He felt a mad desire to grin, even though he knew that would be deemed inappropriate by the lovely, blood-filled humans who surrounded him.

Julius touched Marco's shoulder. "You should be considering the death of your son," he said.

Marco nodded, but he was thinking, *Derek's body and soul died long ago, as did mine.* Marco turned his head and glanced upward into Julius' somber, grieving brow, and the slightest hint of a smile touched his bloodless lips. Everything about his brother seemed to pulse, vivid with life. Marco could smell the faint odor of sweat under his sharp cologne, could hear, dimly, under the patter of rain and the shuffling of feet surrounding the grave site, the gentle thump of his brother's heartbeat. Could see the coursing of blood through Julius' veins that stood out like some glorious road map through his skin.

Marco tried to bring himself under control. The ability to withstand the light of day had also brought with it increased bloodlust. I *must maintain my restraint around Julius. His feelings about my most recent change have not gone unnoticed, but he will understand in time.*

Marco glanced around at those gathered around the grave of his son, all of them listening to the droning of the priest. So purposeful, so intent, all of them. Marco forced down a small chuckle. These petty humans with their stupid ideas about life and death, they thought they were looking at their own mortality in this place, but in reality, their own mortality was busy watching them, seeing nothing more than a delicious feast.

Julius laid his hand on Marco's shoulder, the weight a chafing comfort, as if he could read Marco's thoughts and was trying to help him stay calm. Julius knew of Marco's condition, and supported him, though of late, his support had been more formal, more stiff than ever before. Julius' feelings came through most strongly whenever the subject of the procedure came up. His vehement reaction to Marco's proposal that he himself undergo infection was simply the most obvious change in Julius' attitude.

In time he will be persuaded.

Marco's thoughts shifted slightly, settling on the plan, his plan. The men of Ordo Maximus had made his role in their scheme clear, but they were short-sighted, thinking only of walking in the daylight again and the power it would give them. They seemed oblivious to the next steps, to where that power could take them. To them, he was simply another cog in the wheel, a vampire who would be in the right place at the right time. It had been their idea for the personal protection angle exploited so profitably by Fratellanza, Inc., and it had been their money that had funded it. All so that when the moment came, certain powerful individuals—individuals who might be in position to cause problems for Ordo Maximus—could be quietly disposed of. It angered Marco to think that they could discount him as a simple tool, but soon they would learn of their mistake.

With considerable effort, Marco stifled a surge of anger. "Thank you, brother," he said to Julius.

Sorrow, he thought, *sorrow is what I'm supposed to be feeling.* He looked at the bronze-tinted casket, and forced himself to think about Derek. His son, his heir, his dreams for the future. The casket was normal size, though Marco knew that Derek's body, once so strong, so commanding, only took up a small portion of the casket's interior.

The only way Lone Star had been able to identify the eviscerated, burned thing that now rode inside the plush interior of the metal box was by Derek's credstick, which had been jammed into the blackened, cracked mouth. That mouth had been stretched into an eternal scream of fear and anger. That scream had been so hard, so violent that it had actually unhinged Derek's jawbone.

There were doubts at Lone Star whether the body was actually Derek's, but Marco had known instantly. He'd been expecting news of his son's death ever since the trid chip had been delivered. Silent anger began to build inside as he remembered the trid recording. He felt an itch of madness take hold as the face of Martin de Vries came into his memory—the smug self-assurance in those undead eyes, the casual way a fellow vampire could torture and kill one of his own.

Even now, Marco's men and hired mercs were scouring the city for any sign of the rogue vampire, searching with extreme prejudice to find the man who had murdered the heir apparent to Fratellanza, Inc. And when they found him, Marco would be there.

Now, Marco looked down at the skeletal ruin of his legs,

the vicious twist of his hip bones that spoke of the helix that had been his spine. He looked like a cripple, but Marco knew that if needed, his body would respond in ways that would surprise even another vampire. When the moment came, he would be the one looking down at Martin de Vries' dead-white skin, and de Vries' death would make the murder of Derek look like a mercy killing.

The pressure of Julius' hand increased ever so slightly on Marco's shoulder, and Marco could sense his brother leaning in to whisper in his ear. "There he is. I told you he would make it."

Marco squinted to see into the distance and through the hazy drizzle, he saw the metallic-gray Saab Dynamit in the cemetery's roughrock gateway, idling behind the electrified wrought-iron fencing.

Marco watched as Biggs, a big red-haired ork and one of Fratellanza's best captains, checked Warren for ID. Biggs was in charge of today's security arrangements and had personally taken over the gate. He was ambitious for a meta, and Marco had even considered breaking one of his unspoken rules for the man. No meta had made advancement past captain in Fratellanza, Inc. Biggs might just be the first.

Tires hissed on the wet pavement as the sleek car rumbled through the now-open gate and accelerated up the narrow asphalt path into a forest of granite and marble.

Marco watched as Warren got out and walked across the wet grass to the gravesite, stopping at the outer fringe of mourners.

The young man was dressed in a suit just barely appropriate for the occasion, not nearly somber enough for a member of the family. He stood there, head bowed, his spine rigid and angry.

He is no Derek.

The thought brought just a hint of bitterness to Marco. There had been a time, not so many years ago, when Marco and Julius had discussed Warren as the logical heir to Marco's wealth and power. There had been no doubt that Warren was far more intelligent than Derek, but Warren lacked other qualities that Derek had possessed in spades. Where Warren was soft, Derek had been hard, where Warren was understanding, Derek had been demanding, where Warren was squeamish, Derek had shown delight. Derek had been a warrior, Warren an artist.

Now, the situation had been forced. Warren would have to be the first step on the path to Marco's realizing his dreams, and the thought galled him. Not just because Warren was not his first choice, no, it went deeper than that. What galled him most was that he had been short-sighted. He'd placed so much faith in Derek, who'd seemed so untouchable. Derek had shown himself able to kill, burn, ravage.

Marco had come to believe that Derek would always be around. Now, Warren was untried, untested, and certainly not ready to captain Marco's forces into the upcoming alliance with Don Maurice Bigio that would be the first step in Marco's double-cross of Ordo Maximus. He'd use both of them as long as he could, until the day he had so much power than even they would have to bow to him.

I am to blame for his lack of conditioning. And I must correct this error.

Marco looked across the grave site and tried to picture Warren, not as he saw him now, a delicate creature that pulsed with lifeblood, but as the rest of these fools must see him. He let a small smile creep onto his heavily made-up lips.

Warren was strong, standing tall, his long hair beaded with rain. Despite Warren's seeming gentleness, Marco believed that he could be fashioned into a warrior, molded into something more than the self-absorbed brat Julius had allowed him to become.

If Warren could be made to understand, he might still make a better leader than Derek ever would. Recently, Warren had been going through a rebellious phase, and Julius had given the boy entirely too much slack to pursue his whims. Warren had taken all that slack and had demanded more.

He was even seeing a stripper. Marco knew all about Warren's secret life as Warren Storey. All about the fact that Rachel Harlan, Warren's current quim in residence, knew nothing of Warren's connection to Fratellanza, Inc.

Frag, the boy has convinced her that he's poor.

Marco knew that Warren had been slumming, merely to gain attention from Julius and himself. He would come back around to the corporate way, eventually. Of that Marco was certain, which was why he'd allowed his brother to be so lenient with his son.

Now that Derek was gone, Marco could no longer afford to be so lax. *Derek's death was a setback, but I can't afford to let that affect the plan. I will rule the entire earth one day, with my offspring crushing all opposition in my path.*

Marco knew of one sure way to exorcise all of Warren's faults, without jeopardizing his good qualities. An exorcism involving a vampiric virus tailored by Dr. Olso Wake.

He thought about the day Wake had come to him, telling him that Ordo Maximus believed Marco had potential and should be the first of the vampires to walk in the light of day.

At first, Marco hadn't believed him, but one quick telecom call to London had put Marco's suspicions to rest.

Despite the crippling outcome of the procedure, Marco held no grudge against the man. Marco knew that the leaders of Ordo Maximus had been the ones to rush the procedure, had been the ones to force Wake's hand, even though the doctor had warned them of the risks.

It was worth it, Marco thought as he looked around, seeing his natural prey by the light of day. *I'd do it again in a second. Now how do I convince Warren to undergo Doctor Wake's procedure?*

Where Derek had welcomed the transformation, Marco knew that it would offend all of Warren's tender sensibilities. However, once Warren had been . . . changed, once he saw the world as it really was, once he'd tasted the true fruits the new life had to offer, he would fall into line. Marco had no doubts about that.

Still, there was another possible complication involved there. Julius would never be party to coercing Warren. Julius' love for his son would be his downfall if Marco didn't solve the problem soon. *And it might only widen the rift that's come between us.* That would not do. Julius knew too much, and Marco wanted to avoid any action that might turn Julius definitively against him. Julius could ruin everything.

Marco thought of de Vries and Derek, and then of Warren, and a plan came to mind. It was so simple, so ridiculously simple, that for a moment, he let his smile out in force.

Luckily, none of the mourners happened to be looking in his direction when he made the slip. Because, in that smile, even the simplest person would have realized that there was nothing remotely human hiding behind the mask that was Marco D'imato.

The only person to see that smile stood just outside the high stone wall that marked the perimeter of the cemetery. The high-powered digital camera on the telescoping boom was capturing every moment of the funeral.

Jacked into the camera, Short Eyes saw everything. She shuddered as the camera zoomed in on Marco D'imato's face.

Acting as de Vries' daylight eyes took its toll on her, and the security here was very high. She simply needed to get some good trid of the funeral and then she could call it blowtime.

Since meeting de Vries last year, Short Eyes had felt purpose come back into her life. Before, she'd been nothing more than a second-rate media snoop and a chiphead. Now, she had direction.

She remembered the night she'd met de Vries in the alley behind a club in Amsterdam, the night he was hunting a vampire named Carlson. When Short Eyes first saw him stalking through the club, tall and stooped, chain-smoking his cigarettes, she'd thought he was a chipdream. But then she'd quickly realized what he was, and had followed him. She was the only witness to the magical vampire duel that had taken place in the deserted alleyway behind the club.

As de Vries was taking Carlson's life, she'd tried to get away, but somehow, de Vries had known. He'd cornered her before she'd taken ten steps. She thought she was dead, but instead of draining her blood, de Vries said he wanted to speak with her.

They began to walk and by the end of that fifteen-minute conversation, Short Eyes knew she would follow de Vries anywhere. When he told her he would be headed for UCAS soon, and asked if she would accompany him, she hadn't needed to think twice before accepting. She pledged her life to the cause, and no force of darkness, no matter how terrible, would ever sway her from her course.

Through the boom camera's field of vision, Short Eyes saw that the funeral was over and that Marco D'imato was being wheeled away from the grave as the casket finished its short descent.

The man standing behind Marco stopped for a moment and gestured for a younger man to approach. The latter was the one who'd come speeding up to the funeral gates, his sports car moving like the devil himself were giving chase.

Short Eyes zoomed in to catch a close-up of him, and she didn't have to be a genius to see the physical similarities between the young man and the older one pushing Marco's wheelchair.

Something in the young man's manner caught Short Eyes' attention. Unlike the rest of the mourners, who had approached both of the older men with respect and deference, this one seemed to show Marco cold indifference. That only broke when he shook the hand of the other man, whom she guessed was his father. The respect and admiration were apparent on both of their faces.

They talked for a moment, and Short Eyes wished she had a shotgun mike to catch the conversation.

Finally the man in the wheelchair frowned and motioned with his hand toward the waiting limo. The young man shook his head, and pointed toward his car. The two older ones nodded, reluctantly, and the three separated.

Short Eyes collapsed her equipment and stepped further back into the tree line as the funeral procession began to leave the cemetery. Then she loaded the equipment into the rented Ford Americar and drove it back to the hotel, where de Vries slept the day away.

5

Vampire, sanguisuga europa. *Vampires are not a true species, but rather they are individuals of a human sub-species who have been infected with an agent that causes the vampiric condition. The infection only seems to reach its full virulence in a magic-rich environment, but there are indications that both the Human-Metahuman Vampiric Virus (HMHVV) and vampires were present before the Awakening.*

—from *Dictionary of Parabiology,* edited by Professor Charles Spencer, third edition, MIT&T Press, Cambridge, 2053

Summer had returned with a vengeance to the Seattle sprawl. Even this near midnight, the air was close and humid, the heat still well into the eighties. No breeze stirred the noxious brew, and the night stank of hot desperation.

The normal noises of the city seemed muted and faraway as the sound waves struggled to penetrate the sluggish air.

Two vampires climbed out of a stepvan, leaving it running. They left a third vampire inside the vehicle and walked across the street toward a low tenement. At their signal, the two Fratellanza guards parked in a black Chrysler-Nissan Jack-rabbit near the tenement's front door pulled out onto the street and disappeared around the corner. Within seconds, the sound of the car's motor had faded to nothing.

The two vampires continued on foot and walked up the steps to the door of the doss in the middle of the block.

Behind them, on the roof of the tire retread shop across the street, a clinging shadow disengaged itself like a slice of midnight, and vaulted silently to the ground. What the two vampires didn't realize was that this piece of darkness had been with them ever since they'd left Magnolia Bluff.

Martin de Vries watched the two inhuman monsters dressed in double-breasted suits step lightly across the street, conscious of keeping their movements slow and controlled. De Vries watched carefully, studying them, searching for their strengths and weaknesses.

He knew that to these two vampires, the putrid night was a thing of beauty, something that still held incomparable wonder. These were young bloodsuckers, new to their enhanced senses and fantastic powers. It had only been a month since they'd been mere humans, trusted captains in Fratellanza, Inc.'s corporate structure, with nothing much of distinction to their lives.

Now, the whole city was their playground, and the night was the most magical time they'd ever experienced.

De Vries could sense their hunger, their bloodlust so strong it threatened to consume them. He could tell that they'd stifled it for now. Tonight, they were not abroad to feed, they were on business.

They passed the Honda Viking that was chained to the mangled parking meter, then walked calmly up the stairs to the doorway of the doss. One of them knocked three times.

It took a moment, but finally a man's voice answered, full of suspicion. "Who's there?" De Vries could here it clearly even from across the street.

"Mr. D'imato? It's Max Fein. I've been sent by your uncle. He needs to speak with you, in person. It's very urgent."

"Spirits be fragged!" came the muffled voice through the door. Then, "Don't you know you're not supposed to come here?"

De Vries moved a step closer, wondering at the disappearance of the first pair of Fratellanza guards. These vampires were from Marco D'imato, so why had the guards left? Why weren't they used as travel insurance? Things didn't seem right.

De Vries got his answer as the young man, so familiar from the trid images Short Eyes had obtained, opened the door.

Both of the vampires moved, and with a speed no uninfected could even hope to follow. The young man was knocked unconscious and carried across the street.

De Vries slid backward, blending perfectly into the darkness at his back.

The vampires toted the man's still form to the van, then one of them opened the door.

"We got him, sir."

De Vries heard the grunt of Marco D'imato from where the crippled vampire sat in the back of the stepvan. "Get him loaded. We don't have much time to get to Hell's Kitchen."

De Vries stiffened at the sound of that voice, a voice he had studied and had begun to know so intimately. Then the van was gone, accelerating up the street and taking the corner with precision.

Alone now in the darkness, de Vries stepped from the shadows. A moment later he was joined by Short Eyes.

"Your take on what just happened?" he said.

Short Eyes shrugged. "Body snatch, natch. Chum Boy got an invite he couldn't refuse."

De Vries nodded. "Sloppy work for someone as sharp as D'imato, unless he planned it that way."

The two crossed the street and walked up the stairs to the still open doorway of Warren's doss. Moving silently, de Vries stepped inside.

He let his vision shift into the astral, then gave a low whistle. When viewed in this manner, the entire room seemed to come alive. Small statues glowed with magical light, paintings seemed luminescent.

"Our boy Warren is no ordinary mundane."

Short Eyes, just a step behind de Vries, giggled like a school girl. "Corner of the eye trick?"

De Vries walked over to the table that dominated the center of the room, splinters of stone crunching beneath his boots.

On the table, the crude form of a demon was taking shape in the marble block. De Vries looked straight at the form, and it seemed like nothing more than a statue, but as he shifted his eyes to the astral, the little demon seemed to move, straining to take flight.

As he studied the rest of the carvings, he noticed they all did that. When looked at directly, they seemed like nothing more than exquisitely carved pieces of art, but when viewed from the astral, the pieces seemed to come alive.

"They're flip," said Short Eyes, just a hint of wonder in her voice.

"Yes," said de Vries, knowing that Short Eyes was seeing only one aspect of the sculptures. "It would seem that our boy has a talent of major proportions. I wonder if his uncle knows about this? I wonder if the boy himself even realizes what he can do? Though someone must have noticed it by now."

Short Eyes started talking, but suddenly de Vries was no longer listening, no longer able to breathe. In the corner stood a sculpture unlike the others, slightly smaller, but formed with such care and attention to detail that he almost cried out.

Barely aware of his own movement, he crossed the room and stood there in front of the small stone statue.

It was a woman, reclining on a small divan. Her arm was stretched out, in a beckoning manner, and the slight smile on her face was half playful, half seductive. She was beauty itself.

"Josephine," whispered de Vries. "It's impossible."

Then Short Eyes was at his back, and he heard her sharp intake of breath.

Short Eyes had never known de Vries' wife. The woman

had been killed before Short Eyes was born, but she'd seen holopics.

"What is . . ." But de Vries was already past her, moving through the doss, heading for the bedroom. Short Eyes followed.

In the bedroom, de Vries found what he was looking for. A holopic of Warren and the woman who had obviously been the inspiration for the statue.

By the time Short Eyes had caught up with him, he'd flipped the pic over, and was reading the inscription. "Me and Rachel at Lake Washington." It was dated just a couple of months before.

De Vries flipped it back over and looked at the image closely. In the background, Lake Washington gleamed like a blue-gray crystal. Rachel had her arm around Warren, staring straight into the camera as he kissed her neck.

"She loves him," whispered de Vries.

Short Eyes sighed. "Changes are a comin'."

De Vries glanced up at her as if he'd forgotten she was there. "Changes? Yes, this changes things for me."

"Sensei, plans are laid, and they're golden. Changes now could shuck us to the bone."

De Vries looked back at the pic, at the woman who could have been his dead wife's twin, at the love that was displayed so freely in the image. "You let me worry about that. There's no way I'm going to let Josephine down again."

Short Eyes reached out and touched the holopic with one elongated fingernail. "Not Josephine. Rachel. Not the same thing."

De Vries rubbed a thumb over that perfect face. "Tell that to my heart. We have to make sure that boy doesn't die."

In the dust bowl of Hell's Kitchen, the stepvan plowed along, its headlights cutting through the swirl of volcanic ash that still plagued the area despite the many years since Mount Rainier had last erupted.

The van pulled up to an armored gate, passing the small camp of denizens who were already forming up for the free meal that would be passed out just before dawn.

Marco shifted uncomfortably in his wheelchair and listened as Max and Sonny spoke in the front seat. Max chuckled and looked over at Sonny. "That was us, just a few weeks ago."

Sonny didn't seem to find the memory so humorous. "Yeah, and by tomorrow, some of them will have disappeared. I wonder what happens to the ones who don't turn out?"

Max laughed. "Who gives a frag? The ones who can't cut it get removed. That's life. And death." His own wit caused him to laugh so hard that he almost missed the stop.

Marco was not amused. "Damn you," he said, as the van skidded to a halt. "Pay attention to what you're doing, or you'll find out what happens to fools who *think* they are immortal."

Max keyed his window, letting a swirl of gray dust into the van. The speaker, mounted on a thin post, crackled. "Business?" came a thin, distorted voice.

Max leaned out. "Marco, with a special delivery for Wake."

"See some ID."

Max slid the ID card into the reader below the speaker.

The armored gate slid backward, and Max pulled the van inside. This was the first of two walled partitions that separated the compound from the outside world. Through the swirling dust, Marco could make out the subtle forms that roamed the fifty meters separating the two walls. Cyberdogs and their handlers. But no ordinary dogs. These were beasts, their thin, cadaverous bodies supporting cyber headgear that made them look impossibly top-heavy.

They passed the second checkpoint, where the van was sniffed by a small Doberman with a telescoping cybercamera cut into its head, just behind the dog's ears. Cleared through, they entered the main compound proper. Max backed the van up to the loading bay, then stepped out and set up the ramp for Marco's wheelchair.

As Marco rolled out behind Max and Sonny, who were carrying Warren's limp body from the van, someone Marco had met only once came out onto the loading bay. Dr. Raul Pakow was a short man, with a heavy shock of sable hair that continually threatened to fall into his eyes. He was forever pushing his hair back with an impatient gesture.

"What's going on?" asked Pakow, the low undercurrent of anger in his voice telling volumes about his frustration. "Dr. Wake didn't authorize any new acquisitions."

Marco's anger at the man's tone blazed, and he stood, his twisted hips jutting forward as he maintained his balance with difficulty. "I authorized it. And if Dr. Wake wishes to remain in my good graces, he will do as I request."

Pakow showed neither surprise at Marco's twisted appearance, nor did he back down. "That is something you will have to take up with Dr. Wake, Mr. D'imato."

Marco smiled, and for just a second, Pakow seemed to shrink back. "Oh, I intend to. Now get Wake down here. Time is short."

"I'm already here, Mr. D'imato."

The man had approached so silently that even the vampires were caught unaware. Marco twisted around painfully.

Wake stood on the opposite side of the loading bay. He had risen to his full height, which allowed him to tower above all those present, but his skeletal frame made it seem like a strong wind would carry him upward like some crazy, human kite. His white hair jutted painfully from his head, crowning his look of complete exhaustion. "What is it that I can do for you?"

Marco let his body go, and felt his very atoms begin to flow, until he was nothing but mist. He let his essence guide him until he was in front of Wake, then he willed his body to coalesce again.

Wake continued to look at him casually.

"You know of the troubles of the last few weeks?" Marco said.

Wake nodded. "Of course. I'm very sorry for the loss of your son. Still, I'm confused by what you're doing out here in the middle of the night." He looked over Marco's shoulder at the still form lying on the concrete. "Is this some form of retribution? Or do you have something even more . . . diabolical in mind."

Marco laughed, a short bark completely devoid of humor. "The only thing I have in mind is the continuation of my lineage. I'd have preferred to keep my options more open, but I'll simply have to work with what I've got."

Wake nodded again. "And this young man has something to do with that? I'm sorry if I seem a bit slow, but I was given to understand that you had only one son."

Marco looked behind him, and a fierce grin spread across his face. "That is correct. This is my nephew. I want you to perform the process on him."

Wake looked at the body and his eyes took on the faraway look that told Marco he was peering into the astral. With that distant look still in his eyes, Wake said, "And it would seem that he isn't undertaking the process with the same . . . gusto displayed by your son."

Marco laughed, a low angry sound. "He would have taken some convincing, but unfortunately, I don't have the luxury of the time it would take."

Wake snapped back to the physical world. "Are you also aware of his talent?"

Marco paused for a moment, puzzled. "Are you talking about his sculpting? I've seen some of it. It's not bad, if you like that sort of thing."

Wake smiled, a small thing that refused to reach his eyes. "No, I was speaking of his magical talent."

"He's got no magic."

"In that you are mistaken, I'm afraid. In the astral, his ability is obvious."

"Well, I'll be damned."

Wake laughed. "You already are."

The two vampires at Marco's back joined in the laughter until Marco's glance silenced them.

Marco turned back to Wake. "Your attempts at humor are on the verge of being offensive."

Wake looked into Marco's eyes, as though measuring him somehow. "Is it still your wish that the process be performed?"

"Of course."

"Even though you know that the procedure affects magically active creatures in different ways?"

Marco shook his head. "You don't understand. This is my last chance to keep my legacy within the family."

Wake looked at the body of Warren, who was beginning to stir. He paused for a moment, as if making a decision. Then he nodded. "Dr. Pakow, ready room number three. Put this young man on a saline IV with Syndorphin infusion, and prepare the vat. We have quite a bit of work ahead of us."

Pakow nodded, and stepped up to a wall-mounted telecom next to the bay doors. "Team alpha, report to bay six, priority red."

Marco grinned at Wake. "Make sure he comes through this and I'll triple the monies I've been funneling to you. If he dies, I'll cut you off at the knees."

Wake simply smiled.

A new voice sounded on the loading bay, one groggy and unsure of itself. "Uncle Marco, is that you?"

Wake moved before anyone else. Pulling a patch from his coat, he knelt by the struggling form. "Rest now. You've had an accident, but we're going to take good care of you."

Wake slipped the patch over Warren's jugular, and Marco watched him drift immediately back into oblivion.

6

At its highest levels, Ordo Maximus is the tool of a secret cabal of at least half a dozen vampires—perhaps more—all skilled initiates who use the Ordo's funds and political connections to conduct biomagical research well hidden from the public eye. Their goal is simple and terrifying; they seek to create variant strains of HMHVV, new viruses that will confer the strengths and weaknesses of vampirism at the Ordo's sole discretion.

—Martin de Vries, *Shadows at Noon,* posted to Shadowland BBS, 24 May 2057

The following morning, seagulls swirled in an azure sky over Marco's mansion in Magnolia Bluff, some four kilometers from the heart of downtown Seattle. The area was favored by the sprawl's elite and wealthy, including those who earned their nuyen on both sides of the law. The mansion was surrounded by a three-meter stone fence topped with wrought iron spikes, track-mounted Ares security drones, and trid cameras. This served to deter all but the most well-equipped burglars from even thinking about attempting a break-in.

The mansion grounds were spacious and well-landscaped in Italian-garden style, with roses and olive trees and fountains shaped into the forms of Roman deities. Today, the sun glimmered off the moving water, though Marco, groggy and just awakened from his daily slumber by an irate Julius, could not see it.

The two men were in Marco's inner office. High ceiling fans provided the only movement of air in the completely enclosed room. Even though Marco could now sustain the touch of sunlight, on days like today, with the light so blazing and clear, he would still be severely burned.

Marco shook his head. He hadn't anticipated Julius learning of Warren's disappearance so soon.

"And I'm telling you he's gone!" Julius' voice was like a diamond saw cutting through stone. "Warren's been taken by someone who knew our release codes." Julius turned and paced across the Persian rug.

Marco knew he had to handle this with extreme care. "Maybe he simply went to one of his art shows." He made sure to add just the hint of derision that Julius would expect.

Julius shook his head impatiently. "Impossible. When I tried to get in touch with him this morning, I got no answer. So I checked the guard logs, which showed he was left unattended from just before midnight last night. I went over there personally, and his front door was wide open. There was no sign of forced entry and no sign of a struggle, but Warren is gone. He would've told me if he was planning to leave Seattle."

"And who do you think did this?"

Julius stopped pacing and turned to face his brother. "I've been warning you for months that something like this was bound to happen. Our contract with Don Bigio makes us a target. The yaks, the Seoulpa, it could be anyone. But whoever it was, it looks like they took a page from Derek's killers and decided to get to us through Warren."

Marco suppressed a smile. This anger on his brother's part would serve his purposes nicely. "First off, we have contracts with a number of Mafia families as well as with the yaks. None has ever considered it a conflict of interests, and I don't see why they would start now. Also, if you say there was no sign of forced entry, then it's nothing like what happened to Derek. In case you've forgotten, Derek's car was completely shredded. *If* Warren has been kidnapped, then he must not have put up a fight. Therefore, it might be something you haven't considered, though I don't think you are too far wrong."

Julius' face grew still, and in a soft voice he said, "You're keeping secrets from me."

Marco nodded. "I'm sorry, brother. Derek's death seemed like a personal attack, and it pained me so much, I didn't want to share what I've learned. However, in light of Warren's disappearance, there's something I've got to show you."

Marco crossed the room, his nearly useless legs dragging on the floor as his will carried his misshapen body. Sitting down heavily in the overstuffed chair behind his desk, he pulled the trid recording from the center desk drawer. "Have a look at this."

Julius' face became even more still. "What is it?" His voice was little more than a whisper, the soft buffeting of a breeze through fallen leaves.

"It's from the man who killed Derek."

As if reaching for a live scorpion, Julius took the chip over to a tall bookshelf. He put his face to the hidden retinal scanner that had been placed in an ancient hardcover of *Moby Dick*. Then he stepped back, and the book case recessed and slid down into the floor, revealing a security console and a large trideo rig.

Marco slotted the chip and stood there as Martin de Vries came into view. Julius watched the whole thing without making a sound. When the monitor faded to black, he turned back to Marco.

Julius was nearly shaking with anger. "This explains a few things, like the unusual distribution of our sec forces for the last couple of weeks. You shouldn't have kept this from me."

Marco forced himself to seem contrite. Bowing his head, he said, "You're right, brother. It was short-sighted of me to think that this de Vries was through, that he would only come after me."

"I want him. If he's taken Warren, he'll find that we have ways of making even vampires suffer before they die."

Marco nodded, once again keeping a smile from his lips only by force of will. "Find him. If you can get to him soon enough, Warren might still be alive. Go, use whatever resources you need."

Julius turned and headed for the door. "I will, brother. I will hunt this Martin de Vries, and if he's hurt Warren, then I'll make sure his death is neither clean, nor painless."

Marco squinted at the bit of sunlight that peeked through as Julius opened the door and left. *Be careful, brother. You're still human. At least for a little while longer.*

7

A creature with the power of mist form can transform its physical body into a mist by controlling the molecular cohesion of its cells. The mist can pass through any crack or crevice that is not airtight, even penetrating filtration systems that are proof against gases or pollution.

—from *Paranormal Animals of Europe,* first edition, by Charles Spencer, Department of Parabiology, University of Oxford, 2053

While Short Eyes slept the night away, de Vries hunted. This night's hunt was just part of the long hunt, the kind that required months of tracking, preparation, and that would culminate in violence and death.

Short Eyes was one of only a few humans who understood his hunt. But de Vries had a feeling about this other one, this stripper who looked so much like Josephine. He wanted to believe she would be another, even if it was only to help retrieve the one she loved.

From across the street, he watched her exit The Joy Club. He crouched on the roof of The Headlight Factory, just behind a monstrous set of neon breasts. De Vries took in the sight of her and found himself forgetting to breathe.

With a sharp intake of smog-laden air, he tracked her as she walked through the early evening heat. It was Josephine, and yet it was not. He trembled slightly at the proud way she tossed her head, not letting the heat humble her as it did the other denizens of the district.

She walked through the others like a princess among her subjects. Her see-through plastic micro that clearly showed the hot-pink g-string underneath, her azure blouse that left nothing to the imagination, showing perfect little breasts that swayed naturally—no augmentation there. These things were not Josephine. No, Josephine would never have worn those clothes even in the privacy of their home, let alone out on the street. Also, this girl was muscular where Josephine had been frail.

Still, the tilt of her head, her grace as she dodged the press of foot traffic, these things were Josephine through and through.

He watched her strut, the tips of her stiletto heels dragging sparks from the concrete, her open sexuality taunting those she encountered to do anything other than look, then cast their gaze back down to the filthy pavement.

De Vries knew that this section of downtown was controlled by the yakuza, and considered "safe." Patrols of yak *kumi-in* kept the streets free of gangs and organized violence, but that wouldn't stop sex-starved, drunk corporate slots from attacking a barely clad stripper on her way home.

De Vries knew where she was going, knew it as he knew that she was aroused. The scent of her came to him, strong enough to overcome even the stench of the streets, and he knew she was headed toward Warren's doss. It was only five blocks over, though a dangerous five blocks. Still, she walked without fear, almost as if daring anyone to accost her.

De Vries knew what she would find when she got to Warren's, however. He thought about the night he returned home to find Josephine gone, to find that she had been taken by a dark one. He remembered the sense of void and loss as he searched for her.

As he watched Rachel swagger down the street, he decided

to spare her that pain, even if it meant revealing things she might not want to know.

Silent as a wraith, he crept along the building tops, trailing her, gliding from rooftop to rooftop as she crossed the streets. Finally, she turned down the one leading to Warren's doss. Here, the shadows would make her more cautious, but would give him the cover he needed before revealing himself.

Still, he found himself hesitating.

Then he smiled to himself in the darkness. He was the vampire, and a caster of spells, yet this mortal creature had captured him with a spell far more powerful than any magic at his own disposal.

He took a deep breath, pulled a pack of Platinum Selects from his pocket and gently swooped to the ground, almost half a block in front of her, just meters from Warren's front door.

De Vries watched her approach, only remembering his cigarette when she was close enough for him to catch her scent. The scent of roses.

She flinched a little when he touched flame to his smoke, but didn't pause in her stride.

"Miss Harlan, a moment of your time?"

She kept on walking, and only someone whose eyes were bred to the dark, as his were, would have caught the slight lengthening of her stride, the defensive swing of her arms.

"Rachel?"

"Frag off." Her tone was a quiet rasp, no fear, no anger, just the words, spoken with enough edge to give a normal human pause.

He smiled to himself again, knowing that Josephine would never use that kind of language, but then again, Josephine had been sheltered from the dark, dangerous world this beautiful creature took for granted.

"He's not home."

She passed him by, the subtle shift of her stride the only indication that she was attempting to place herself outside the edge of his grasp. If he had been a normal human, she would have succeeded nicely.

He made no move. "Miss Harlan, please. You won't find him there, and we need to talk. There is much you don't know, and if Warren is to survive what's going to happen, there's not a moment to waste."

Without warning, she spun on him, a heavy Seco LD-120 pistol emerging from her purse.

Her aggressive stance caught de Vries off guard. "Back off," she said.

Her hand was going for something else in her purse, and de Vries recognized the shape of a screamer alarm.

If she sets that thing off, the yaks will be here any minute. He needed more time than that.

He stepped to the side, too fast for her to track. She didn't shoot, though she shifted her stance, trying to keep her aim.

De Vries pulled the electronic screamer from her hand before her finger could touch the button.

Rachel spun around again, trying to find her elusive assailant. When she found him again, her eyes locked onto his face. Whatever went through her mind, it only lasted an instant. The next moment her decision was made.

She raced toward Warren's doss.

De Vries' smile turned into a full-fledged grin of admiration, watching the line of her back, that rapid undulation of her buttocks, the way she managed to get up so much speed, wearing heels. That was the part that made him smile.

De Vries let her make it to the stairs, then up to the door, which she was trying, vainly, to unlock. Then he spoke a word. The birthplace of that word had died thousands of years before, in a tiny little village just north of what would one day be Pompeii, but he spoke it now, and felt the cool fire build in his back and in his arms.

Time dilated, and Rachel seemed to slow until she looked more like a waxen figure than a human, and the sounds of traffic faded to a dull wash of lazy noise. De Vries moved.

When he was a step or so behind her, he let his body slow down, and Rachel resumed her pounding on the door.

"Miss Harlan, I told you, he's not here and his father has changed the locks on the door. Your key won't work, and if you keep pounding you'll only attract the wrong kind of attention."

Rachel turned quickly, pressing her back to the door. Her eyes moved quickly to the left and the right, judging her options.

De Vries saw the look of quiet acceptance as she realized she had no options, not even the ghost of an option.

"Who are you, and what do you want?" Her voice was breathy, but the note of resignation it carried made de Vries sad. Such a beautiful creature, such strength, but with an air of fatality that made her seem tragic at the same time.

De Vries took a step back. "Miss Harlan, my name is Martin de Vries, and I know what has happened to Warren. You and I need to talk."

A look of deep suspicion took its place on her fine-boned features. "What have you done to Warren?"

De Vries smiled. "I have done nothing to him. But I know what will happen to him if I don't help him. All I'm asking for is a moment of your time."

Rachel shook her head. "Why would anyone want to harm Warren? He hasn't done anything."

De Vries laughed. "Of course he hasn't. People want to do things to him because of who he is, not because of what he does."

Again, her eyes shifted from the left to the right. "You're crazy. Warren is a good guy who spends all his time trying to be an artist. Why would anyone want to hurt him for that?"

Suddenly it dawned on de Vries. "You don't know, do you?"

"Know what?"

De Vries let a slow, tired laugh escape his lips. "I should have guessed. You have no clue who Warren D'imato really is."

Rachel began to slowly edge to the left, and her intentions were clear to de Vries. If she could vault the low railing, she could hit the street running, maybe get away. "Now I know you're crazy. Warren's last name is Storey, not D'imato."

De Vries shook his head. "Miss Harlan. First off, let me clear up something for you. Even if you could jump over the rail without breaking an ankle in those shoes, it would be a simple task for me to catch you before you took more than a step. I suggest we go inside before others take too much of an interest in this meeting."

Rachel laughed, and it was a rasping, ugly sound. "Yeah, right. Even if I could open the door, you think I'm insane? You get me in there, and I'm never coming out alive."

De Vries moved again, faster than the normal eye could follow, and he watched as Rachel stifled a scream when he seemed to suddenly appear, his nose just millimeters from her own. She shrank back against the door as if she were trying to worm her way through its molecules.

"Believe me, Miss Harlan, if harming you had been my intention, you would never have seen me, and my breathing as I drained the life out of you would have been the last sound you ever heard. I don't mean to frighten you, but time is very short, and there is much you need to know."

De Vries reached out with his left hand and stroked the new lock on the door. Once, twice, and on the third pass, he felt the lock give way. The door swung inward, and Rachel would have fallen to the floor if de Vries hadn't caught her.

He picked her up gingerly, and walked her into the doss, gently kicking the door closed behind him. He set her on the futon, then thumbed the switch for the small lamp on the work table.

He turned and Rachel gasped. "What . . . what are you?"

De Vries smiled, feeling his curved incisors dimpling his bottom lip. "I think you know exactly what I am, Miss Harlan, but for now, what you must understand is that I am the only friend you have in the world. The only person who is in a position to help Warren."

Rachel struggled to sit upright, and after a moment she made it. "What is going on?"

De Vries opened his duster and pulled out his pack of Selects. He offered her one, and she took it with a trembling hand. He lit it for her and then one for himself. Taking a deep drag, he let the smoke drift out of his nostrils. "Let's take things one step at a time. If I had known your ignorance of even the basic facts involved in your situation, I might have approached you somewhat differently, but there you have it."

Rachel looked at the cigarette in her hand as if she couldn't remember how it had gotten there. Finally, she put it to her lips and took a long pull, holding the smoke as if it was the very air of life in her lungs. Finally she exhaled, and when she spoke, her voice had calmed considerably. "All right, I don't accept this, but because this is my delusional episode, I'll play along. You're a vampire. Am I correct in assuming that?"

De Vries smiled and nodded.

"Okay, now that I'm sure I've fallen over the deep end, just go ahead and lay it on me. What have you got to do with Warren, and why did you call him by the wrong name?"

De Vries was silent for a moment. "Miss Harlan, there are things I wish I could spare you, but I want you to listen to everything I have to say and to keep an open mind. The man you know as Warren Storey, a very talented artist, is actually Warren D'imato, and he is something else entirely."

Rachel sighed. "Why would he lie?"

Once again, de Vries was surprised. "You aren't familiar with the name D'imato?"

She shrugged. "Should I be?"

De Vries sat next to her and was impressed when she didn't shrink away from him. "This is going to seem a bit far-fetched to you, but your Warren is a very rich man and the son of a powerful corporate honcho. He is also the nephew of Marco D'imato, who is head of the D'imato family. The D'imatos are sole owners of Fratellanza, Inc., a provider of private security in Seattle and other cities across UCAS. They're not Knight Errant by any stretch of the imagination, but that hasn't prevented them from making Fratellanza immensely profitable. Warren is a rich, rich man."

Rachel laughed. "Far-fetched? That's a huge understatement. You must be mistaken."

"Miss Harlan, understand this, I'm neither mistaken, nor crazy. It's obvious that Warren has been hiding these facts from you. Most likely in an effort to shield you from a very ugly situation."

"What situation?" She took another drag on her cigarette, and de Vries noticed that the slight tremble had returned to her hand.

"You must have heard something about the mob war that went on here in Seattle? The trid was full of it."

She sat up straight. "Are you trying to tell me Warren was involved in all that bloodshed? You really are crazy."

De Vries shook his head. "No." He stood, and walked to the center of the room. "One of the reasons I'm here is that I've done some checking on your Warren D'imato. He wasn't an easy nut to crack, because his self-extraction and cover were immaculately pulled off. The only advantage I had was in knowing both identities."

De Vries shook his head again. "No, even though Fratellanza did phenomenal business during the recent mob infighting, Warren was not personally involved. In fact, he has tried to isolate himself from the family business for some time. His uncle and his father have permitted him to disguise his identity and live apart from it all. However, I would guess that he was trying to protect you from learning things that would endanger your life."

De Vries leaned over, stubbed out his cigarette, and pulled the holopics from his pocket. "Warren attended a funeral yesterday. Were you aware of that?"

Rachel nodded, looking at the pics in de Vries' hand as if he were holding a viper. As if she knew what was coming and wished to avoid any proof that what de Vries said was the truth.

"Here, take a look at this." He handed her the top picture, one of Warren is his sharkskin suit.

Rachel took it, looked at it, and flipped it onto futon between them. "So Warren owns a nice suit, so what?"

De Vries showed her the rest of the pics, explaining each one. He finished up with a close-up of Marco D'imato smiling. "And this is his uncle, the man who had Warren kidnapped."

Rachel shuddered visibly at the look of animal cunning on that ravaged face. "Is he like you?"

De Vries took the holopic back and placed the bundle of them in his pocket. "Yes, and no. I am simply a creature of the night. He is an abomination, even compared to my kind. He plans to do to Warren what he has done to himself. If he succeeds, Warren will no longer be human, will no longer be the man you love. Do you understand this?"

Rachel slumped over, and put her head in her hands.

"Miss Harlan?"

Without looking up, she said, "Just give me a damn minute, will you? This is a lot for me to absorb in a short amount of time."

"I wish I could give you the time you need, but time is the one thing we don't have right now. By my calculations, we have until morning to extract Warren from the place in Hell's Kitchen where he's being held, or it will be too late. Once started, I understand the process is irreversible."

Rachel looked up at him, and there were tears in her eyes. "Well, then, we must go and get him. What are we waiting for?"

De Vries smiled gently. "Slow down, Miss Harlan. It isn't quite that simple. If it was, I'd have gotten Warren out of there and delivered him back safely without involving you in any way. No, the reason I *am* involving you is that the place is too well-defended. I could get inside, but there's no way I'd get out again with Warren intact. It's going to take a full team."

Rachel thought for a moment, then said, "I know some runners who might be looking for work, but I could never afford to pay them."

De Vries stood and turned from her, looking around the room at all the pieces waiting to be finished. "I was hoping you would, and I've got a few contacts of my own here in Seattle. But for this job, we'll need all the help we can get."

Rachel gave a sigh of great weariness. "This is all so unbelievable. Even if I could convince them to do it, they cost big nuyen. They've been known to do favors for a chummer, but not anything like this. I could never cop up the nuyen they'd want."

De Vries turned back to her. "You just get them to agree. I'll take care of the rest."

8

The vampire may appear human, but the resemblance stops at the beast's cold, clammy skin. Once infected, the human or metahuman victim of vampirism is dead. In the victim's place is born a devil from the darkest heart of Creation, a thing reared in darkness and nurtured on innocent blood.

—Martin de Vries, *Shadows at Noon*, posted to Shadowland BBS, 24 May 2057

As Rachel stepped through the door to The Joy Club, her senses were assaulted. She came into the strobing black lights in a daze, the scent of incense choking her, and the music—scant decibels from being ear-shattering—hit her like a physical blow.

Just inside the entrance, to the right, the long bar stretched back into the darkness. To the left, Lindsey was doing her thing on the main stage, her high, elven features making her look a bit vulpine in the flashing colored lights. Lindsey was the only elf who danced, and she usually went home with the most nuyen. Norms of both sexes loved having her for lap dances, thinking they were getting something exotic as well as erotic.

Rachel knew that Lindsey was far from the best dancer there, but it seemed that few could resist that extra twinge of strange that accompanied her wide, sensuous mouth and platinum-tipped ears.

Screams from backstage attracted Rachel's fogged attention for a moment. It was Mia.

Rachel frowned. Mia must need nuyen bad if she was going into her act this early in the week.

Mia sat, naked, in a chair center stage, her back arched, sweat dripping from her forehead as a young ork pushed the head of a large golden pin through her soft flesh. Mia whipped her head around, her shoulder-length black hair covering her face in sticky strands, her scream drowned out by the roar of twenty male voices, as blood welled around the pin.

At fifty nuyen a pin, Mia was working on pretty close to a thousand nuyen for this set, but Rachel knew, no matter what painkillers Mia was dosing, she wouldn't make it more than another set or two. Not to mention if some customer wanted a little more intimate lap dance. However, that seldom happened to Mia, because she charged five hundred for a table dance. All for the customer to have the privilege of actually drinking any of the blood they shed from her body.

Before tonight, Rachel had found the blood-drinking thing a bit disturbing, but now it made her shiver, imagining what de Vries could do to Mia with those sharp teeth of his. She turned back to the bar and walked down toward the end as the music came to an ear-rending crescendo, barely drowning out Mia's screams.

Suddenly, Rachel felt two small hands slip under her shirt and cup her breasts. She turned and saw Celone standing there, a wide grin on her sensuous mouth. Celone was the tallest of the night girls, with brown hair just past her shoulder blades and incredibly long legs. She was also the nastiest dancer.

"Hey, you working a double?" Celone yelled.

Rachel shook her head, still in a fog.

Celone's grin turned to a frown. "Devon and I got a guy who wants a three-girl shower show. He asked for you."

Rachel's eyes tracked to the back of the bar where the shower slash hot tub set-up rested. Devon, a tiny girl with muscular thighs, over-sized breasts, and long, dirty-blonde hair, was already in the shower, letting jets of neon-colored body paint spatter her body.

The customer was just getting undressed, smiling at Rachel and trying to suck in his hairy gut.

Rachel shook her head. "You know I don't do the live sex thing."

Celone smiled. "He promised no touching, so it would just be you, me, and Devon. Sex with girls isn't the same thing."

Rachel frowned. "Sex is sex, no matter who you do it with, and I don't do it for nuyen."

Celone frowned. "Hey, that's not fair to Devon and me. Besides, when was the last time you made five hundred nuyen in under ten minutes?"

Rachel shook her head again. "Sorry, I've got to find Flak. You seen him?"

Celone's frown turned into a full-fledged pout. "Come on, Rachel. I'd do it for you."

Rachel doubted that, but she just smiled. "Why don't you ask him if he wants Jessica? Everybody says we look like sisters."

Celone's big brown eyes widened. "Rocket. He probably won't even know the diff." Then she started to turn around as the music began to wind its way back upward.

Rachel grabbed her arm. "Have you seen Flak? I've gotta talk to him." Her frustration bled through into her voice.

Celone turned, and pointed behind the bar. "In the office, with Lucus." Then she was gone into the smoky depths of the bar.

Rachel turned back to the bar, and saw who she was looking for.

Flak, the bartender-doorman, stepped from the gloom at the rear of the club, and walked toward her with a smile on his face. That smile had been known to make norms weep with fear. Flak stood over two meters, small for a troll, but there was no mistaking the sheer power in the ripcord twist of his muscles. His massive head was shaved, and his knobby left arm was covered with a huge tattoo that he'd once told Rachel was a Special Forces tat.

"Rachel!" he bellowed over the music. "What're you doin' here?"

Rachel gestured toward the back, behind the bar, and screamed, "I need to talk to you!"

With a nod, Flak led her back through the tiny kitchen area, and past a storeroom to the cramped office.

Lucus, the owner was just getting up. He was an older man, turning heavy, but with the most gorgeous mane of salt and pepper hair Rachel had ever seen.

"Boss," said Flak, "can I use the office for a minute?"

Lucus looked at Flak, then at Rachel, and for just a moment, his eyes narrowed. Then he looked more closely at Rachel and grunted. "Yeah, but make it fast."

After he was gone, Rachel sat down in front of the desk, while Flak tried to fit his bulk up onto the side of the desk itself.

"What's on your mind, Rach?" Flak's voice was soft, gentle, and completely out of place coming from that mouth full of tusks.

Rachel looked up into the huge man's eyes, and she realized for the first time that they were black, with absolutely no delineation between where the pupil ended and the iris began. It had never occurred to her before, even in their workout and training sessions, but now she wondered if they were natural or augmented in some way.

"How did the run go?" she asked.

Flak grimaced. "We had some minor frag-ups," he said. "Pretty standard really."

"Did you convince Carlos to stop beating Corinna?"

Flak gave a harsh laugh. "You could say that. Carlos won't be beating anyone anymore. For the rest of forever."

"Oh," was all Rachel could say. She had no sympathy for Carlos, and if anyone deserved to die, he was her number one candidate.

"Why?" Flak asked. "You got another job for us?" He started to smile, but it faded the moment he saw the look on her face.

Rachel felt the laugh bubble up in her throat and it came out dry and brittle, the laughter of someone who's seen too much and gone quietly insane. The sound of it scared her.

Flak's expression didn't change, but his voice took on a hard tone Rachel had never heard in it before. "Why don't you tell me about it?"

Rachel laughed again, trying to hold back the tide of emotion running through her. "What do you know about vampires, Flak?"

Flak's eyebrow arched, but he didn't laugh at her, and for that Rachel was grateful. "Not as much as some people, but more than you might think. Why do you ask?"

Rachel took a deep breath as Flak reached his mammoth paw into the desk drawer and pulled out a bottle of Petron tequila and two shot glasses. "You look like you could use one." He poured the drinks, and handed one to her.

Without a word, they slammed the liquor at the same time.

Rachel let the smooth, bitter liquor slide down her throat like a tiny bit of molten lava. It was real tequila, not the synth stuff, and started a small warm glow as it hit her stomach.

Flak smiled as he took the glass from her. "Better?"

She nodded. "You remember my man, Warren?"

Flak's small eyes narrowed. "He do something to you?"

Rachel laughed again, and was relieved to hear it come out sounding normal. "No. No, I think something's happened to him."

"Go on."

Rachel pulled a smoke from her small purse, and before it was even to her lips, Flak had magically produced a small golden lighter.

She took a deep drag. "I got off work tonight and headed over to his place. We always get together on Wednesdays. Just before I got there, I met this guy. He told me Warren was gone, and that the people who had taken him away were going to do horrible things to him if we didn't get some help."

Flak leaned forward. "You know this guy?"

Rachel shook her head. "No. He said his name was DeVreece, or de Vriss, something like that."

Flak rocked back on the desk. "*Martin* de Vries?"

Rachel started. "You know him?"

Flak shook his head, and let out a long breath that sounded like a balloon being slowly deflated. "Know him? No. I know *of* him, though, provided this slag really is de Vries. The guy's a fragging legend."

Rachel's voice turned bitter. "He's a fragging vampire."

Flak chuckled. "I've heard that. But what he's famous for is hunting other vampires."

Rachel took another drag from her cigarette. "Well, this de Vries says he knows where Warren is, and can get to him, but can't pull him out without help. When I told him I knew some people, he said that was one of the reasons he was telling me any of this."

Flak nodded thoughtfully, and reached out to lay one of his huge hands on Rachel's shoulder. "Where's this de Vries now?"

"He's still at Warren's place. He said he'd wait there for your answer."

Suddenly, there was a pounding on the door, and Lucus' voice yelling, "Flak? We got a situation here!"

Flak moved so fast that to Rachel, he suddenly blurred out of sight. The door banged open, and the sounds of shouting invaded the office.

Rachel leapt to her feet and ran out of the office, through the kitchen and into the bar, just in time to see Flak, over by the shower area, pulling the naked customer out of the hot tub by his hair.

Flak dragged the dripping man grimly toward the door, while Devon, also naked and trailing splatterings of neon body paints behind her, followed after the two, pausing every couple of steps to kick the customer as hard as she could. With every kick, the man let out a short, high-pitched scream.

As he passed Rachel, Flak yelled, "I get off in an hour. I'll talk to some people and meet you at Warren's in an hour and a half."

Rachel turned, catching the fierce light in Flak's eyes. "You know where it is?"

Flak smiled. "Don't worry. I'll find it."

Then he was gone, still dragging the man toward the front door.

Rachel used the ensuing confusion to slip quietly out the back.

9

I've been monitoring some closed-door proceedings here at UniOmni, and there is a certain research scientist who might be of interest. He fits our profile, and his expertise is unparalleled. I think we may have struck orichalcum . . .

—Email transmission, J. B. Darl, Communications Support Team, Universal Omnitech, New York City, to blind account, London, England, 19 September 2051

Dr. Oslo Wake walked through the decon unit on level 7, beta wing. The decon area had been shut down ever since he and Pakow had converted beta into the stasis floor.

Passing row after row of long, rectangular canisters, Wake checked the status of each vampire stockpiled there. It had been Pakow's idea to store the vampires when they weren't needed. It was a brilliant idea and easy to implement. Depriving vampires of air put them into a coma state, shutting down their physiological functions. That meant all he and Pakow had to do was keep them comatose, which let them house as many as two hundred at virtually no cost.

As Wake checked their status, he also double-checked the datajacks inserted into each unit. When Pakow had suggested the stasis chambers, a light had come on in Wake's mind. In the early days of the Terminus Experiment, he'd been plagued with the problem of how to keep independent and very powerful creatures from taking matters into their own hands once they'd served their purpose as test subjects. Several of those first vampires had managed to escape their holding cells, and had to be killed.

Now, Wake had each subject implanted with both a datajack and a chipjack before undertaking any other procedure. The chip Wake had decided to use was strictly psychotropic in nature, and guaranteed that the compound's experimental vampires looked on Wake and Pakow with a kind of blind love and adoration. They would do anything either man commanded. The datajack simplified how the vampires would be controlled. Depending on what tasks the comatose vampires were required to do upon waking, the datajack allowed Wake to instantly download instructions to scores of them without any effort.

The plan had worked perfectly.

Wake paused for a moment, feeling the exhaustion deep in the backs of his legs and in his shoulders. He concentrated for a moment, willing his muscles to relax. As he did, his mind drifted to the path he'd taken in the last six years. He turned his head to the left and the right, looking down the line of long canisters, and he let a small smile touch his lips. *They should have known,* he thought. *Those fools at UniOmni should have known nothing could stop me, that every obstacle only sharpened my resolve. They should have realized they couldn't deny me my destiny.*

Wake's tall frame was wrapped in the second skin of his envirohazard suit, and he refitted his face mask. The suit was merely a precaution, because without the special chemical bath, the contaminants in the room couldn't find purchase on the human form. Still, better safe than sorry.

Wake yawned, suddenly finding himself exhausted. He bent to check the computer readouts again, satisfying himself that all was as it should be. Then he went over to the large stainless steel tank that dominated the far end of the large room.

The subject, one Warren D'imato, seemed to be taking the

first step of the procedure well, his vitals strong, his brain patterns registering as normal.

Behind him, he heard Pakow shift in his chair and call out the reading. "One-oh-one . . . one-oh-two . . ."

Wake ignored him. It wasn't that he didn't appreciate Pakow's attention to detail. It was more that he was so tired that the other man was beginning to become distracting.

Finally, when the body temperature was close enough for them to begin pumping the first of the chemical compounds into the tank, Wake let himself relax.

"I know him," Pakow said abruptly.

For a moment Wake wasn't sure if Pakow had actually spoken, or if his tired imagination was playing tricks on him. The words were uttered so softly, and Pakow wasn't one to make idle conversation. He turned to his assistant. "Did you say something?"

Pakow didn't look up from his work, but spoke again. "I know him."

Wake was confused for just a moment, then he understood. "You mean the subject?"

Pakow nodded.

"A friend of yours?" Wake could not imagine that Pakow would have refrained from speaking up before this, but they were still in the first stages of the process, and no damage had yet been done to the subject. In fact, it would be another twenty hours before Warren D'imato would be prepped enough for the actual transition to take place.

Pakow shook his head. "No, but I'm a big fan of his work." He looked up and met Wake's eyes, and for just a moment Wake caught something in the other man's gaze, something vaguely disturbing, but then it was gone, and Wake wasn't sure if he'd seen it at all.

"A fan?" Wake laughed. "You don't strike me as the fan type, Dr. Pakow."

Pakow frowned. "That's because you've never seen this man's sculptures."

Despite his exhaustion, Wake found himself interested. It wasn't that he cared about getting to know Pakow on a personal level. In fact, Wake could foresee a time when he would have to eliminate Pakow to cover his own tracks. Still, this display of emotion was so uncharacteristic that Wake couldn't help but be intrigued.

"So he's good?"

Pakow looked back down at his console. "I wasn't completely sure it was him, because I only met him once at a show of his work a couple of years ago. And the name he was using then was Warren Storey. But the work was unforgettable. I even bought one of his pieces."

Wake walked over to the smaller man. "An appreciation of the finer things in life is commendable, but I'm not sure what you're getting at here."

Pakow fidgeted. "The piece I bought is an African tribal warrior killing a lion. The craftsmanship is so fine and detailed that it took my breath away, but that wasn't why I bought it."

Wake continued to stare, but said nothing.

"The reason I bought it was because of what I seemed to see inside it."

Wake kept his voice soft, almost a whisper. "And what was that?"

Pakow looked up, and there was a quiet pleading in his eyes. "When you look at the piece, it's obviously a marvelous stone sculpture, but if you stare at it long enough, the marble almost seems to come to life."

Wake smiled. "Really?"

Pakow nodded vigorously. "All his things are like that, all exquisite, but when you begin to watch them, they seem to literally live and breathe. You can almost see the lion preparing to leap, and you can feel the deep fear of the hunter."

Wake placed a long forefinger to the side of his mouth. "Sounds amazing, though I'm still not sure why you're telling me all this."

Pakow looked back down, and squirmed for another moment. "I know you're planning to use HMHVV-Charlie on him, and I worry."

Suddenly it all made sense to Wake. "You're concerned about the anomalies we've discovered when using Charlie on magically potent creatures?"

Pakow nodded. "I know we've taken steps to reduce the risk, but I . . . I think it would be a mistake to allow any risk to his talent. It would be a shame if this man lost his ability."

Wake thought about it for a moment. "And what do you suggest we do instead? You know what the Beta strain would do to him."

Pakow shuddered visibly, then swallowed. "I guess I just don't understand why we have to do this at all."

Wake frowned. "We are at a very delicate juncture. If something were to interrupt the work, we could lose valuable time trying to back-track. Marco D'imato's our most successful subject so far, and I'm not ready to lose him. We may need to study him further. All we've got to do is keep him placated a little while longer. After that, D'imato's inevitable deterioration will no longer make him a problem for us."

Pakow's shoulders sagged just a bit, but his face remained defiant. "Then I suggest we use the Delta strain."

Wake laughed, throwing back his head. "By the gods, Dr. Pakow, those are words I never thought to hear coming out of your mouth, especially with Delta being virtually untested."

Pakow leaned forward, his forehead covered with a sheen of sweat. "We know that Delta *should* have no adverse affects on his talent, and if Delta proves out, then he would be the first to be unaffected by bloodlust, the first to be able to eat normal food. If this man is the kind of person I think he is, I know he would rather have his life endangered than to risk losing his art."

Wake's smile widened, "That is, of course, if strain Delta proves out."

Pakow nodded. "I understand the possible ramifications, as

well as the potential for something unforeseen happening. God knows we don't want another Marco on our hands, but I think he would rather—"

Wake held up his hand to silence the other man, and turned to look at the tank. He thought about it for a moment. Finally he turned back to Pakow and clapped one skeletal hand on the small man's arm. "You make a good point, though it's not so much that which sways me. No, you've shown me something else. If Delta doesn't prove out, the young man will die. No exceptions. However, if Delta works, then our problems with Marco D'imato may vanish."

He laughed again. "All right, Dr. Pakow, you have my permission. However, before we administer the treatment, I want a full battery run on Delta, from RNA reversion to white cell count. The works. You're going to have to bust your hump to have all that ready by the time he's finally prepped."

The relief on Pakow's face made Wake a trifle uncomfortable, but he let it pass. "I'll do it all, no problem," Pakow said, and even managed a smile.

Wake looked at him for just a moment longer before getting up to leave the room. As he waited for the contamination seal to begin unlocking, he spoke over his shoulder. "This man's work must be extraordinary. Remind me to come to your home to see it some time."

In the glass, Wake caught Pakow's shudder of revulsion, but his voice was steady. "Of course, Dr. Wake. I would be most pleased for you to come over and see it."

Wake walked through the door and headed for his personal quarters, two levels down.

10

Susceptibility to sunlight is the only thing preventing vampires from becoming the dominant life form on this planet. If Ordo Maximus succeeds in creating an HMHVV strain without that weakness, vampires will no longer be detectable except by sophisticated blood tests, and this new anonymity will enable them to take over every institution in society with no one the wiser until it is far too late. Humans and metahumans will be doomed, save for those few kept alive to breed the vampires' food supply.

—Martin de Vries, *Shadows at Noon,* posted to Shadowland BBS, 24 May 2057

By the time Rachel had walked the five blocks back to Warren's doss, the anticipation of the upcoming meeting was making her giddy with excitement. Finally, she was going to meet Flak's team of runners.

She was worried about Warren, but she had confidence in Flak; his team's rep was among the best. Also, de Vries was obviously a creature of uncanny power and resources. How could Warren's captors hope to succeed? They had no idea who and what they were up against.

Rachel tried to calm herself, but the excitement that kept grabbing hold also kept her from paying attention to what she was doing. She'd already walked the final half-block to Warren's doss before she realized something was different, and by then it was too late.

A Toyota Elite limousine idled in front of Warren's place, its huge engine making just the slightest vibration in the muggy air.

Rachel was so busy wondering why de Vries had ordered a limo that she didn't even notice the two armed men standing in the shadows near the doorway until she was only steps away.

She took a deep breath to keep from screaming, and continued walking past the doss. Her mind kicked into overdrive, and the only thing she could think was what a fool she'd been to trust de Vries. He was obviously in cahoots with the sick vampire from the picture. Who else but a corporate boss would roll around in a car like that and have huge bodyguards with such obvious mods?

She was just past the doorway when one of the guards stepped up to block her path. He was human, standing just shy of two meters, and was impossibly wide. His brown suit fit awkwardly over his misshapen frame, and the gleam of metal in the socket of his left eye gave him a corpse-like expression.

"Miss Harlan," he said. "Where are you going?" He smiled, but that did nothing to quell the bolt of fear that shot through Rachel, turning her bowels to water.

"You got the wrong chica, chummer." She tried to sidestep him, but he moved easily to block her.

"Please, Miss Harlan, no harm will come to you. We were told to expect you, and Wolf and Mister de Vries are waiting."

That stopped her. "Wolf?"

"Yes, he's inside, and he is somewhat pressed for time."

Rachel knew about Wolf and Raven. What runner didn't? They were like the Robin Hoods of the Seattle sprawl, like white rumors starving mothers might tell their children when the little ones had to go to sleep hungry. Something like, "Go to sleep and maybe tomorrow Wolf and Raven will stop by. Then everything will be all right. But if you're bad, Kid Stealth will come with his metal feet."

Rachel had heard about them too often, and from people she trusted, for there not to be something behind the tales.

Still, she couldn't believe that the man she was about to meet could possibly be the same person.

She turned and climbed the stairs to the door, then went inside. Warren's doss was better lit than it had been last time she'd been here, and she could smell fresh coffee. Not soykaf, but real, honest-to-god coffee. The smell made her mouth water. She'd only had real coffee once, and the taste was unforgettable, so rich and dark and strong. It made soykaf taste like bitter swill.

Rachel became aware of low voices as she stepped into the living room.

"Welcome back, Miss Harlan. Did everything go well?" It was de Vries. He was sitting with his back to her, not even bothering to turn to see if it really was her. She shrugged the thought away. If he was so powerful, he would have known she was coming even before she entered the doss.

Still, de Vries wasn't what held her attention.

The man sitting opposite him was small, but exuded power, a brutal physical magnetism that at once attracted and repelled her. He was older by a good twenty years, going gray around the muzzle and on the sides of his full head of hair, but his face was smooth. Except where scars tracked its surface.

He wore a gray flannel suit that showed off his powerful physique without sacrificing class. His back was straight and proud, and in one hand, he had a cane. Its tip rested on the floor as he twisted the silver wolf's-head handle in a lazy circle.

Even as all these things registered, she caught his eye, and for just that instant, she knew how a wild thing must feel when caught in the glare of headlights. Fascination and fear threatened to overwhelm her, and she thought she would just stand there, mid-stride, and stare into those killer eyes until he casually walked over and ripped out her throat.

The second passed, and suddenly she was looking into a normal pair of eyes again, pleasant brown with flecks of gray.

The man smiled and stood up, leaning heavily on his cane for support. His grin was the most comforting thing she'd seen that night.

"Good evening, Miss Harlan. My name is Wolfgang Kies. I'm sorry if I startled you."

Rachel swallowed and forced herself to continue into the room. "It's a pleasure to meet you . . . Mister Kies." This was more than she could ever have imagined. In all those nights, lying awake and thinking about the shadows, thinking about what it would be like to run them, she'd never imagined that one day she would be face to face with the man known as Wolf. The tremor of excitement she'd felt walking back to the doss was replaced with a *quake* of excitement, and for the briefest instant, she let herself forget why she was here, forget the reason behind Wolf's visit.

He walked painfully over to her, favoring his left leg, but the smile never left his face. He took her hand gently in his, and led her to the chair he'd just vacated. "Please sit. Martin was just filling me in on what's been going on. I sympathize with your situation, Miss Harlan, but—"

"Rachel."

Wolf turned to her with a look of mild surprise, as if he were unused to being interrupted. "Excuse me?"

"My name is Rachel. Everybody keeps calling me 'Miss Harlan' tonight, and it's making me uncomfortable. Miss Harlan was my mother."

Wolf turned to de Vries, who smiled as Wolf let out a small laugh. "You're right, Martin. I like her." He turned back to Rachel. "As I was saying, I just got the scan on your situation, and I was telling Martin I wish I could help. Unfortunately, my own team's got some big problems right now."

De Vries laughed softly. "I must admit, I was surprised to see you in a limo, let alone with bodyguards."

Wolf's smile faded slightly, "Raven's orders. Until this whole matter is settled, no one in the organization is to travel without protection. It chafes a bit, but I understand his reasoning. And that, of course, is the same reason I can't give you much help at this moment."

De Vries sighed, but Rachel didn't think he looked especially surprised. "I thought you might say that, but I had to ask. I know you've got your plate pretty full right now. I could probably convince you that this situation is big enough to warrant you leaving off whatever else you're doing and help us, but I won't put you in that position. Still, I thank you for coming down on such short notice."

Wolf's smile faded completely for the first time since Rachel had entered the room, and a look of infinite sadness crept into those deadly eyes. "Of course, Martin. It's been too long, and I know you wouldn't have called if the situation weren't dire. I simply don't have the resources to back your play right now. After what happened to Kid Stealth, we've been up to our neck in this thing."

De Vries nodded. "Will he pull through?"

Wolf smiled again, but now it was a tight thing, one just barely holding back the anger. "Yes. But it's put us in a very awkward situation, and Raven's out for blood."

De Vries stood, in a swift motion that made Rachel wince involuntarily, but that seemed to have no effect on Wolf. The two shook hands, and she got the feeling they had once been very close.

"My friend," said Wolf softly, "don't let it be so long next time. The rest of us age a lot faster than you do."

De Vries laughed. "If I live through this, I promise we'll head to the country and do some night hunting. Swear."

Wolf held de Vries' grip for a moment more, then dropped his hand and began to limp to the door. At the door he turned, as if he'd just remembered something. "The least I can do is arrange safe transport through Hell's Kitchen for you. We don't want things to go south on you before you even get to where you're going."

De Vries nodded without saying anything.

Wolf smiled, and pulled a card out of his jacket. "Call this number when you're ready to go in. Use my name and you won't have any problems."

"Goodbye, my friend."

"Goodbye." Wolf turned his gaze to Rachel again, and gave her a brief, sad smile. "It was a pleasure meeting you, Rachel. What you're up against isn't going to be pretty, but trust Martin. He knows what he's doing, and despite how he looks, he really is one of the good guys."

Rachel watched silently as the man left, feeling as if she'd understood only about a quarter of what had just transpired.

De Vries turned back to the room and smiled, but unlike Wolf's good-natured grin, the vampire's made her shiver. "Well, I wasn't actually expecting his help, but it never hurts to ask. How did things go on your end?"

Rachel pulled a smoke out of her bag, and lit it. She checked the clock on the trid rig. "Flak'll be here in about an hour. He and his friends will hear you out, then decide."

De Vries' smile grew even wider. "Excellent."

11

You're telling me that after all I've done for you, after I've discovered a procedure that will net you billions in nuyen, you now have the audacity to question my methods? The Léonization process is the pinnacle of life-lengthening procedures, and you now seek grounds to dismiss me? Are you mad?

—Oslo Wake, defending his use of metahuman subjects before the Board of Ethics and Review, Universal Omnitech, New York City. Transcript #ETH678, p. 347, 20 September 2051

Raul Pakow pulled the needle from Warren D'imato's arm and set it on the small metal tray. Warren looked up at him, dazed. He'd come to in the operating theater, where Pakow was carrying out various preparatory procedures. Pakow was trying to tell him quickly what was going on.

"Which piece did you buy?" Warren asked.

"I purchased 'Past Battles' at a show of your work a year or so ago. Down in the U District."

Warren's look of confusion turned to one of distant pleasure. He was about to speak but Pakow cut him off. "That piece of stone is the only thing keeping you alive right now. Like I said, the man who owns this place has plans for you that you couldn't imagine in your worst nightmares. I was blind for awhile, but not anymore. Now, I know I've got to try and stop this madness, but if Wake were to find out what I've done, there's no telling what might happen. I've put my whole family at risk trying to help you. Something's happened to him, and it gets worse everyday. He was always strange, but now he seems downright certifiable."

Pakow looked down at Warren, whose eyes had become unfocused. "You rest now. Someone should be coming soon to help you. I make no promises, but I'll do what I can to get you out of here."

Pakow put the protective straps back in place, then went over to the deck on the console. Jacking into the Matrix, he followed a series of maneuvers he'd been using for almost four months, and found himself in a small drop box.

As quickly as he could, he left a message. *I've bought us some more time, but not much. You must pick up the package within forty-eight hours, or else it will be spoiled.*

Pakow didn't bother putting a name to the message. He knew that de Vries would figure it out. Jacking out, he took one last look at Warren D'imato, and shuddered. He hoped the vampire hunter was as good as his word, because he suddenly felt as if he'd put all of his chips into one slot, and if that slot didn't hold, he wouldn't survive.

12

De Vries uses a variety of strategies when hunting vampires. He prefers to battle them hand-to-hand, draining blood and essence from his targets. A curious magical artifact he discovered on an Indonesian trip in 2045 is said to give him an edge in such duels, though its nature is unknown. However, in the case of an exceptionally dangerous opponent, he has been known to hire samurai with extreme capabilities—explosives and frag-lethal fire and blast results.

—Posted to Shadowland BBS by Doktor Freeman and the Deathcore Kid, 22 March 2055

Rachel paced her way around the living room for what seemed the thousandth time. Then she walked over to the now-overflowing ashtray and stubbed out her cigarette with a fierce jabbing motion.

Seated on the blue futon, de Vries reached into his duster and pulled out his pack of Platinum Selects. Rachel had run out of smokes almost thirty minutes ago, and they had fallen into a pattern. She would pace, gulping coffee and smoking until she'd finished her cigarette, at which time de Vries, without being asked, would give her another. Then the process would repeat while he himself continued to chain-smoke.

"If you don't mind my saying so, Rachel, if you have one more cup of coffee, I think your head might explode. That is, if your lungs don't collapse first."

Rachel turned to him angrily. "I do mind." She took a deep drag of her cigarette.

De Vries laughed. "Well, it's nice to see that you no longer have any fear of me. But you might want to consider being more polite. After all, I'm the one doing you a favor."

There was a small beep, and de Vries looked at his wristphone. "If you'll excuse me for a moment." He answered the call. Rachel watched him talk quietly, expecting bad news, but suddenly his face brightened. "That is good news. You're sure of the origin of the message? Excellent."

He disconnected, and looked up at Rachel with a small smile. "It would appear that we've been given a little more time than I'd originally thought. Still, it isn't as much as I'd have liked."

Rachel turned toward the door again, and her frustration boiled to the surface. "Where in the hell are they? They should have been here already."

She turned to look at de Vries, who had a faraway look in his eyes. "Your friends are very close, my dear. Very close, indeed. In fact, I'm quite impressed."

Rachel's forehead suddenly prickled with sweat. "What are you talking about?"

De Vries' eyes snapped back into focus. "Your friends are most cunning. Tricky, tricky, tricky. They'll be here in a few moments, so I suggest you have a seat. It wouldn't do for them to get over-anxious, so why don't you come and sit next to me?"

Rachel continued to look at him without comprehension.

"My dear," said de Vries again. "What I'm trying to tell you is that you're about to be treated to a sight few people not connected with the military ever get to see. So, sit down. Now."

Almost without realizing she was doing it, Rachel crossed the room and sat down shoulder to shoulder with de Vries.

As she relaxed into the sofa cushions, the lights in the

apartment seemed to dim, flickered twice, and then came back up.

Rachel jumped as the figure of Flak seemed to materialize suddenly in the center of the living room. Towering only a few steps away, Flak had changed out of his work outfit, and was now dressed in heavy camos that seemed to shift and swirl in the light, making it hard for Rachel to look at them. He wore a hood she recognized as a balaclava, even though it was pushed back up on his forehead. She could just make out the handle of a big gun strapped to Flak's back, but near his hip, where the barrel should have been, she could see six small barrels, configured in a circle. She'd never seen anything like it, and just the sight of such a piece of hardware sent a small thrill through her.

"There won't be any show," said the troll, opening his hands to show they were empty.

"What the hell is going on?" said Rachel, her voice too loud in the ensuing silence.

Flak ignored her. "Mister de Vries, if that is who you are, please be so good as to remain seated, with your hands grasping your knees. It would be appreciated."

Rachel turned to de Vries, who wore a small grin, but did as he was told.

"Now, Rachel, if you will slowly rise to your feet, and walk directly to your left."

"Flak? What's going on?"

"Rach, just do it."

Rachel stood, and moved to her left as Flak said, "Very good. As you probably already know, you're being covered from four different directions, and even though only an idiot might not be able to tell that you're a vampire, I trust you understand that every weapon trained on you is capable of killing you. Even if you managed to dodge, or deflect the first volley, eventually one will find its mark and you'll be yesterday's news. Are we clear on this?"

Rachel turned her head, but she couldn't see anyone but de Vries, herself, and Flak in the room.

De Vries laughed, a soft, deep sound that seemed to fill the room like thunder.

"Is there something about this situation that you find amusing, Deadman?" The low growl in Flak's voice made the hair on the back of Rachel's neck stand on end.

De Vries' laugh died to a chuckle. "Absolutely not. I'm impressed. I thought you and your compatriots were going to put on the full pageant for us. It shows an encouraging amount of self-control for you to handle things this way."

Rachel shook her head. "Will somebody please tell me what the frag is going on here?"

De Vries turned his head in her direction, but his eyes never left Flak. "Your friend is very concerned about your safety, and obviously knows enough about me to comprehend that I could use a spell to influence your thoughts, or make you lie to him, or do whatever I desired. So he's decided that until he has a better grasp on the situation, he's going to remove you from the equation, at the same time limiting any possible retribution I might bring into play. Provided, of course, that I'm not who I've claimed to be, or that I mean you any harm. Does that about sum it up?"

Rachel looked to Flak, who gave her a tight, quick smile. "Close enough, Deadman."

"Fine," said de Vries, standing slowly. "Now, if you'll be so good as to let the rest of your team come out of their hiding places, we can get down to business. I've been able to smell them since they came in, and I know exactly where every one of them is. I can also hear that the heartbeat of your elven mage has just increased slightly in tempo. Your human physical adept is holding steady, though I believe she will find that her weapon is useless against the barrier I have erected."

De Vries sighed. "But I didn't really ask Rachel to invite you for banter like this. Time is short, and while I'm sure you could easily spend the next twenty minutes trying to determine if I'm on the level, I think that would be less than prudent. So I propose we dispense with the preliminaries."

For the first time since Flak had appeared in the room, Rachel saw a look of unease cross his face. "Just what did you have in mind?"

Though de Vries seemed not to move so much as a muscle, a small card appeared in his hand. "This is the private number of a person you know very well and whom you trust completely. He's expecting your call."

With a flick of the wrist, de Vries sent the card spinning toward Flak, who snatched it out of the air in a lightning motion, never taking his eyes off de Vries.

From off to her right, near the doorway of the kitchen, Rachel heard a soft, female voice say, "I got him, Flak."

Rachel turned, but she couldn't see where the voice came from. "Hey," she said. "This is starting to freak me out a bit, all right, and just when I was beginning to think that nothing was ever going to freak me out again. So could we just knock it off with all this macho bulldrek and get down to business?"

Once again, Flak ignored her. He turned the card over in his hand, and Rachel saw his eyes go wide. "Wolf?" He looked back up at de Vries, who nodded.

"All right, everybody. Unpack." Without another word, he slipped the card into his camouflage vest, as if he were returning a holy relic to its resting place.

Rachel turned just in time to see one person step in from the kitchen, one from near the front door, and one from the bedroom. How they had all gotten there without making any noise boggled her mind. All three were dressed like Flak, in camos and ski masks that hid their faces from view. All three carried high-tensile crossbows and tacticom gear.

De Vries smiled, as he looked around the room. "Excellent, my children. Everybody make yourself comfortable. The young lady and I have a very long story and a very short amount of time. According to information I've just received, we've been given another forty-eight hours, but beyond that, I cannot promise the survivability of the person we are going to rescue."

13

Julius D'imato is officially listed as the number two man at Fratellanza, Inc. (see FBI File #894-656LY), though evidence suggests he is actually the brains behind much of the outfit's success. During the two months his brother Marco D'imato (see FBI File #894-666LM) was recovering from the "accident" that left him a cripple, Julius D'imato managed to improve Fratellanza's profit margin by forty-two percent.

—FBI File Access #894-676LM, Subject: Julius D'imato. Codeword: Brotherhood. Clearance: Classified Top Secret. Transmission intercept by Fratellanza deckers, 01 January 2059

Dust filled the high, cavernous ceiling of the huge Fratellanza-owned warehouse near Devil's Lake in Redmond. Early morning sunlight, streaming through the high, dirty windows, caught the motes of dust and made them dance in the air.

Throughout the warehouse, a small corporate army of fifty men hurried around equipment, servicing weapons and the five large vehicles that dominated the center of the warehouse.

Julius D'imato stood in the center of all the activity, but was hardly aware of the men yelling to one another as they loaded four Citymaster riot vehicles. The main truck, an Ares Mobmaster Command and Control vehicle, sat closest to the wall of the warehouse as four men finished arc-welding a massive steel wedge to the front.

Where are you? thought Julius. In his mind, he pictured Warren as he'd last seen him, at the funeral, his broad shoulders fixed, his jaw set in that angry line that always seemed to appear during family events. *I should have made my move against Marco sooner. Marco's vampirism has put my son's life in danger . . . that, and my lack of foresight.*

Julius shook his head. This kind of self-recrimination wasn't going to get him anywhere, and it certainly wasn't going to get Warren back. When Warren was safely returned, then and only then would he consider how his own actions might have put his son's life in danger.

Since the death of his wife, Rolanda, almost sixteen years before, Julius had done everything in his power to make sure Warren was safe and happy. Even as a teenager, Warren had felt an aversion to the family business and made no bones about it. The "covert warfare business," he called it. And so the only way to make Warren happy was for Julius to allow him to become separate from the family and Fratellanza, Inc.

For just a moment, Julius let himself hate his brother. Ever since Marco's infection, he'd become a different man. Though always ruthless, he'd also shown at least a modicum of familial sentiment. Now, even with Julius' help to keep things under wraps, Marco was like a machine. Caring about nothing but his own needs and designs. He hadn't waited even a day after Derek's death to begin badgering Julius about making Warren the next heir.

Julius had been concerned about the future of Fratellanza for some time now. Someone had to worry about the legacy of the family business. What with Marco's increasing instability, Julius didn't know what would happen next. Anyway, it was all in the hands of the lawyers now, and they were the best money could buy.

There was a shout from the back of the warehouse, in the direction of the soundproof room where Killian, Julius' personal mage, had secreted himself almost five hours before.

It had been a long shot, trying ritual magic to find Warren, and Julius was still skeptical. However, he was also desperate. Every feeler he'd put out on the street had come back null.

Julius walked quickly back to the far end of the warehouse, stepping around men in street armor who were loading guns and ammo into the back of the other vehicles.

Killian was a short man, with wire-rim glasses and a balding head that made him look more like a highschool English teacher than a gifted magician. He was being supported by two guards and his face was covered with dirt and sweat, but there was no mistaking the look of triumph on the little man's face.

"Got him." Killian's voice was deep, a rumble that seemed completely out of place with his timid demeanor. "He's still alive, and he's close."

Julius felt a loose trembling hit his stomach first, then spread to the rest of his limbs. He hadn't realized how tense he'd been, until that moment. For a second he didn't say anything, and Killian looked at him strangely, the look of triumph replaced by one of concern.

"Where?" It was all Julius could manage, his voice strangled in his throat.

Killian shook off the two men who were supporting him, and came over to Julius. In a quiet voice he said, "You all right?"

Julius nodded, suddenly impatient with everything but struggling to keep his cool. "Where?" he repeated.

Killian nodded. "In the astral, street signs are impossible to read, but there was no mistaking the geography. He's in some kind of research compound in Hell's Kitchen, which puts him about two hours from here, counting checkpoints and the like. I couldn't get too close. The place is guarded like nothing I've ever seen before. Everything from alarms to paranormals. The background count there is nothing short of explosive. I got a headache just scanning the place. It's going to take everything you got to bust him out."

Julius nodded again, and felt the strength flow back into his body. Now that he had a concrete objective, an actual enemy to face, he was on track. It was the waiting that had almost killed him.

He nodded. "I want you to get together with Biggs. He's in charge of the decker. Narrow his range of search for him, and get me as much info as you can on this place, everything from tactical to shipping requirements. I want to know what kind of deliveries they get, how much food they eat, and what they use to wipe their hoops. Everything. And I want it an hour ago."

Even through Killian's smile, Julius could see the exhaustion. Julius put a hand on the smaller man's shoulder. "Good work. After you've talked to Biggs, get yourself some rest."

Julius turned to the men all around him in the warehouse. "All right, everybody! Listen up!"

The raucous noise calmed quickly, until the only sound filling the room was the dull whine of the portable generators.

"We got a locale, and within the hour, we should have more tech info. If this place pans out the way I think it will, we'll hit them tonight, under cover of dark. I want all vehicles running silent by noon. We'll take them quick and quiet, and hit them so hard and fast they won't even know we're there until they're already dead."

Silence was the only reply. These men had been hand-picked by Julius, and they were all professionals who knew the risks. But they were also the most loyal men Julius knew. There wasn't one of them who wouldn't lay down his life for this job, because each one knew that if the tables were turned, the same effort would be made to rescue him.

Julius gazed around at his men once again, and wondered how many of them wouldn't be coming back. If the place was fortified the way Killian said, this whole thing might end up being a blood bath. Still, these were competent warriors with skill and experience. If anybody could pull this off, it was them.

"All right, that's it. Back to work."

With that, the warehouse exploded back into activity.

14

In his younger days, Martin de Vries was known as an exceptional mage who became an initiate of Ordo Maximus while completing his hermetic studies at Oxford. Then he dropped out and began to finance his own researches into magical threats. His contemporaries found him paranoid, antisocial, and obsessive, but de Vries was convinced a secret society of vampires was planning to take over the whole world for their own insane purposes. Despite the ridicule he met at every turn, he undertook a series of one-man vampire hunts in Europe between 2040 and 2051. Then he completely vanished from sight for some eighteen months.

—Posted to Shadowland BBS by Doktor Freeman
and the Deathcore Kid, 22 March 2055

Just inside the perimeter of Hell's Kitchen, with the dim pool of the only working street light showing dry, gray dust swirling over her feet, Sinunu Sol stood to one side of the stepvan, painting her albino flesh with a multicolored camo stick. With each angry stroke of the stick across the flesh of her face, she had to up-end the stick and look into the small mirror on the stick's bottom. The scars on her face tended to cause the camo to bunch up and leave tracks that might give her heat signature away to anyone peeking into the thermal spectrum.

"Damn it," she said.

Out of the back of the van, Truxa Fin poked her head around the corner. Her long brown hair was pulled back into a tight French braid, showing off her delicately pointed ears. Truxa was dressed similarly to Sinunu, swirling desert blacks that seemed to shift into shades of gray with each movement, and down around her neck rested a face-covering balaclava hood with built-in air filter and tacticom gear. Truxa was small for an elf, one of the things Sinunu liked about her. Somehow, Truxa made the androgynous battle wear seem feminine, almost sexy. "Sin, baby, what's wrong?"

Sinunu looked up, and couldn't help but smile. It was like that every time she saw Truxa. A calm, giddy feeling Sinunu had no control over. "Nothing. Just a little bent about having to babysit the bimbo. She shouldn't even be coming along."

Truxa smiled and leaned down, kissing Sinunu firmly on the lips, letting her soft tongue slide gently into the bigger woman's mouth. After a second, Truxa pulled back. "We all know how you feel, baby, but Sandman is almost in, and you need to be quiet, 'kay?"

Suddenly, Sinunu felt something stir deep in her gut, something black and ugly. More ugly than any of her teachers at the White Oak Foundation would ever have been able to put there. It was an instinct that was undeniable. With an almost vicious gesture, Sinunu grabbed Truxa by the shoulder and lifted her easily. Pulling her close, Sinunu kissed her, hard. She poured everything she felt into that kiss, everything she had never really been able to put into words about how much she loved Truxa.

After a second, Truxa melted into her embrace, and returned the kiss with just as much passion. When Sinunu finally broke away, Truxa said, "Damn, girl. What was that for?"

Sinunu just shrugged, setting Truxa back on her feet. "I won't be covering your six tonight, and I guess it's got me worried. You watch your back." Which was the truth, but not nearly close to how desperate Sinunu was beginning to feel. Something was going to go wrong, and somebody was going to get hurt, she knew it, just as surely as she knew her own name.

Truxa reached up with a long, delicate hand, and gently stroked some of Sinunu's camo back into place. "You just worry about yourself, baby. You're the one with all the extra baggage tonight."

Sinunu nodded. "I just hope the recon information is steady. There's no way I'm going to let that biff frag us."

Truxa smiled. "Chill, baby. The recon's tight. You know Flak wouldn't let us walk in without it."

From inside the stepvan, they heard Sandman's whisper coming over the small speaker mounted on the inside wall of the van. "I'm in," he said. "Damn, this guy's good."

Truxa and Sinunu turned in the direction of the back doors, but came up short as the tall, stooped figure of Martin de Vries seemed to materialize in front of them. There was a grave expression on his face. "It looks like we have luck on our side tonight."

Sinunu felt her face tighten. Maybe it was because for the first time in her life, she had to deal with someone who actually frightened her. Or maybe it was the fact that with his pale skin and lifeless eyes, Martin de Vries looked like her. Like an albino. It made her think that maybe they had more in common than she liked to consider. Still, she fought against her feelings. He was a Johnson, like so many others before him, and he was paying them ridiculously well for what seemed like a straightforward, if very dangerous, assignment.

"Yeah, lucky us." Sinunu started to step around him, but de Vries put up a hand.

"If you would be so good as to have a word with me, in private?"

The vampire addressed Sinunu, but the apologetic smile he gave Truxa gave Sinunu an immediate urge to smash his face. For just a second, the idea that the woman she loved and this creature should ever have come into contact seemed so repulsive and despicable that she had to do a quick four-breath to find her center and control her emotions.

Truxa, however, seemed to have none of her feelings. Smiling sweetly, she said, "Of course, Mister de Vries." With that, she circled around him and up into the van.

Left alone with the vampire, Sinunu felt her anger drain out, leaving her hollow and empty. "What do you want?"

De Vries stood there for a moment, looking at her with such empathy that Sinunu was immediately uncomfortable again. "If you've got nothing to say, then I need to be finishing up."

De Vries looked out across the desolation that was Hell's Kitchen, the sweeping volcanic dust that only seemed to settle when there was a torrential downpour. When he spoke, his voice was so soft that Sinunu had to strain to make out the words. "Have you ever read about yourself? Listened to what others were saying about you without their knowing you where eavesdropping?"

Sinunu shook her head. "I don't care what people say about me, and unlike you, I try to keep a lower profile."

De Vries laughed softly, and turned to look at her. "I'm going to tell you something that no one else knows."

Sinunu rolled her pink eyes. "Oh, joy."

De Vries went on as if he hadn't heard her. "Before my life took its current course, I was married. Did you know that?"

Sinunu shrugged. "Didn't know, didn't care. You going for some sort of point here?"

De Vries smiled softly, and for just a moment, Sinunu was sorry she'd responded so callously. "Yes, I was married, to a wonderful woman named Josephine. I'd just finished up my doctorate in hermetic studies, and it looked as if I was on top of the world. Of course, I gave no thought to the fact that things like vampires and wendigos were running around the earth again. And even if I had, it wouldn't have caused me any concern."

Grunting, Sinunu said, "Yeah, ignorance can be a real killer."

De Vries smiled again. "Exactly. Well, Josephine got pregnant, and I was going to be a father. She was only five months along, but she was a delicate woman and the pregnancy was hard on her. I was called to a faculty meeting one night, and it ran late."

Suddenly the short, white hairs on the back of Sinunu's neck stood up straight. She realized she didn't want to hear the rest of what de Vries was going to say, didn't want to feel any sympathy for this creature, but his eyes held her.

"I came home to an empty house. Josephine had simply vanished. I contacted the police, and they searched. For six days I went out of my mind. I couldn't eat, I couldn't sleep, I sat by the telecom in that big empty house, and I prayed."

Sinunu thought about her days at White Oak, those hateful days when she was being groomed to become the great mother of all white humanity. Prayer had been a big thing at White Oak, and she had come to despise all the pitiful wishing and pleading that seemed to go hand in hand with bowing to some higher god. Still, when de Vries spoke of it, she felt the desperation he must have known during that time. Sinunu turned to look out into the hot darkness as de Vries continued.

"On the seventh night, I was sleeping fitfully in my chair in the living room. I suppose if I'd been able to sleep well, I would be dead now."

De Vries paused, and despite herself, Sinunu said, "Josephine?"

"Actually, no. Not at first. I woke feeling something crawling up my leg. I thought I might still be dreaming, because when I looked down, there was a tiny, white thing hanging off my trousers. Malformed and hideous, it was no more than twenty centimeters long, white as a ghost, still covered in a sticky red slime. Its tiny arms were digging into the fabric of my pants, and as I looked down, the thing looked up with bright red eyes."

Sinunu knew what was coming, and for the first time in years, she felt nauseous.

"That's when Josephine came in. And in a flash, I knew what had happened. I knew. Josephine stood there in the doorway with the dim light behind her, like some kind of dark angel. But she wasn't looking at me. She was looking at the thing on my leg, calling to it, like any normal mother whose child has crawled too far for her to be comfortable."

Sinunu turned to him. "Your child?"

De Vries nodded. "Yes. I understand what happened now. When Josephine was infected with the virus, and her body died, it rejected anything of flesh that was not its own. It purged itself of the little fetus. Unfortunately, the fetus was also now infected, so in a fashion, it survived the miscarriage."

Sinunu thought her heart was going to break at the thought. "What did you do."

De Vries shrugged. "I staked them. Josephine didn't even resist. She simply begged that I look out for her baby after she was gone."

Sinunu found herself taking a step back from de Vries. The utter coldness in his voice chilled her to the bone.

"They were the first. After that, I managed to find the creature who had done this to my family, and I staked him as well. My life was changed from that moment on, and it has led me down paths so dark and frightening that very little of the man I once was remains."

Sinunu felt anger rise in her like a volcano, heaving and out of control. "Why are you telling me this?"

De Vries' eyes softened. "I said very little of that man remains, but enough for me to understand how you feel about tonight. Enough for me to realize the care you have for the elf and the concerns you have about bringing Rachel along."

"So?"

De Vries stepped in close, and it took everything in Sinunu's power not to fling herself backward. "Just this. There is more to Rachel than you can guess, and she stands to lose as much as you tonight, so in one sense, she had a right to insist on coming along. Also, if things go wrong, and our target is damaged in any way, we need her there. He'll need to see a familiar face, or else he might screw the whole thing up.

"But I didn't tell you that story to justify my backing Rachel's desire to come along. I simply wanted you to know that I understand your concern and now it is mine as well. If everything goes right, then we'll all get out safely, a little wiser about how dark the night can be, but otherwise no worse for the wear. But if things go wrong, I'll make you this promise. I will do everything in my power to keep you from having to go through the same pain I went through all those years ago."

Through tight lips, Sinunu asked, "That supposed to make me feel better?"

De Vries smiled. "It should. Over the years, I have become more powerful than you could possibly imagine. I will use every trick, every skill I possess to make sure your love comes through tonight intact."

Sinunu smiled, a tight, ugly thing. "And if she doesn't?"

De Vries stepped back. "Then I will help you put her out of her misery."

15

Of course, the procedure was radical and involved incredible risks. Surely, you realize that the potential benefits outweighed those risks. That's why I was using SINless, rather than citizens. After all, it's not like they would be missed.

—Oslo Wake, defending his use of metahuman subjects before the Board of Ethics and Review, Universal Omnitech, New York City. Transcript #ETH678, p. 678, 21 September 2051

Oslo Wake's office was a small, private place buried deep beneath the main compound. Rough rock walls contrasted sharply with the soft lighting and the rich Persian rugs that covered the floor. The air in the office was warm and damp, heated naturally by a thermal spring in the bedrock, and it smelled slightly of sulfur.

Sitting at his antique oak desk, which had begun to warp from the sultry atmosphere, Wake slipped the small dermal patch into the crook of his right elbow, and hissed as the shaking tension immediately eased up. He rolled his sleeve down to cover the patch as well as his emaciated arms. In the last two years, Wake hadn't slept more than three hours a night. For a while, it had been the work that kept him awake, kept him at his deck trying to crack the secret of the virus metagene. But after a time, despair had invaded the work.

That was when the drugs had become a necessity. The goal

was close now, so close he could almost smell success, but there was still so much ground to cover if his plan to save metahumanity was to work. He would not rest until all metahumans could be infected without any deleterious side effects, and that presented complications that still boggled Wake's mind.

He was very close to a breakthrough on normal humans. They were the easiest to work with, and not just because there was so much more information available on them, but because the HMHVV strains acted fairly consistently on humans. With metas, Wake had discovered the hard way that each strain not only affected the individual species differently, but there had also been marked differences in how each strain affected each test subject. Most variants were due to magical ability, but with some strains of the virus, there were variables that Wake hadn't even come close to pinning down.

He put his head in his hands, rubbing the heels of his palms into his eyes. Then he took a deep breath, the light from his touch screen playing over his face. There were times he wished he could risk getting a datajack. It would make his work so much easier, but he also knew what it would do to his magical ability. Even a trode rig had the nasty habit of giving him a headache. Flatscreens had sufficed for years, and they would continue to do so.

He had been working on this one genetic sequence for almost a week now, and he was nowhere closer to figuring where the nips and tucks should go than when he'd started.

Wake took a deep, shuddering breath, rubbed his watering eyes, and tried to calm himself. "All right," he said softly to himself. "The metagene seems variably activated, depending upon background mana levels. So what I need is a scale to accurately measure the mana at a particular time and place. It must be kept constant."

He squinted and leaned in close to the screen, which was filled with a scrolling mass of nucleotide sequences and a modeling of which ones would be activated at a given mana level.

Suddenly, his private line beeped. "Go ahead," he said, without taking his eyes from the information rolling in front of him.

Just to the left and at the bottom of his screen, a small square opened, showing the heavily made-up face of Marco D'imato. Wake suppressed a vicious grin. The pushy bastard just wasn't going to learn.

"What can I do for you, Mr. D'imato?" Wake kept his voice neutral, and went back to studying the DNA sequence.

"We might have a situation on our hands."

Wake touched the screen, and the flow of information came to a halt. "Do tell."

Marco paused, and for just a moment, Wake got the impression that the vampire was uncomfortable. "First, let me ask you a question. How is the progress on Warren?"

Wake leaned back, actually intrigued now. This game of cat and mouse wasn't usually Marco's style. Wake steepled his fingers under his chin. "Excellent, actually. We are using the latest strain of the virus, which should allow for more improvements on the original model than even you had hoped for."

Marco's eyes shifted, but Wake knew that was simply an effect of the contacts sliding slightly. Still, it only made him look more nervous. "Good, good. Keep up the work. When can we expect Warren to be finished with the process and ready to make a public appearance?"

Wake smiled, though he hid it with his fingers. "I'd estimate about a week."

Now Marco's discomfort became apparent. "Not any sooner? There is no way you can push the process along?"

This time Wake laughed outright. "We are not making a cup of soykaf, here, Mister D'imato. We are performing an experimental procedure that is probably the most delicate blend of science and magic this side of Aztlan's delta clinics. Or, to be more succinct, no, I cannot rush this."

The vampire sighed, and then nodded. "Just had to ask. I think I might have been a bit too hasty."

Wake steepled his fingers again. "Oh?"

Marco nodded. "I had intended to kill two birds with one stone. My brother is an extremely calm man, except when it comes to family. I had thought to convert Warren to the cause and use his father's natural protective nature to eliminate a potential problem. Not to mention getting vengeance on the man who has interfered with my plans."

Marco paused, and Wake, smiling softly, said, "And things did not turn out quite the way you expected them too?"

Marco grimaced. "I underestimated my brother's determination. I fully expected him to find my son's killer, which is well within his abilities, and I even had a high degree of confidence that he would be able to dispose of the killer with little problem. However, I was a bit too slow."

Wake leaned forward. "How do you mean?"

Marco shrugged, looking like a little boy who's just broken his mother's favorite vase. "I intended to destroy the small scrap of Warren's genetic information before my brother could try ritual magic. Unfortunately, he beat me to it."

Wake settled back slowly, letting the cracked leather of the chair comfort him. "You realize that this is a bad thing, of course."

For a moment, anger flared on Marco's face, but it died quickly. "Yes, and coupled with the fact that I can't reach him . . . well, frankly, it has me worried."

Wake shook his head slowly. "Assuming your brother has a mage competent enough to penetrate my magical defenses, what kind of force can he bring to bear?"

Marco shrugged again. "Actually, your best bet is the fact that Julius has no idea who you are, or where you are. I kept him in the dark about everything to do with you, as per our agreement. Also, if he still believes that my son's killer is the one behind his son's disappearance, then he might underestimate your compound's particular capabilities.

"However, if he has any decent recon info, then I would suggest you find a way to get out of there. Julius can bring enough firepower to bear to wipe out the entire area."

Wake nodded. "And what exactly do you expect me to do?"

Marco paused, as if he had been about to say something, then changed his mind. "About Julius, he's expendable. I'd rather he was captured, but if there is no alternative, then he can be replaced. As far as the rest of the men are concerned, they are disposable."

Wake nodded. "Very good. You continue trying to stop him from your end, and I'll make sure he doesn't get through from this end."

Marco shook his head. "You don't understand. If I can't reach him and stop him, he will roll over you and your defenses like they don't even exist."

Wake smiled, letting his grin go wide. For the first time since he and Marco had met almost a year and a half ago, he saw something close to fear on the vampire's face. "Don't underestimate me. Your brother will not make it past my first barrier. Do you honestly think I would be foolish enough to show you all of my capabilities? Don't flatter yourself. If you value your brother's life at all, then I suggest you redouble your efforts to stop him. If he comes after me, I will destroy him."

Marco took a deep breath, and let it out. "Of course. I'll do my best."

"As will I."

Suddenly, Wake touched his screen and Marco's face sprang to life-size. A nervous tick was causing the vampire's left eye to jump. "Show me your hands," Wake said.

Marco looked troubled, and his left eye jumped even more frantically. "Why?"

"Just hold them up in front of the telecom."

With a frown, Marco did as he was told. His hands, also

coated with dusky make-up, twitched and fluttered as if they had a life of their own.

"When did the tremors start?"

Marco looked down at his hands as if they had betrayed him. "Almost two weeks ago. However, it's nothing. It passes quickly."

Wake cursed. "Why didn't you inform me?"

Marco shrugged again. "I told you, it's nothing."

Wake shook his head. "With a procedure as delicate and radical as the one you underwent, there is no room for posturing. I should have been informed immediately."

Suddenly there was concern in Marco's eyes, and because Wake had never seen it there before, it took him a moment to recognize it for what it was.

"Is it something I should worry about?"

Wake considered his response for a moment. "I'm not sure. I'm going to conduct a few tests with the tissue samples I took from you after the procedure. I'll let you know if I find anything. However, for now, try to identify the times when the tremors hit, and what triggers them. That could be very important. It might be something we can easily correct."

Marco nodded. "All right, I will. And I'll try to find Julius again."

Wake nodded and cut the connection.

He sat back in his chair and rolled up his sleeve again. Pulling another dermal from his desk drawer, he slid it into position next to the first.

Things are getting messy here, he thought, as the drug soothed him. He touched his screen again, and Pakow's dark features filled it. The man looked exhausted and wary. His thick hair was greasy, and a line of grime clung to the side of his forehead. "Pakow here."

"We might have a situation on our hands. Go to code seven-red. We should ready thirty of the controlled troops, and bring another thirty onto standby. Deploy the hounds as well."

Pakow's thick eyebrows shot upward. "You're expecting an assault?" His voice broke on the last word.

Wake shook his head, half in pity, half in disgust. "Get a grip on yourself. There's a possibility that our friend D'imato may have led the wolf straight to our door. However, I don't think it's anything we can't handle. If D'imato is correct, it will be an assault of the frontal variety."

Something very much like relief spread across Pakow's face. "Certainly. I'll call up for seven-red immediately."

Wake rolled his neck, hearing his vertebrae crack back into alignment. "Excellent. I'll be working here all night. I want hourly reports. Also, it would appear that Mister D'imato's deterioration is progressing well ahead of schedule. I want you to run a full battery on the gene sequences we still have on him, and find out if we've missed something, or if his condition is an anomaly."

"Of course."

Wake cut the connection, and keyed his console to show him the trid views of the grounds. It would be interesting to watch and see just how effective his creations were. He smiled. This might just work out nicely.

16

After de Vries resurfaced, it became apparent that he himself had somehow contracted vampirism. It is unlikely any vampire would have willingly given him this dubious gift had he known de Vries' purposes and identity. Some European runners claim he deliberately offered himself for infection, intent on learning more about his prey by becoming one of them. However it happened, de Vries became a paradox: a vampire who maintains his own essence by feeding on other vampires. Only in utter desperation does he prey on any other targets.

—Posted to Shadowland BBS by Doktor Freeman and the Deathcore Kid, 22 March 2055

Sinunu sat in the back of the stepvan, listening to the distorted rumbling of the six Honda Vikings that were acting as escort. She had no idea where the go-gangers had come from, and didn't care. All she knew was that with the gangers riding wing, her team wouldn't be hassled by anyone as they made their way through Hell's Kitchen.

Sinunu looked to her left, where Truxa sat, calmly staring straight ahead. Without turning, or even seeming to know she was being watched, Truxa slipped her hand into Sinunu's and squeezed.

Sinunu squeezed back, then turned her attention to the rest of the van's occupants. Flak was driving, quietly cursing the swirling dust that made it difficult to see clearly, even with his enhanced vision.

Just behind the driver's seat, Sandman rested in his sway-couch seat. The seat, a circular couch made up of plastic tubing and tie-down straps, had been installed by Sandman and Flak. Once securely fastened in, Sandman could jack into their satlink system without having to worry about keeping either himself or his deck steady when they were on the fly. Sandman was riding the Matrix right now, eyes closed, mouth half-forming words as he continued his efforts to navigate the potentially lethal minefield of their target's computer system.

Even with the codes provided by the vampire's inside man, Sandman was having the fight of his life trying to get inside their target's defenses. He'd jacked out, just before they started to roll, sweat streaming down his face, the strain evident in the bags already showing under his eyes. He told them the target system was guarded by drek-hot IC, countermeasures Sandman had never seen before and hoped like hell he never would again.

Sinunu, however, had caught the gleam in his eye. Sandman was one of the best deckers in the sprawl. Not only was he enjoying the challenge of this run, but he seemed almost in awe of what he was up against. If the team came out of this thing in one piece, their own defensive measures would surely get quite a boost.

Next to Sandman was the vampire. He hadn't so much as glanced at Sinunu since their conversation, and he seemed to be meditating. Sinunu knew better. After two years with Truxa, she recognized a magician's pose when she saw one. He was looking beyond, as Truxa would say. Gathering his mojo, and discovering what needed to be done.

Sinunu noticed that she was seeing him differently now, and wasn't sure how she felt about that. There was none of the revulsion she'd experienced before their little chat, and she even noticed a bit of sympathy.

Beside him was the biff. Sinunu frowned. The biff was

everything she detested in a woman. Beautiful, yes, but with a strength to her that surprised Sinunu. That was part of the problem. For a woman of strength to bother hiding it just so males would find her less threatening made Sinunu physically ill. The biff was also a stripper, and that was another thing Sinunu had a problem with. A woman who would degrade herself in front of men just to cop a little nuyen.

The biff caught her staring, and smiled. For just a second, Sinunu felt her breath catch in her throat. When the biff smiled, it was as if the whole van lit up. That smile was so genuine, so warm, and at the same time with just enough fear behind it that Sinunu doubled back on her thinking. In that moment, she thought she understood some of the vampire's concern for this woman. Thought she might even *want* to take care of her, to keep her from harm.

What's happening to me? First I find pity for a vamp. Then I find myself liking a biff. What's next? Open a clinic for emotionally depressed ghouls?

Truxa squeezed her hand again, and Sinunu looked at her. The little elf was watching her closely, a small smile on her delicately featured face.

"What?"

The smile widened, and Truxa leaned in close. "You can't go through life wondering why you *shouldn't* hate someone, my love. Sometimes you have to look at people and wonder why you shouldn't *care* about them."

Sinunu smiled, and felt some of her tension melt away. "Point taken."

She turned, and leaned forward, extending her hand to the biff. "They call me Sin."

The biff smiled again, turning the wattage way up. "Rachel Harlan." And shook Sinunu's hand.

Sinunu was surprised by the grip. She'd expected something soft and pliant; instead, it was firm and hard. The kind of handshake she'd expect from a warrior.

"I'll be looking after you tonight, so just stick tight to me and do what I do and what I say, and we'll come out of this together, *capiche*?"

The smile faded from Rachel's face. "You guys don't want me here and I know that. You think I'm putting an extra strain on you, but trust me, I'll take care of myself."

Sinunu frowned. "Flak vouches for you, but that's not the point. This is a team, and we're still kicking because we work like a team. You're a new player who doesn't know the signs, doesn't know the calls, and hasn't read the playbook. If Flak says you're good enough, then I believe him, but I worry that you'll zig when you should zag, and it'll get us all killed."

Rachel looked down for a moment, and Sinunu had to lean forward to catch her next words. "I won't. I promise. But I couldn't just sit on my hoop when someone I love is in danger."

Sinunu frowned again. She didn't really want this mission to become so personal. She preferred runs to be clinical insertions without any emotional entanglements, but it seemed that everyone was determined to make her care about them on this one. She knew that could work against her at the wrong moment. Sometimes caring too much made you *think* when you needed to *act*. It made her uneasy.

Sinunu sat back. "It's understood, Rachel. Rest easy, though. We'll do everything to get your man back in one piece."

Rachel lifted her head, and there was that thousand-watt smile again. "You don't know how much I appreciate your help, especially since I can't afford to pay you."

That caught Sinunu off guard. Rachel seemed to think they were doing this as a favor to her, maybe because she and Flak were acquainted or because of that Corinna biz. She seemed to have absolutely no clue that the vampire had already deposited mondo nuyen into their Cayman account.

Despite herself, she leaned forward again. "I got to ask, and you don't have to answer if you don't want to, but how did you get mixed up with"—she nodded in the direction of de Vries—"him?"

Rachel looked startled for a moment. "I don't know what you mean. I've only known him for about two hours longer than I've known you. He found me. Without him, I'd probably still be sitting in Warren's apartment waiting for him to come home."

Sinunu couldn't help a small start of surprise. "You mean you didn't seek him out? He just showed up and offered to help you?"

Rachel shrugged. "Yeah, pretty much like that."

Sinunu sat back and digested this. The vamp shows up to help the lady in distress, pays out major nuyen without even telling her, and lets her come along on a very dangerous run. It didn't scan. She looked at the vamp again, wondering what angle he was running. Then she thought about what Truxa had said. *Was it possible he was doing this out of the goodness of whatever heart he had left?*

Sinunu shook her head. Maybe Truxa was right. She was certainly finding it harder and harder not to like the creature sitting so calmly across from her.

Suddenly, the rumble of the Vikings, which had become like distant white noise, screamed to a higher pitch, and then was gone as if they had never been there.

"Heads up," said Flak from the front. "Escort away. It's party time."

Through the mounted speaker over Sinunu's head, Sandman's voice was distant, making him sound like a strung-out chip head. "I'm home free. All systems running like clockwork, but there's some sort of internal cycle on all the ice in this place. It's being constantly replaced by different defensive lines. I give us a half an hour, max, from insertion to extraction, before I have to fight this system again. So let's light it up."

Sinunu pulled her hood down over her face, fitting the air

filter into place. She pulled her Heckler and Koch MP-5 TX, checked the load again, and strapped it to her back.

From under the seat, she took the compound crossbow, complete with forty real wood quarrels, that she'd used the night before to cover de Vries in the apartment. The quarrels had cost a mint, and she would have to be careful not to waste them. Not to mention that the crossbow wasn't a weapon she'd normally have opted for. Still, she found herself liking its simplicity, as well as its silence. If only they made a faster repeater for the thing. As it was, she only had six rounds before she had to reload. Still, if she was careful, and if she was centered, it would do nicely.

De Vries had told them their target was full of vampires, and the team had been briefed on how to kill them. He'd told them vampires were as allergic to wood as to sunlight. He'd said that if a vampire's spine were damaged, it would kill him. He also told them the place was full of vampires with augmentation, something no one had ever heard of before now. They'd have to cross that bridge when they came to it.

After making sure all of her hand-to-hand weapons were in place and ready, Sinunu turned her attention inward. Focusing on her breathing, she let her mind wander through her body, loosening any tensions, focusing her chi into her belly to center her power.

When she was ready, she opened her eyes and looked at the world with new eyes. Everything seemed to be connected by lilting lines, and she could see how the slightest action or movement of one person or thing affected everything else. Sinunu knew instinctively how an action on her part would cause those lines to waver and snap. She felt perfectly at peace, and ultimately capable.

She knew, even before it began to happen, that the van had reached its destination and would be coming to a halt.

"Last stop. Everybody out," said Flak, his low voice coming through the tacticom built in to Sinunu's head gear. She was at the door, gracefully pushing it open and stepping out, before anyone else had even moved.

Dropping to a crouch, she scanned the area. The place looked like they'd suddenly been transported to the dark side of the moon. The night sky was black, and the only light came from behind her, at the front of the van. The light was orange, and cast the whole landscape into hellish relief.

Even with the air filter on, the smell of the place was overwhelming. Dry and noxious, with just the hint of spoiled eggs over the top. It was the scent of death and decay. The stench of age-old battlefields where the dead have not rested easily.

To her left, a small collection of haphazardly erected structures formed a small shanty town. She knew this was where the locals had set up camp when the compound had first opened its soup kitchen. That was, of course, before many of the occupants of the little town had began to disappear with alarming regularity.

Since then, even offers of free food had failed to bring the hungry of Hell's Kitchen back with any regularity. Sinunu knew that some of the area's more desperate denizens still came at odd intervals, but now the camp was deserted.

She felt Truxa's distinctive movement behind her even before she actually landed beside her. Truxa was practically crackling with magical energy. Something Sinunu could only sense when she was completely centered.

Satisfied that their six o'clock was clear, Sinunu rounded the left side of the van as Truxa took the right. Flak, the only person on the team who could match Sinunu's speed, was already standing in front of the van.

The big Vindicator looked like a toy in his hands. Its trigger housing and grip had been modified to fit his huge hands, as had the belt-driven ammo pack mounted on his back. The Vindicator's six rotating barrels gleamed dully in the soft light.

They were just about to move, when an unfamiliar voice at their backs said, "Rocket, *muya.* Dig the party atmosphere."

Sinunu was faster than Flak on the spin. She did a pirouette that dropped her almost prone, the H&K leaping into her hand like a live thing.

Reflexes jacked to the max, she put the whole picture into focus.

A small figure stood behind her, at a distance of approximately ten meters, gray duster flapping gently around her ankles, her dark skinsuit looking more like dolphin hide than synthleather. Her face was a gentle V-shape, with five datajacks lining her right temple.

To her side, Sinunu could hear the telltale whine of Flak's Vindicator start up as he too slipped into a defensive posture.

But before they could start the rock and roll, the little one in front held up one hand, palm outward. "Keep it chilly, compadres. I got invites to this bash."

Then, faster than even Sinunu's jacked reflexes could see, de Vries was standing between them and the intruder. "Stop," he said.

There was a tableau that lasted almost two heartbeats—nearly an eternity—before Sinunu felt Flak relax his stance.

De Vries smiled. "My apologies. I should have warned you that she would be meeting us."

Flak stood up to his full height, and even though short for a troll, he still towered over the rest. "De Vries, this is getting serious. You're footing the bill here, but if you don't keep us on the scan, someone's going to get hurt."

De Vries smiled. "Once again, I apologize. This is a companion of mine, Short Eyes. She's been with me for almost two years. She is my personal secretary, of sorts. She's been here throughout the day, keeping an eye out. She has become very good at what she does, and seems to have a natural skill at detecting vampires." De Vries turned to the young woman and Sinunu caught his smile. "After all, she picked me out of a crowd, and I was actually doing a passable job at staying hidden."

The one called Short Eyes smiled back, showing uneven,

grimy teeth. "Gotcha all right. Get 'em all if they get too close."

Sinunu shook her head at whatever the private joke was between de Vries and his chummer. Now was not the time, nor the place.

Flak grunted, and Sinunu's face pulled into a scowl. Short Eyes smiled at them and said, "Tension's high, I can do without the stimuli." Then she laughed.

"She will not accompany us inside," de Vries continued as if Short Eyes hadn't spoken. "Once I realized how this was going to work out, I thought it best if no harm came to your man in the Matrix. He's a bit vulnerable out here, and there's no else one to guard him. Without him it's unlikely many of us would get out alive, so I figured Short Eyes could stay here with him."

Sinunu turned to Flak, about to object, but the dark look on the troll's face stopped her.

"Listen, de Vries," Flak said. "We got this down to a science. We got no need of, or desire for, anyone else to come along to frag this up." He turned to Rachel, who was just stepping out of the van. "No offense, Rach, but enough's enough."

Rachel smiled, and said, "None taken."

De Vries stepped close, and said something Sinunu couldn't quite catch.

"All right," Flak said finally. "You made your point. She stays."

De Vries smiled again, "Excellent. Then I would suggest we get underway. As your Sandman said, we have precious little time."

With a jerk of his head, Flak directed Sinunu back toward the wall. When they were out of earshot, Sinunu touched his arm. "You gone whack, completely?"

Flak looked at her. "No. He just asked me how many times any of us have heard him approach. He said the little one will know if any of those vamps come within a hundred meters of the van."

Sinunu shook her head. "What, she got some special vampire sniffer? This is just over the edge, Flak."

Flak nodded. "It's way borderline, but de Vries says that's something close to what she's got. Says she can pick out vamps sometimes before he can. I got the feeling he doesn't even know how she does it."

Sinunu was about to say something else, but Flak raised his hand. "Let it ride, Sin. You're wasting your breath."

They had made their way to the front of the van again, and Sinunu pulled herself together. She would be on point for the first part of this run.

Flak looked at Sinunu, only his eyes visible now that his hood was in place. No words were needed. They had worked together too long for there to be anything but perfect communication between them. With the possible exception of Sandman, Flak was the only male Sinunu trusted. After the things that had happened to her at White Oak, that trust had not come cheap.

She turned and surveyed the scene before her. The stone and wire fence stood almost four meters high, and was topped with concertina wire. Every ten meters, she could make out the distinctive outline of chain-mounted miniguns topped with motion sensors. All of which hung low, obviously deactivated. Above each, mounted on long metal poles, were the orange floods.

Sinunu knew they were at the rear of the compound, a direct one-eighty from the front gate. She also knew this was where the compound's best defenses were concentrated. She just hoped that whoever de Vries was trusting on the inside had taken care of things as promised. If not, then this was going to get real ugly, real quick.

She strapped her bow to her back and bounded across the shallow ditch, and up to the closest rock section. The rock was mostly jagged volcanic, and she scaled it quickly.

As she went up, the flood directly above her went dark. Cresting the top, she got a view of the first fifty-meter expanse they were going to have to cross. She was glad Sandman had been able to deactivate the miniguns. The space was uniformly flat, with absolutely no cover, and nothing to stop the miniguns from laying down an incredible lethal crossfire. Across the distance, she could see the second fence. The far one was completely mesh, and was sure to be electrified.

As she started to swing over, a crawling instinct made her freeze, hugging the top of the rock wall, the concertina wire digging into the small of her back.

Just to her left, about thirty meters out, something moved.

She watched it out of the corner of her eye, and for just a moment, she couldn't figure out what it was or what it was doing.

As it moved closer, she felt a sense of unreality, as well as something very close to shocked amusement. It was a dog. That much should have been obvious, but it was the distended head that had her confused. The thing was wired up, some tech contraption attached to its head. Then she realized that the creature was busy chasing its own tail. At any other time it might have been funny.

Growling viciously, the animal moved like a dervish anxiously snapping at its tail with each spin. It wasn't until it came a little closer that Sinunu realized that it had obviously caught its tail more than once. The tail was a ripped, bloody mess, mangled with each bite the dog delivered.

She shuddered, suddenly afraid. What had they done to this animal to make it mutilate itself like that?

Suddenly, the dog straightened, growling low in its throat, and sniffing in Sinunu's direction. Moving silently, she slipped the crossbow off her back and was just starting to aim, when the dog barked once and began to charge her, a dirty brown streak covering the dusty ground in space-eating bounds.

Moving as quickly as possible, she took aim, when a swirl of what she had mistaken for dust condensed directly in front of the animal. It was de Vries.

Without a hitch, the dog changed its angle of attack and

leapt for de Vries' throat. As it reached the top of its arc, something seemed to sprout from its throat, a barbed cyber-tongue that swept in a tight curve straight for de Vries' head. With a graceful sidestep too fast for even Sinunu to follow, de Vries ducked the lashing tongue and snagged the dog out of mid-air, one-handed.

A truncated *whoff* came from the animal as de Vries snapped the animal's neck with ease.

Dropping the still-twitching carcass to the ground, de Vries looked up at her and smiled slightly. Then he beckoned her with one hand.

Sinunu thought about de Vries saying he was more powerful than any of them could imagine. Somehow, this display of that power made her feel less comfortable, not more.

She swung over the top of the fence, then gently lowered herself to the ground. Checking her one-eighty as far as she could see, Sinunu detected no movement. She knew that there were all sorts of nasty surprises dotting the extent of this no man's land, but hopefully the animal guard was the only one Sandman hadn't been able to counteract.

Satisfied that everything was as calm as it could be under the circumstances, she approached the wire mesh section of the fence, and waved Flak forward.

Slinging the Vindicator over his shoulder, the big troll hunkered down at the fence and began quickly cutting. Within a second he had a hole big enough for him to squeeze through and plenty large enough for everybody else.

Everybody moved through, Truxa giving Sinunu an anxious wink as she stepped lightly through.

As Sinunu turned to look at de Vries again, her tacticom crackled. "Otay, kiddies," came Sandman's soft voice. "Now that we've paid admission to the circus, it's time for the obstacle course."

Flak's voice cut in. "Any more guard dogs?"

"They're everywhere, boss. Everywhere, except here. This is the only section not on hot alert. I guess de Vries' contact has a bit of pull. That dog seemed to be more for show than anything else."

With hand gestures, Flak lined everybody up. Sinunu in the lead, followed by Rachel. Then Truxa and Flak. Sinunu smiled a little to see that Flak didn't even bother with de Vries. Evidently, he thought as she did. The vamp didn't need any of them, and therefore, they didn't need to bother themselves about him.

"Sin Sister," said Sandman, "you got to be precise about this, or you're going to wind up dead, you scan? I've shut down everything I could, but I found a schematic for mods on this place, and not everything is hooked up to the system. So just do everything I say, and I should be able to lead you through this mess just fine. If something goes wrong, you'll hear a small whine of trap doors opening. After that, you're hosed."

Sinunu smiled inside her hood. "Thanks for the vote of confidence, Sandy."

"Any time, Sin. All right, if the girl scout troop is ready to roll, take eight steps forward from where you are right now."

Sinunu turned to Rachel, and leaned close. "Just do what I do, and step where I step, and keep as quiet as a mouse. Comprende?"

Rachel looked back at her, those blue eyes wide with excitement, but she nodded.

Sinunu turned back to the no man's land, took a deep breath and started forward.

For the next six minutes, the group tracked a convoluted course across the ground toward the second barrier. At one point, their meandering trek took them within just a few meters of the dead dog. Sinunu took one look at it, then turned away. Whoever had modified that dog deserved to die slowly and painfully.

After what seemed like hours of being exposed and vulnerable, the group finally reached the opposite wall.

"Now that was fun, wasn't it, kids?"

"All right, Sandman," came Flak's voice. "Everybody's a bit tense out here, so just get on with it."

"Gotcha. Well, the obstacle course is over. Now it's time for the fun house. Flak, you'll want to handle this. The fence is electrified, and its power source is in a closed circuit operated from a generator up near the front gate, so go with plan bravo."

Sinunu dug into the pack at her waist, and pulled out the thin cables with wire jaws at each end. As Flak moved past her, she tossed him the cables, which he snagged over his shoulder without looking.

Sinunu immediately took up position watching their six o'clock. Truxa came up beside her. "Something's very wrong here," Truxa said.

Sinunu didn't take her eyes off their rear, but asked, "You mean aside from the obvious?"

"Yes. This place is protected from magic just as heavily as it is from things mundane, but for all my effort, I've only been able to detect minimal life here. It looks more like a tomb than a research facility. The astral is so incredibly cloudy and polluted."

Sinunu felt the hackles on her neck stand high. "Toxics?"

Truxa shook her head. "This would be a perfect place for them, but someone has gone to a great deal of trouble to keep anything like that out of here. There's magical energy of incredible proportions being used here. Someone with phenomenal talent and a very refined style has been doing things I can't even begin to guess at. This place is giving me the heebie-jeebies."

"What you sense," came de Vries' low whisper, startling both of them, "is the process for creating a new breed of infected. From what I've been able to determine, it's a process so complicated, and containing such a mixture of magic and technology, that there are only about five people in the entire world who could do it. And only two of them who could carry it out single-handedly. The man behind this place could easily be the most dangerous person on the entire planet."

Then he was gone again, leaving Sinunu to wonder how de Vries could possibly have heard their whispered conversation.

"All right," said Flak, "I'm in. Let's roll."

"Okay. Loading bay number three is located fifty meters to your right. Everything is green, but time's running out. So let's hump it up."

Flak took point, as they had planned, and the team fanned out in an arrowhead formation. Sinunu on the left, Rachel just behind and to her right, and Truxa taking the far wing. De Vries shadowed Truxa, and somehow, Sinunu found his placement comforting.

Moving in set stages, they covered the ground quickly, taking cover as best they could, until they reached the loading bay.

The building was a low-slung dome, longer than it was wide, and stretched off into the darkness. The loading bays were at the end of a short paved road that circled around to the front of the building.

The bay was empty and they swung up the short stairway, noting the dead cameras at the entrance. The double doors at the end of the bay were locked as Flak stepped up to them.

"All right, this part is tricky," came Sandman's voice over the tacticom. "If I unlock it, an auto alarm will sound. It's retinal ID only, along with an eight-digit code."

"Damn," said Flak. "Why didn't you say something before?"

"Take it easy, big guy. Just put your eye to the scanner. I couldn't open it myself, but that didn't stop me from changing the codes."

Flak grunted, and lowered his face to the scanner. There was a small beep, and a tiny panel near the door slid out to reveal a numbered keypad.

"It's coded for your birthday, then five-five."

Using his thumb nail, Flak entered the code, and for a

moment nothing happened. Then the lock clicked as the panel slid back into place.

"Like taking candy from a baby," came Sandman's voice.

The team stepped into a long, dimly lit hallway. "All right," Sandman said, "our target is three floors down. The elevator is out of the question. No way for me to reroute the programming without letting the whole place know we're here. But the emergency stairs are just peachy."

They were just starting to move, when de Vries appeared at Sinunu's side. "I've got a bit of business to finish before we get there," he told her. "I'll meet you at the target."

Before she could say anything, de Vries dissolved into a cloud of mist that floated softly down a small vent.

17

Science has already discovered that the HMHVV virus, and its numerous variants, have wildly differing effects on different metatypes. The vampires of Ordo Maximus intend to isolate these and use them to create monsters of their own devising. Humans, elves, and orks retain normal intelligence after infection with HMHVV; dwarfs and trolls do not. If the Ordo can determine the reason some metatypes retain their mental faculties and others don't, they can convey intelligence on infected dwarfs and trolls . . . or take it away from infected humans, elves, and orks, creating mindless feeding machines or powerful creatures with malign intelligence at their whim.

—Martin de Vries, *Shadows at Noon,* posted to Shadowland BBS, 24 May 2057

Pakow sat at the main console of the operating theater, cushioned by his overstuffed chair. Below him, framed by the octagonal-shaped, slanted plexiglass walls, stood the huge stainless steel containment chamber. Two of his assistants, both barely more than automatons, moved about their programmed assignments, filling the vats with the glowing blue fluid Doctor Wake had developed.

Pakow wiped away a trickle of sweat that dripped from his hairline and ran down his forehead. Things were getting messy, and it was scaring him.

He leaned down and spoke into a microphone that sprouted

from the top of the console. "Number Two, set temperature at thirty-one point three, then exit."

Pakow watched as the misshapen creature stepped onto the engraved white and green pentagram that gridded the floor, shambled to the huge container, and did as it was told. Once the setting had been entered, the thing that had once been a man made his way to the lift platform that would lower him out of the chamber. Pakow knew it would take him down into the decontamination section, where he hoped the small glitch in the decon program would go unnoticed. If it didn't, the computer would realize that Number Two didn't have any contaminants on him at all. And if that happened, the game would be up.

Another trickle of sweat followed the first, and Pakow wiped at it in frustration. He was exhausted and frightened. He didn't like all this intrigue, wasn't used to the stress it caused, and was seriously worried that he was going to crack before the night was over.

"Number One, transfer the patient to the tank."

The other occupant of the room, an ork who had been one of the first metas to undergo the procedure, shook slightly, then started in the wrong direction before stopping, turning, and heading over to a large hatch in the side of the theater. This ork had been part of a test group for an omega strain Pakow had designed, one intended to transform members of the various metatypes into vampires, without also conferring the disadvantages HMHVV usually bestowed on their metatype.

Pakow shook his head. He hated using Number One. In fact, he hated everything about Number One. He shuddered as he thought back on the night he and Wake had finished the procedure on the poor creature.

Instead of the fully intelligent and magically capable being they'd hoped to engineer, the ork had come off the table a drooling, homicidal thing devoid of any ability whatsoever. They'd implanted the psychotropic chip, but the ork's metagene reacted with the virus in such a way that the chip seemed to have no effect.

Only after they'd given it a frontal lobotomy did Number One settle down to where it was manageable. They had spent almost three hours inside the thing's skull, selectively searing neurons until they'd found the right combination.

However, whatever talents the ork might have had were also deleted, making it fit for nothing more than high-risk, decon-proof tasks that didn't require any brain power. Still, tonight, that was exactly what Pakow needed. Even if things didn't go quite as planned, there was no way Wake could learn anything from this creature, not even using his formidable magical skill. The only magical manifestation Number One showed was a profound resistance to anything magical. Something that Wake thought of as a success of sorts.

As Number One opened the sliding hatch and clumsily lifted the body waiting there, Pakow turned to the large monitor at the front of the console. Everything was ready. The room showed no sign of contamination, and the vat itself was now filled with a simple saline solution instead of the DMSO-saturated liquid required for the process. The DMSO facilitated the subject tissue's absorption of the chemicals necessary to start the conversion process.

Number One placed the limp form into the vat, and stepped back.

"Initiate sedation."

Number One shook again, but this time got the order right on the first try. A small needle attached to an articulated mechanical arm stretched out from the side of the vat and slid into the side of the patient's neck. Pakow smiled. Anybody watching the trid replay would see that everything was going according to standard operating procedure. However, instead of sedating the patient, he was being injected with a chemical that would actually counteract most of the drugs he'd been given in the last twelve hours.

Pakow sat back and took a deep breath. "Number One, exit."

It took Number One two tries to get to the lift, but when he was safely gone, Pakow felt tension bleed out of his shoulders. His part in this was over for the moment. Now it was up to de Vries and whoever he had with him to do their part. Hopefully de Vries had found the package he'd left for him. Pakow had done everything within his power to prevent any slip-ups, but all this cloak and dagger was definitely out of his league. It was too late for regrets, but he couldn't help fervently wishing he'd never heard of Oslo Wake or the Terminus Experiment.

Pakow reached into his pocket and pulled out a small holopic of Shiva and their little girl, Kirstan. The reasons he was here in the first place. And the reasons he'd decided to turn on Wake.

He shook his head and a grim smile touched the edges of his mouth.

"I hope," he whispered to the still image, "that I haven't jeopardized your lives." He looked at Shiva's dark-skinned face smiling up at him, feeling tears begin to well at the corners of his eyes. "I'm so sorry. I know I've let you down."

Shiva, a woman of vast heart and incredible strength of character would never have condoned what he'd been involved in here. Would never have understood the choices he'd been offered. He knew without even thinking about it that Shiva would rather have died than to see her husband a part of this abomination.

Pakow shook his head quickly as if he could shake off the guilt he felt. Guilt at lying to her about where he was, guilt at doing something she would find reprehensible, guilt at not being with her. Guilt at not being man enough to protect her.

He checked the clock on the console. De Vries had a fifteen-minute window, and Pakow hoped that whoever de Vries had decking the system was good enough to get past the intricate Matrix defenses Wake had paid so much to put in place.

He leaned forward and tapped in an extension on the keypad next to the microphone base. After a second, Wake's voice filtered out of the speaker. "What is it, Dr. Pakow?"

"The subject is in the vat, and I've begun the process," Pakow said. "I'm going to head down to the cafeteria and pick up some coffee. We won't need you for another four hours. Also, I finished up the tests on Marco D'imato's gene coding. He's an anomaly, as far as I can tell, but you're right about the deterioration progressing much faster than we expected. He's on the verge of coming apart."

There was a long pause, and Pakow found himself sweating again.

"All right, thank you," came Wake's voice. "I'm nearly finished with my preparations, except for a few final details. Keep me informed of the subject's progress, and also keep me updated on the security matter we discussed earlier. I've noticed some excess magical activity in the area. Somebody gave us a quick scan about an hour ago. I think it was a follow-up on the astral scan we got this morning. Keep your head up."

"Yes."

Pakow disconnected, and then stood. He jacked into the system quickly, and delivered the program he'd put together just that morning. If things went well, it would give anyone snooping security the impression that all was as it should be here in the operating room. He jacked out again. As he looked down at the vat, which still remained unsealed, he saw movement.

Surprised, Pakow leaned forward, his face only millimeters from the thick safety glass.

Sure enough, the young man was moving. Slowly, sluggishly, trying to return to consciousness. Pakow was amazed. He would have thought this kind of activity impossible for at least another couple of hours.

Pakow watched in complete fascination as the man pulled himself up over the lip of the vat, and then fell to the floor, hitting his head.

Pakow winced at that, but there was nothing he could do. His program was running, and he had a five-second window to get himself out of the room before any anomalies in the trid would become obvious.

Pakow checked the clock again. Almost time. He turned, and without looking back, hurried up the carpeted steps, and out of the theater.

Deep in his underground office, Oslo Wake watched Pakow on the touchscreen monitor. As the other man hurried from the operating theater, Wake smiled. With the stroke of his finger, Oslo changed the view to bring up the stasis wing. The display showed him Number Two, just then placing the body of a young man with infinite care into a vat identical to the one Pakow had just left behind.

Oslo nodded to himself. *Pakow, Pakow, Pakow. A valiant effort, but I just can't allow your delicate sensibilities to jeopardize my plan.*

He spoke into the small microphone next to the monitor. "Number Two, begin the restart process."

With that, he touched the screen again, and the view faded to black.

18

This work brings me to the verge of a technological, magical breakthrough such as the world has never seen. The mating of magical creatures with cyberware is a feat most scientists don't even dream of.

—Oslo Wake, laboratory notes, test series OV13652, 02 November 2053

Julius D'imato sat in the corner of the warehouse, fitting the boot straps of his heavy armor in place. He cinched the last strap, and pulled his helmet from the bench next to him.

The activity in the warehouse had become quieter, but also more intense. His men knew that D-hour was fast approaching, and there was a crackle of nervous energy underlying their every action.

Weapons were loaded, checked, broken down, then reassembled and loaded again. All the men were in heavy armor now, their bodies faintly resembling beetles scurrying about.

Julius took a deep breath and let it out. It had been a long time since he'd seen real action. Fratellanza, Inc. had been plenty busy providing security during the recent mob war, but Julius hadn't taken any part in the street fighting. His role, for many years now, had been more that of general than foot soldier. Like any corp, Fratellanza did have its own combat section, though Julius knew those soldiers would be stretched to the limit by this operation.

They were professional enough. That wasn't the problem.

Some had served in the Desert Wars, some in the Eurowars, and almost all had been corporate military at one time or other. But there were only fifty of them.

Julius had thought about pulling up some of the reserves from different places, but had decided against it. Pulling employees like that would have caused a stir, and if they were going to get through this without alerting people like Knight Errant and Lone Star, they were going to have to move like cats until the actual moment to strike.

He smiled to himself as he thought about the big two. His deckers had found no registered security provider on record in the compound's files, which, of course, meant two things. One, Julius wouldn't have to deal with interference from Lone Star or Knight Errant, because his people had simply changed the record to show Fratellanza, Inc. as the compound's sec provider. That way, when Julius started to roll, the signal would automatically go out that Fratellanza was responding to a legitimate emergency. Unfortunately, the other ramification of having no sec provider of record usually signified that the place must have internal defenses of a very high caliber.

Julius hoped he was up to this. He would hate to let Warren down again. Just the thought of his son strengthened his resolve. If Warren could be saved, he would do it. If Warren was already gone, then whoever was responsible would pay big and hard. Julius would make certain of that.

"Biggs!" he bellowed.

Biggs snapped to at the telecom, where he'd been taking notes. His curly red hair and little boy freckles made the fangs in his mouth look completely out of place. "Boss?"

"Status report? We can't wait all night."

The big ork ripped a sheet of paper off the pad on which he'd been writing, and disconnected from the telecom. He strode over to Julius with the confident walk of one who knows himself, who knows exactly what he is capable of doing.

"Things ain't right and they ain't normal," Biggs said. "And if it weren't for what you told us earlier, I'da thought every contact I had in Hell's Kitchen had started chippin'."

Julius nodded. "Spill it."

Biggs looked down at the paper and scratched his head, as if he were having trouble deciphering his own writing. "Okay, but this is gonna sound a bit strange."

He cleared his throat. "First contact I talked to is a guy who's usually reliable. He didn't know that much, only that somebody bought up a former Fuchi processing plant in Hell's Kitchen about three years ago. A month or so later, whoever bought it turned it into a soup kitchen. Free food, and no forced sermons like they have at the mission. So they was pretty popular.

"My contact said he never went there, but he'd heard that anyone who was down and out could show up and get a hot meal and a blanket. In winter, the Hell's Kitchen folk put up a little encampment out there. He says that's about the time people started disappearin'."

Julius looked up. "Disappearing? Did he say why?"

Biggs shook his head. "Naw, he just says that after that, everybody was afraid of the place. In fact, some of the folk won't even go back there to get their stuff from the camp. And when yer talkin' about people who got little or nothin' to start with, they gotta be pretty damn scared to leave anything behind."

Julius nodded. "That it?"

Biggs paused, and Julius could tell he was weighing his answer. "Well, no. That's only the start of it."

Julius nodded again. "Go on."

"The next guy I talked to swore up and down it was a secret ghoul . . . enclave? Is that right? I think that means that a bunch of ghouls are holed up there. He says that's why people are disappearing, 'cause the ghouls are eating them. But I figure that's just paranoia, 'cause nobody's seen any of the usual signs, and if ghouls are out there, they've been keepin' to themselves for the last coupla months. I dealt with ghouls before. No matter how many people they mighta snagged a few months ago, they'd be getting pretty hungry by now."

Julius nodded. "It's not ghouls, so skip the rest of that."

Biggs licked his lips and glanced again at his notes. "The next one's somebody I used to trust, but she's been known to go benders the last couple of years, so take this with a big rock of salt. She's not sure, but her guess is that the place is a chop shop for body parts. She says that in the first month, before they opened the soup kitchen, there was lots of medical supplies delivered in unmarked vans. She knows, 'cause she got the registration number off one of the trucks and decked into the DMV. The truck was registered to Zulu BioGen, a small, but very high-tech firm out of Atlanta, but with branches all over the world."

Something nagged at the back of Julius' mind. That name rang a bell. Biggs started to go on, but Julius held up a hand. "Zulu BioGen, why do I know that name?"

Biggs shrugged. "Dunno, but I can have the decker boys check it out for you."

Julius nodded slowly, feeling as if he was missing something, but couldn't quite get it. Finally, he sighed. "Yes. Track it. If something goes wrong tonight, and we don't get the bad guy, we're going to want any shred of information that might help us. I want Zulu's logs of what they sent here, and who bought it, and if you run into dummy corps, or anything like that, I want you to double your efforts."

"You wanna hear the rest of this?" For the first time, the big ork seemed unsure of himself.

Julius nodded.

Biggs shifted his weight from foot to foot, and Julius could tell he was uncomfortable. "Come on, Biggs. I haven't laughed at you yet, so spill it."

"Well, the last part is so crazy I wouldn't even waste your time with it, except the source I got it from has never let me down. Ever. She tells me she did an astral fly-by about two months ago. The place is protected up the yin-yang, but she managed to find a few cracks in its armor. She says they got monsters in there. Things she never saw before, things that shouldn't exist. She also says everything inside that place is crazy, with this fragged-up, unnatural kinda aura like she's never seen before."

Julius felt the muscles in his neck go tense. "Talk to me."

Biggs scratched his warty chin with one huge hand. "She told me somebody is doing very bad things to animals and people. That something or somebody was turning them into things that shouldn't exist. She also said she mighta been able to tell me more if she hadn't been astral, but that something . . . not sure exactly what she called it . . ." He stopped to think for a moment. "Oh yeah, I think she called it the background count, said it was too high and frizzing up her view."

Julius nodded slowly, and took a deep breath. "Anything else?"

Biggs nodded. "Just one last thing. She said some of these things were wired to the hilt. They had more dead spaces on 'em than half an army of street sams."

Julius stood and reached up to put one hand on Biggs' shoulder. "Thanks. This has been a big help. At least now we know what we're facing in there."

The look on Biggs' face would have been comical at any other time. "You telling me this is what we're up against?"

Julius forced himself to smile. "Plan for the worst, and you'll always be pleasantly surprised."

19

We reckon there are three hermetic organizations that know cybermantic magic in enough depth to produce mages who can cheat death: the Ordo Maximus, Aztechnology, and the Azanian Heavenherds. . . . We know the Azzies use sacrifice and blood spirits to cope with the drain. I've heard similar stories about Ordo Maximus, except for the part about blood spirits. The Azanians know the formulae and rituals for cybermantic magic, but they do not practice it. It's anathema to them.

—From encrypted telecom transcripts posted to Shadowland BBS by Captain Chaos, 11 December 2056. Identity of speakers not definitively verified.

Following Sandman's lead over the tacticom, the team had made it through the loading dock entrance, then down a number of levels to a large room, tiled in green and reeking of industrial disinfectant. Along one side of the room a long row of biohazard suits hung neatly from steel pegs. On the other side, a low-slung bench lined a series of lockers.

At the far end was a round door that looked more like a portal on a submarine than anything Rachel had ever seen before.

That was where she'd been looking a second before, when the door had suddenly swung open. Rachel stood frozen in her tracks, utterly paralyzed by fear.

The infernal thing shambling through that doorway was something out of a nightmare. She'd seen enough orks on the street to know that this used to be one, but somebody had sheared its horns close to the skull. One side of its head was a simple metal plate. The entire left side of the ork's body was gone, replaced by a steel cylinder with eight small appendages sprouting at various angles. The bottom of the cylinder, where the ork's left leg should have been, was an articulated foot that looked impossibly thin to bear up under that much weight.

The ork's eyes were gone and in their place was a steel grid that completely encircled its shaved head, attaching to the metal plate for support.

Rachel had seen something like this once. It was supposed to give the person a three-sixty view of the world. They hadn't been very popular, because most people couldn't adjust to having that much visual field. Just above the viewing bar, to the side of the metal plate, the ork had the words "NUMBER ONE" tattooed into the skin of its forehead.

All these things she could have dealt with. She had seen body mods before, though these were clumsier and more obvious. No, the thing that made her body seize up on her was the ork's mouth.

The mouth was filled with needle teeth that didn't quite mesh. They had broken off in places and some of the splinters jutted through the dead flesh of the ork's lips.

"Down! Now!"

It was Sin, right behind Rachel. Then Sin's hand was on her shoulder, gripping with a strength Rachel wouldn't have dreamed, shoving her violently to the floor.

Above her head, she heard two soft twangs, and watched as the ork developed dual feathered hafts in its throat.

The thing let out a strangled cry, and turned a half-circle to stumble into the frame of the round door. It landed on its right side, mechanical leg peddling against empty air while its flesh leg twitched uncontrollably.

More twangs followed the first, and as two more crossbow bolts buried themselves in the thing's body, the twitching of the flesh leg stilled. Even so, the chrome leg spasmed twice more before it finally jerked once and then dropped. As if someone had just cut the power.

Sinunu's hand was still on Rachel's shoulder as Flak's huge form did a low, curled vault over her, landed on one foot, and spun to the side of the doorway, the Vindicator going into its warm-up whine as he jammed it through the circular opening.

"Twelve o'clock clear." Flak voice was soft.

"Six clear." It was Truxa's voice from somewhere behind Rachel.

"You solid?" Sinunu touched the side of Rachel's face, pulling her gaze from the downed monstrosity in front of her. "I said, 'you solid?' "

Rachel nodded.

"Package secure," said Sinunu.

Rachel pushed Sinunu's hand off her shoulder and stood. She wasn't exactly proud of her reaction to the situation, but she wasn't going to be called a "package" if she could help it.

From just behind her, she could hear Truxa say, "I didn't think it was possible. There's no way that thing should be able to exist." The wonder and fear in her voice made Rachel feel just a bit better about how she'd reacted.

Over the headset they'd given her, she heard Flak say, "Talk to me, Sandman. What the hell was that all about?"

There was a pause, then, "Whoever's helping us out has gone to a lot of sweat pulling this particular room off-line. I didn't notice, because they covered their tracks pretty well. It looks like they didn't want anyone finding out that the decon tanks shut down just as your newly dead pal came through them. Sorry. I'd just noticed myself when he surprised you."

Flak took a moment to look down at the dead ork. "That's some seriously sad cyber. Looks like a wind-up toy."

It was Sandman who responded. "Actually, if that's Number One, he's got some SOTA cyber, but from what I can see, they had to make mods to his wetware. Actually, from the schematics I just pulled up, your dead boy is brainfry. They got a direct neural digitizer hooked up to his network. He only responds to specific verbal stimulation. In fact, my guess is that if you'd all just held real still, he would have walked right past you."

"All right, enough about our pal. Two questions, any more like him between here and our objective? And how we doing on time?"

"Good news is you got nothing between you and our boy. Bad news is that I got some minor activity on the home front here. Everything just went on red alert. I think you got about eleven minutes until your position is completely compromised."

"All right, boys and girls," Flak grunted. "Time to hump and earn our pay." With one hand, he lifted the ork's body and shoved it under the bench next to the lockers, then covered it with a biohazard suit. It wouldn't fool anybody who actually entered the room, but it might keep from alerting someone merely walking past.

The rest of the team were taking up their positions again, but Rachel felt Sinunu's hand on her arm. She turned to face the pink eyes beaming out of her balaclava hood. "Next time, don't move unless I tell you to," Sinunu said. "Barging straight into a room like that might have gotten you killed, and I got a deal with a certain someone to try and bring you back alive. Got that?"

Rachel swallowed her response and nodded.

"Good. At my left shoulder, one pace back." Sinunu held Rachel's eyes for a moment. "You got a gun?"

Rachel nodded again, then pulled out her Seco LD-120.

Sinunu snorted, then reached down to her ankle. She drew a much larger, squared-off pistol from a velcroed holster. "Seco makes a good weapon, but it tends to jam if it runs too hot, and the load is way too light for what we got going on here. Here, take my Manhunter. It's got sixteen shots, and the safety is here. But I don't want you firing it unless things get out of control, and then, I don't want you firing it anywhere near me. Understand?"

Rachel shook her head to show she didn't. "Then why are you giving it to me?"

Those pink eyes seemed to bore into her for a second. " 'Cause if I'd just seen what you saw and didn't have a real weapon, I think I'd have lost it. Just be careful with it."

Rachel nodded and pulled the weapon, popped the clip to check her rounds, and then reholstered it. She velcroed the pistol to the small of her back, where it would be out of the way, but within easy reach.

Sinunu nodded in approval.

"All right, ladies," said Flak, who had finished stowing the body of Number One, "hate to bust this up, but we're trying to beat the clock." He handed the four crossbow quarrels back to Sinunu.

"You might want to be careful of the blood on those." He turned and looked at the covered body of Number One. "There's no telling what kind of monster made that thing, or what nasty ingredients went into the soup, if you know what I mean."

Sinunu nodded at him, then turned and gave Rachel a wink. "Papa Flak, just looking out for me."

As they moved through the round door into an entirely white chamber, Rachel watched Sinunu wipe the black fluid from the ends of the bolts, then reload them into her crossbow. The room they came into was almost five meters in length by three meters wide, with a line of nozzles ringing it.

At the far end was a small corrugated steel platform with handrails. Big enough to hold all of them, it ran on shiny plastic pulleys up into the ceiling.

"This is it," said Sandman over the tacticom. "That platform should lead right to the money boy's room. Be on the alert. Once you hit the room, it's ringed with windows, so some dirty peeper could be watching you without my knowing it."

"What?" Flak growled. "You can't get a trid feed of the room above?"

"Sorry, Flakman. Somebody did a digital loop, and I don't want to interrupt it. If it's our insider, then he's done it to cover his own tracks. If it's not, well, you'll know in just a minute."

Flak grunted. "Thanks a lot."

He turned to the group. "Okay, it's showtime. Everybody keep it tight. Sin, give the package body-cover if necessary. You'll have the ground level one-eighty. Trux, you'll take the sky one-eighty." He pulled out a modified Predator II from a holster at his belt. The big gun looked tiny in his grip. "I'll take both ground level and skyward zero. Let's move."

They stepped onto the platform, Sinunu pushing Rachel gently into a crouch in the center of the group. From there she could cover Rachel as well as her field of fire without obstruction.

Rachel watched as the small elven woman pulled a slim, golden rod from a long pouch at her back.

Then they were on the lift, and without any of them doing anything, it rose quickly and silently into the air.

Her first thought as they came out of the darkness and into the light was that they were on stage. For just an instant, it reminded her of some of the rooms at The Tiger's Lair, where she had worked most of her teenage years as a cocktail server. Woo Ling, madame of the Lair, had paid a truckload of nuyen to have a circular room constructed where the girls performed with each other and with any customers who were into exhibitionism. People could walk around the outside and watch through the glass, picking the girls they liked or just enjoying the show.

That was what went through her head as the platform came to rest.

"Sky one-eighty clear!"

"Ground one-eighty clear!"

"All clear!"

The others had moved off the platform, and were continuing to cover their fields of fire, but Rachel had stopped noticing them, had in fact stopped breathing. She stared at the still form on the floor, at the tiny trickle of blood seeping from the back of his head.

Scrambling out from under Sinunu's protective stance, she moved forward on her hands and knees until she was over the body. She pulled him to her. "Warren?"

Rachel looked down at the unfamiliar face, and then up at the runners. "Hey, this isn't Warren."

Flak stepped toward her. "What are you talking about?"

Rachel pushed the man away from her. "This isn't Warren. Can I make it any plainer?"

Sinunu stepped up behind Flak. "You sure?"

Rachel felt frustration bubble up through her. "Am I sure? You gotta be kidding. I've seen Warren naked almost every night for the last six months. You think I wouldn't know him?"

"Fraggit!" said Flak. "Sandman, what kind of drek is this? The target's been switched."

Sandman's voice sounded hollow over the tacticom. "You're drekking me."

"Does it sound like I'm fragging drekking you? Find him, and find him now."

It only took a few moments, during which time Truxa took a look at the still form. "He's actually in pretty good shape," she said. "What do we do with him?"

Just then Sandman's voice came back. "Sorry, Flakman. I can't find your boyo anywhere else. You sure that's not him?"

"Positive."

"Then I suggest you get the hell out of there, because things are getting hot."

Rachel thought her heart was going to burst when she

heard that. "We can't go. Not when we're this close. We've got to find him."

Sinunu was at her shoulder. "It's no good. We got no recon, we got no intel, we got nowhere to even start looking. Best to pull back and try the run again from another angle."

Rachel knew Sinunu was right, but it still hurt.

Everyone hustled toward the lift, when a voice from above them said, "Aren't you forgetting something?"

20

Just got the go-ahead from D'imato, and I've seen the prelims. It looks like we're going to be able to pull the whole operation out from under Marco's nose before he even knows what's happened. Julius thinks we can use that as further evidence that his brother should be committed. Just between you and me, I couldn't agree more. I had a talk with the bastard by telecom yesterday, and frankly he scared the drek out of me. The sooner they lock him up the better.

—Interoffice email, John Bonavear to Calvin Justran re: *D'imato vs D'imato*. Fillips, Bonavear, and Justran, Attorneys at Law, Seattle, 07 August 2060

The men had done an excellent job, there was no doubt about that. Even the Mobmaster was running completely silent, its welded, crash-bar wedge plowing trash and dust out of the way as the convoy rolled through Hell's Kitchen.

Julius sat next to Biggs, who sat directly behind the rigger running the Mobmaster. Biggs wore his heavy combat helmet, its dark visor pulled down for thermographic vision. With the blowing dust, Julius couldn't make out a thing around them, and knew he had to trust the rigger's skills.

Julius wasn't interested in the scenery anyway. He was staring at the tiny image on his portable telecom, and the anger surging through him was making the screen shake.

"And you listen to me, brother," he said. "I don't know

what you have in mind here, but I know where my son is, and I'm going to get him. You don't like that, we can talk about what the hell you're up to when I get back. Until then, there isn't anything you can say to make me change my mind."

The face on the screen looked grim. "Julius, listen to reason. I'm telling you, somebody is playing you for a fool. Warren isn't out in Hell's Kitchen. He's somewhere dockside. Come back, and let's do this right, not go off half-cocked to flatten some little facility out in the middle of nowhere, full of people who have no clue why you're coming after them."

Despite himself, Julius had to smile at the image. "Tell you what, if I've made a mistake, I'll apologize. However, I know I haven't made a mistake."

From beside him, Biggs spoke, "Sir, the decker's got site layouts. They're coming up on the front screen now."

Julius looked at Marco again. "Got to go. We're almost on top of the target, and we're just getting last-minute details."

"Wait! There are things you don't know—"

Julius watched as the entire left side of Marco's face seemed to expand and contract violently, and a line of white spittle trailed from his mouth to leave a track of blackness down his chin. Marco's neck muscles bulged until it looked as if they were going erupt right through his skin.

"Damn it, Marco! Are you all right?"

Even on the small screen, Julius could tell that his brother's entire body was shaking and trembling. "Marco, talk to me."

After a few seconds, the tremor passed as quickly as it had come. Marco slumped toward the screen for a second, then righted himself with obvious effort. "Damn," he said, in a suddenly tired voice. "That was a bad one."

Julius looked closely. Marco's left eye was filled with black blood that spilled over his lid and tracked down his cheek. He wiped at it with a curled fist, like a child wiping away a tear.

"Marco, I told you that needed to be checked, and now it's

getting worse. You need to call that doctor of yours. Tell him what's going on. Find out if there's anything he can do."

Marco shook his head. "I already have, and he's looking into it. But let's get back to the point before you do something that will jeopardize our operation here."

Suddenly Julius was sick of talking to his brother, sick of everything to do with the family, with the corporation. The only thing he cared about was Warren and getting him back safely.

"Marco, shut up."

The look of shock and anger on Marco's face was frightening. In a low, cold tone, he said, "I think the stress has made you forget yourself, little brother."

Julius laughed. "I haven't forgotten anything, big brother. I haven't forgotten that if it wasn't for you, my son wouldn't be out here in the middle of nowhere, with some insane thing that wants him dead just to hurt you. Remember the trideo recording? This whole thing is because of you. So just shut up. I'm going in, and this conversation is over. You want to try and stop me, you go right ahead. You'll find out just how far I'm willing to take this. And considering your delicate position, I think you just better sit tight and let me do whatever I want. Is that clear?"

If Marco's tone was cold before, it was positively arctic now. "Are you threatening me? Do you have any idea what you're doing?"

Julius thought about the night Marco had come to him, changed into a vampire, and asked for his help. "*I* should have asked *you* that eight years ago, just after your little 'accident,' but I didn't. Or maybe you should have asked me that when you came to me two years back and told me things were going to be different, and again asked me to back your play. You've taken everything I've ever loved and ruined it, including the brother I used to have. Well, I'm taking some of mine back. Now."

With that, Julius disconnected. Hitting a button that rolled down the bullet-proof glass, he tossed the telecom out the window.

Julius turned to Biggs, who had lifted his visor and was watching him with a raised eyebrow. Julius smiled. "All right, let's take a look at those layouts and see if we can make tonight go a bit easier."

21

Imagine a troll infected with a custom strain of HMHVV. In addition to his already fearsome size and strength, the troll could be endowed with the classic vampire's abilities to transform into mist and regenerate damage, the formorian's resistance to magic, the goblin's tolerance for fire, and the bandersnatch's adaptive coloration and high reproductive rate. Such a monstrosity—virtually impervious to harm, ravening for blood, and able to reproduce—would cut a swath of destruction wherever it went.

—Martin de Vries, *Shadows at Noon,* posted to Shadowland BBS, 24 May 2057

"Aren't you forgetting something?"

As the voice from above echoed in the operating theater, Sinunu reacted even without thinking. Pushing Rachel to the floor, she spun into a kneeling position, bringing both her crossbow and HK MP-5TX on target simultaneously.

The crossbow twanged as soon as she had a viable target—the dark, strangely deformed figure standing at the top of the short stairway just to the side of the huge pentagram. The steps led to a supply elevator.

Then everything clicked into slow motion as she realized what she'd done. Sinunu watched as the arrow streaked toward the figure she now recognized as de Vries. The reason he looked deformed was because he had something slung across his shoulders.

As suddenly as the realization hit her, de Vries moved gingerly down a step, and to the left. He reached out with his free hand, easily snagging the wooden bolt from mid-air.

"Frag!" Sinunu was on her feet, her regret turning to anger the instant she understood the vampire was safe.

De Vries smiled down on her, gently twirling the feathered shaft in his fingers as if it were some kind of cheerleader's baton. "You seem to be a bit on edge, my dear."

He quickly descended the steps to the floor.

Sinunu felt a small hand on her shoulder. She turned and saw Truxa standing there, a smile on her full lips. "Baby, don't get mad. You reacted, that's all."

Sinunu felt her hands unclench.

Flak was still staring at de Vries. "What the hell are you doing? Where the hell did you go? And who the hell is that?" He pointed at the dark-haired man over de Vries' shoulder.

De Vries smiled. "Not enough time for a full explanation, but this man is going to be our decoy. If Marco D'imato were to learn that his nephew had been rescued, he'd simply grab him again and we'd never find him."

Rachel pushed to her feet beside Sinunu. "This isn't Warren," she said. "We got the wrong chamber or something."

De Vries stepped over to the vat and looked at the body on the floor. Then he dumped the body of the man he carried next to the one who'd crawled out of the vat. He was shaking his head. "Bloody hell," he said, for an instant going into what Sinunu guessed was a trance.

"What now?" Flak said, breaking de Vries' reverie. "We don't have time to change tactics and search for our target. Your mole gave you faulty intel and now we're on the verge of being fragged for no gain."

"We bail," Sinunu said. "We'll have to regroup, and come back after we get better intel."

From behind her, she heard Flak grunt again. "Good idea, chica. Let's get the frag out of here."

De Vries lifted the decoy's body and led the group to the

platform. Even under the combined weight of the entire team, the gleaming platform drifted silently downward. Then they were back in the tiled chamber again.

Sinunu looked at de Vries, who stood next to her, the decoy like a limp, naked rag over his shoulder. "What are you going to do with him?"

De Vries shrugged, the movement causing the unconscious man's body to bounce up and down. "I'm not entirely sure. I don't like the idea of leaving him here, so I guess I'll take him as far as I can, and then decide."

Sinunu nodded. It made sense. When you were on a run, you did what you could, and then you did what you had to.

They were just passing through the door of the decon chamber when Sandman's voice came over the tacticom. "We got uninvited guests. The system bumped to full alert. The whole compound just lit up like a Christmas tree, and the grounds are swarming with people."

"Frag it!" said Flak into the tacticom as they moved quietly into the locker room. "What did we trip?"

There was a short pause, then Sandman said, "Nothing. It wasn't us. Evidently the bad guys are expecting some heavy-duty party crashers. They're setting up some serious drek out there."

Quickly, and quietly, they began to move down the hallway, Sinunu and Flak switching point at every hallway juncture.

"What's the easiest way back to the van?"

Another pause from Sandman, this one much longer. "You're not gonna like this, Flak. They got the back buttoned up even tighter than the front. According to Short Eyes, this place is full of vampires and they got wind of us. We're rolling, even as we speak."

"Drek. All right, can you stay in the system?"

"Null sheen. Hold tight for a few ticks while I work out your best exit route and how we can meet up. You solid with that?"

Sinunu stopped listening at that moment. From around the

dimly lit corner, she saw movement, shadowy outlines against the wall.

"Action on our twelve," she whispered into her tacticom. "Fade back?"

"Negative," came Flak's reply. "We got to get the frag out of here. Let's light 'em up."

The shadow figures seemed to glide swiftly from left to right, and for just a moment, Sinunu couldn't tell what they were doing, then it hit her. They were checking all the doors, making sure they were locked.

She heard a soft shuffle behind her, and could tell from his subtle odor that Flak was at her back.

Suddenly the shadows stiffened, going completely still.

"Now," came Flak's whisper.

From her left, Sinunu heard Truxa mutter a quiet chant, then give a soft clap, setting off a spell. Sinunu rolled onto the floor just as a gout of greenish-brown fluid shot over her shoulder and down the hallway. She came to a crouch as the shadowy things leapt out of the way. There were three of them, and the furthest one didn't move fast enough.

The green acid completely engulfed it, rending flesh parts in a putrid explosion.

Sinunu didn't have time to care. There were two of the things left, and for the first time, she had a good idea just what they were up against. If Sandman was right, these were vampires and made Number One look like a child's toy.

The closest was a human male. She could tell by his features that he'd been black at one time, though now his dark skin was a dusky color that contrasted with the short dreds crowning his head.

He stood almost two meters, and wore only a pair of synthleather pants. His upper torso was covered in spiked studs that had surely been implanted, making him look like some vampiric porcupine. She watched as two twenty-centimeter razors snicked from his forearms. He smiled, showing his fangs.

Just behind him, tiny by comparison, was a vampire woman. A mishmash of scars lined her face, making her lips form a lopsided vee shape where the bottom lip had been crudely sewn back together.

Unlike the first vampire, she seemed completely unmodified until she held up her small hands and ten-centimeter scalpels slid from beneath her fingers.

"It's time to play," said the woman, and suddenly they were moving. Fast.

The man streaked down the hall, an inarticulate howl coming from his lips as Sinunu took aim with the crossbow. Three bolts flew, but the man deflected them with the spurs on his arms.

Sinunu started to roll backward, knowing that the vampire would overwhelm her before she could bring her machine pistol to bear.

The monster crossed the last few meters, leaping into the air to land on top of her, when a huge, gnarled hand flashed out of the hallway.

Flak snagged the vampire just below the left spur, at the wrist. Letting his weight act as a fulcrum, Flak spun the thing face-first into the wall. There was a sickening crunch, and the vampire sank to the ground, leaving a trail of black ichor oozing down the wall.

The woman shifted her target, howling for Flak's back, which was momentarily exposed. Sinunu yelled for him to look out, but she might have saved her breath. De Vries was there, standing tall between Flak and the leaping woman.

Just as the dog had tried to do outside the compound, the woman tried to change course when she realized she was up against one of her own kind. She screamed and slashed with ten scalpels.

Before she could complete the maneuver, de Vries' hands shot out, gripping her on both sides of the head. Driving the hapless vampire back against the wall, de Vries rammed his thumbs into her eye sockets, burying them deep into the brain.

The female vampire howled, and Sinunu watched as the life seemed to drain out of her, along with the blood that spurted from her ravaged eye sockets to trail down her scarred face.

De Vries pulled his thumbs free and turned to look Sinunu in the eye. He wiped fluid and tissue from his hands on the female vampire's skin as she sank to the floor.

He winked at Sinunu, then nodded to the vampire Flak had downed. "You might want to stick that one. He's about ready to come back around."

Head spinning from what she'd just witnessed, Sinunu nodded back and fired a bolt into the body of the prone vampire. She made sure to miss the spikes, which she could now tell were deeply imbedded into the man's skin. He convulsed once, then was still.

There was silence in the hallway for the briefest instant, then Flak's gruff voice came over the com. "All right, kiddies. Looks like the drek is going to hit the fan in a very serious way, so let's keep things chilly and by the numbers."

Without a word, everybody formed up again. Sinunu looked at the crossbow with disgust. She'd thought it would be the perfect weapon to use against vampires, but now it seemed more like a useless toy.

She tossed the bow onto the dead man's body and was about to turn away, when a small hand touched her arm. It was Rachel.

"I don't mean to tell you your business, but don't you think you should keep that?"

Anger bled through Sinunu's voice. "Why? It's useless."

Rachel nodded. "Maybe for direct confrontation, but if we're going to get out of here alive, direct confrontation might not be the way to go. Besides, even if you just use it for sticking them once the vampires are down, you won't have to get so close to them to do it."

Sinunu looked at her for a moment, and then let out a shaky laugh. "Well, well, well. Being given lessons by a newbie." She shook her head and reached down to retrieve the crossbow. "Looks like Flak was right about you."

Sinunu watched as Rachel flushed slightly, her eyes lighting up with a strange gleam.

"Okay," came Sandman's voice over the tacticom, "now you've done it. You got enemy converging on you from all points. Take the right corridor as fast as you can."

Sinunu grabbed Rachel and began hustling her down the hall. At the end of it was a doorway marked "Stairs." She was just throwing it open, when a howl came from behind her.

"It's party time!" yelled Flak. "Let's show these bastards we've come with our boogie shoes on."

The quiet corridor filled with roaring gunfire.

Sinunu pushed Rachel into the stairwell, then turned, letting the door close behind her.

At first guess, she might have estimated twenty vampires streaming down the hallway, but because of how fast they were moving, it could have been twice that number.

The vampires seemed to come in all shapes and sizes, most of them human, but she could make out two orks and a stubby dwarf who seemed to be having a hard time keeping up with the rest of their companions. If what she remembered was correct, vampiric dwarfs should look like goblins, and vampiric orks were huge, white-furred monsters. These, except for the cyber on some of them, still looked like orks and dwarfs. She just hoped they died the same way regular vampires did.

She had just started to move forward, when the vampires ran full speed into Flak and de Vries. The sound was like a small clap of thunder.

The first vampire was a gangly human boy, who looked fifteen at most, but who attacked with utter abandon, fingers curled into claws reaching for the troll's eyes and driving Flak back for a moment. Catching both of the boy's hands in one of his massive paws, Flak used his free hand to pull the kid's head from his shoulders in a gout of blood that blinded the vampire coming up behind.

De Vries had managed to snag one of the two orks, a dark-haired woman with knobby, scarred skin. She had come to a stop just in front of him, and Sinunu could have sworn the creature was still trying to get off a spell when de Vries pulled out her heart.

Whatever the spell had been went off in the wrong direction, blowing the woman's body apart, and sending a sheet of flame back toward the other vampires.

Vampire bodies began to come apart in the fire, but it didn't touch all of them.

Sinunu watched as the dwarf stumbled through the flames and the dying vampires. He shook his grizzled head and tamped out the part of his red beard that had caught fire. He was past de Vries and Flak, who were playing clean-up, and in a moment, he focused on Truxa.

Roaring, he leapt for her throat, spurs pushing from his forearms and shins.

Sinunu fired her MP-5 and saw the leaping dwarf's face come apart under the force of the blow. Truxa knelt gracefully as the dwarf, suddenly without direction, sailed over her head.

As the thing hit the floor, Sinunu stepped forward and kicked it in the side of the head with all the strength she had. The head snapped to the side and she heard the sound of its neck breaking, even over the noise of the fighting.

Sinunu was just about to head back to the fray when she heard shots in the stairwell. Cursing, she swung back to the doorway and crashed through it.

There were six of them, three vampires up the stairwell, three below. And they were advancing.

She saw Rachel standing with her back to the wall, the huge Manhunter in her right hand and the smaller LD-120 in her left. Her face was surprisingly calm as she sighted first on the closest of the vampires above her and fired the Manhunter, which roared in the enclosed space.

The bullet tore open the vampire's throat, even as it tried to dodge.

Without even waiting to see if she'd hit, Rachel switched her aim to the LD-120, which was sighted at the vampires below her, and fired.

With a small popping sound compared to the Manhunter's roar, the bullet from the smaller gun ripped into the vampire's head, spraying bone and blood on the two vampires behind.

Sinunu put her back to the wall beside the other girl. Without taking her eyes from her task, Rachel said, "Head shots are about the only thing that seems to slow them down. Anything less, and they just keep coming."

"Sin," came Sandman's voice on the tacticom. "Get past the guys on top. If you can, you got a pretty clear shot to the surface."

"Six clear!" Flak shouted through the doorway.

"Activity on twelve," said Sinunu, as she and Rachel simultaneously fired, Sinunu at the top vamps, Rachel at the bottom. Rachel was using both pistols at the same time now.

Then de Vries was there, standing in the doorway to Sinunu's right. Striding forward, like some evil god, he laughed. "My brothers, you have been deceived. Let these two pass. They are nothing to you. The one who deserves your hatred is the man who created you. Turn your hunger on him."

Sinunu knew he was trying some kind of spell, and for a moment she thought it might work. The vampires hesitated, hissing, their dead eyes filled with something that Sinunu could only read as fear and respect.

Then the lead vampire snarled, and leapt at de Vries with a howl. The vamp never even came close. De Vries made a casual pass with one hand, and it was like invisible blades slashing through the air, slicing into the approaching vampire's flesh, cutting through bone. The vampire quickly came apart in a cloud of black blood and tissue.

De Vries turned to Sinunu, and with a small smile said, "Well, it was worth a try, and it should have worked. These vampires are being controlled somehow."

With that move, the rest of the vampires attacked in force.

Suddenly, the high whine of the Vindicator rolled through the narrow stairwell as Flak joined the fray. Deafening thunder shattered the quiet.

Pieces of vampire flesh flew everywhere, splattering the walls and stairs. The Vindicator tore them to pieces.

As a group, the runners moved up the stairway, Truxa and Sinunu taking the lead.

"Bad news," came Sandman's voice over the tacticom. "Your boys have managed a flanking maneuver somehow." He sounded concerned. "They're waiting for you just at the top of the next landing."

"Beautiful," muttered Truxa, then turned to look up at Sinunu. "You tag them, I'll bag them."

22

The only thing more amazing than the quantum leaps we've taken in advancing technology are the advances promised by our researches into the possibility of combining technology and magic. I foresee a future where the line between the two will blur to the point of indistinction. We stand on the brink of the next great leap in evolution.

—Oslo Wake, defending his use of metahuman subjects before Board of Ethics and Review, Universal Omnitech, New York City. Transcript #ETH678, p. 892, 21 September 2051

Julius felt the Mobmaster's rigger rev the big engine, cranking up its speed to ram the oncoming barrier.

"Brace for impact," yelled Julius.

The Mobmaster hit the reinforced steel gate of the Hell's Kitchen compound and ripped it off its hinges. Rolling over the tire shredders that popped up, the Mobmaster's runflat tires took no notice.

The huge vehicle rocked gently as explosions shattered stone formations to the left and the right, raining deadly shrapnel against the unyielding sides of the truck.

"Our deckers report land mines coming active!" yelled Biggs. "This ride's about to get bumpy."

Julius looked out the window at the distinctive shapes of miniguns along the fence line. He turned to Biggs. "Why aren't they using the miniguns?"

Biggs shook his head for a moment, then looked up. "Decker says they've been taken off line. He doesn't know why, but he can't get to them. He's been locked out."

Julius nodded. He'd have preferred to be able to use the miniguns for his own ends, but as long as the bad guys couldn't use them either, he'd take what he could get. He looked over his shoulder at the men standing behind him, hanging on to the support eyelets.

"Gun rigger, fire at will," Biggs said, rapping out orders over the tacticom, sending them directly to each soldier's helmet. "Mages, establish astral recon. Prepare spirits for combat. Infantry, we disembark in three."

The Mobmaster rocked more violently as the rigger accelerated, rolling over as many land mines as he could. The Mobmaster could withstand damage that would have disabled, if not destroyed, the lighter trucks following. Explosion after explosion lit up the night, and for the first time, Julius got a good look at what they were up against.

"Holy mother of God," Julius breathed.

From behind him, he heard the gun rigger yell, "What in the hell are those things?"

Julius continued to look out the window, but said loudly, "Keep it steady. They're just heavily modified troops. Keep a rock on back there."

The gun rigger yelled his affirmative, sounding a bit calmer. These men had seen heavy mods on troops before, and even though the things coming toward them were so far beyond the pale they were into the black, Julius knew his men would adjust.

"Recon, give me a count!" Biggs shouted.

From inside his headset, Julius heard the rigger piloting the recon drone say, "Thirty, at least, not counting the animals. I'd say we're running against fifty targets."

Sounds of gunfire filled the air as the gunners at the Mobmaster's .50 caliber guns and autocannons let go. Julius watched as the closest figure exploded, the big rounds cutting it in half and sending the two separate sections sprawling away from each other.

The Mobmaster slowed a bit as it rounded the first curve, and that was all it took.

A scream from the top gunner was the first sign that the monstrous things had managed to swarm up the back of the truck.

Julius turned to the back just in time to see a metal hand, more a collection of curved razors than a hand, slice through the Mobmaster's armor.

"Down!" Julius shouted, lifting his chopped Remington twelve-gauge. He sighted at the metal hand's wrist joint, and pulled the trigger.

The roar in the cabin was deafening, but the weapon's solid-core slug took the hand off at the wrist, then flattened itself against the Mobmaster's armored wall. The hand skittered across the floor, bouncing against one of the men's feet. With a look of disgust, the man kicked the still twitching thing away from him.

"You all right, Charlie?" asked Biggs.

"I'm fine," the top gunner shouted, "but you got about six stowaways weighing you down."

Biggs looked at Julius, who said, "Fry them."

"Everybody clear!" yelled Biggs, just before he stroked the small icon on the Mobmaster's touchscreen console.

There was a crackle, and the Mobmaster's power cut out for a moment, as ten thousand volts rippled through the vehicle's conductive shielding.

Screams from the rear of the vehicle spoke of the shock's effectiveness.

They made the next curve in the road, and the rigger hit the accelerator again, bringing the huge truck up to ramming speed.

Directly in front of the Mobmaster, another massive, wrought iron gate loomed five meters off the ground. Reinforced with concrete and steel girders, it looked forbidding and impenetrable.

"Trucks two through five, report," said Julius.

"Two, rolling."

"Three, rolling."

"Four, rolling, but Five is gone. Request permission to back up and locate them."

"Recon," said Julius.

"Recon here."

"Give me status on Citymaster Five."

There was a pause, then, "It looks like they hit a mine, just inside the perimeter. They're stalled, and they've got six targets converging."

The gate rushed rapidly toward them as the rigger pushed the Mobmaster to its limit.

Julius spoke again. "Copy, Citymaster Four. Regroup with five and keep our back door open."

"Brace yourselves," said Biggs.

They hit the fence, guns blazing, the front scoop of the Mobmaster ripping through the heavy metal like it was paper.

The fence top smashed down onto the roof of the truck, cracking the bulletproof glass. Then it bounced high, describing a long arc up and to the left, where the hinges finally gave away, sending the fence flying off into the night.

Julius caught one glimpse of it, as it sheared off a light pole at the base, plunging the near area into darkness. All around them, the darkness seemed to be moving. Undulating and swaying like a field of tall black grass on a moonless night.

Julius switched his helmet to infrared. The crimson-tinged view was not much clearer, but at least now he could see them. Crowds of creatures, their IR silhouettes dim and twisted, impregnated by cold cyber.

Julius only got a glimpse, but it was enough to send fear down his spine like an icy razor.

"Recon here, Mobmaster One. It looks as if the fifty targets are getting some reinforcements from the compound."

"Check," said Julius. "Begin your aerial attack now. Mages, let's turn up the heat."

Then the things were on them.

23

Vampires feed on more than just blood; it is the actual life energy of the victim that sustains them. The bloodletting is just the simplest way to extract that life energy. As a vampire feeds, the energy that sustained the victim is transferred to the vampire, infusing him with strength and well being.

—Martin de Vries, *Shadows at Noon,* posted to Shadowland BBS, 24 May 2057

Sandman had been right. They had reached the next landing and all hell had broken loose. The runners had blasted their way through vamp after vamp, until they were almost to the top.

Just then, a huge woman who looked as if her entire body was covered with grease, and who hung by her feet from the railing above, reached down with her massive hands to grasp Rachel by the armpits and pull her upward.

Flak shouted a warning, but a moment too late. Rachel was suddenly lifted off the floor, pain wracking through her rib cage.

She looked up, wondering how this immensely fat woman could possibly be hanging that way. She didn't have much time to wonder, because the woman opened her mouth in a vicious grin, showing stained fangs. Rachel could smell the vampire's charnel-house breath and nearly retched.

That mouth came closer and closer, and for a moment,

Rachel thought this was it. She was going to die, and she was going to let everybody down.

"Rachel, the pistol! Use it!" Sinunu screamed at her.

Suddenly jerked back into focus, Rachel kicked back with her legs, which let her bring up her right arm.

The hot barrel of the Manhunter fit nicely into the vampire's mouth.

Rachel pulled the trigger twice, then suddenly both she and the fat woman were falling back toward the stairs.

She knew she would be crushed under the woman's huge weight, and tried to spin, tried to maneuver, but it was no use.

Out of nowhere, a giant arm wrapped around her. It was Flak pulling her to his blood-soaked chest. "Gotcha," he said, as the fat vampire hit the ground with a thud and started to roll down the stairs. De Vries stopped the body with one booted foot, as easily as if he were stopping a rolling ball.

"Nicely done, dear," said de Vries, as he drove his fist deep into the woman's chest and pulled out her black, ichor-slick heart.

Gunfire sounded from above, and Flak was gone.

Rachel moved as fast as she could around the turn in the stairs and slipped in the dark, vampire blood covering the floor. She would have gone down, except for a strong hand catching her again. She turned, and found herself looking into the cold, dead eyes of Martin de Vries. He had a small, sad smile on his face. "Careful there. The footing is bad and going to get worse."

They were on the top landing, and ready to make the assault into the hallway that would lead them to loading dock number four. It was the closest dock to the front entrance, which Sandman reported as under assault by troops who looked like they were military. At the very least, they had equipment that bespoke a bigger budget than anybody but Lone Star could bring to bear.

Nobody knew exactly what was going on, but at the moment the attack came, the resistance to their departure had all but evaporated. Small pockets of vampires, usually just two or three at a time, still plagued them, but they weren't of the same deadly caliber that they'd first encountered. Most of them were small and lightly cybered, nor had they encountered any with magical abilities for almost five minutes of climbing.

As Rachel gained the top landing, she looked around at the rest of the runners. Flak stood tall and silent, the Vindicator cradled in his arms like a child. He was breathing easily, despite the blood running from four separate wounds on his arms and chest.

Truxa had done what she could for him, but she'd also been wounded. Her left arm was broken and although she'd healed herself, the bone wasn't completely mended and the wound hampered her magical ability. She'd been forced to take the fall-back position. Wielding Sinunu's crossbow, she was in charge of making sure that whatever the rest of the team knocked down stayed down.

Sinunu had pulled up her balaclava hood to reveal a bloodied mouth, missing two teeth where a dying vampire had smashed her face-first into the wall, seconds before de Vries had broken the thing's spine. She was also walking with a limp, favoring her right hip. From the fire in her eyes, though, Rachel guessed Sinunu was riding on a killing wave and didn't notice any pain.

Rachel found herself smiling. Even though she'd gotten hit a couple of times, the bullet that had grazed her thigh had been a ricochet. She put a hand to her left shoulder and felt blood there. Evidently, the fat woman had managed to get her licks in before Rachel had shot the back of her head off. Still, Rachel didn't feel it either. Her body was humming with intense excitement. Part of her was angry and scared, angry that they hadn't found Warren, and afraid for what might have been done to him. That was a small part, however. She was alive. Truly alive for the first time in her life. It was as if everything had come down to this, fighting alongside people who trusted you with their lives, and knowing that you would kill or die to not let them down. Dancing that razor's edge.

She looked around again, and a huge swelling of pride filled her. This small team was going up against incredible odds, against some of the darkest creatures the Sixth World had ever seen. They'd been bloodied, but were unbowed. They were hurt, but they were still deadly, and any vampire who crossed their path would find out just how deadly.

The only one who remained uninjured was de Vries. He was a whirlwind of destruction, and seemed to take a perverse glee in killing vampires that had made Rachel queasy the first few times. Now, she understood his reaction. The only time de Vries had seemed sad since the fighting had begun was when he'd been forced to hurl the still unconscious body of the decoy at the vampires approaching from below. And though it had bought their escape, she'd heard him muttering, "I'm sorry. I'm sorry."

"Talk to me, Sandman. We're almost out of ammo, and I don't think we can take too many more hits." Flak's voice sounded calm over the tacticom, but Rachel thought she could detect a hint of strain, maybe even fear.

"There's not much I *can* tell you," came Sandman's voice in her ear. "The fighting outside is pretty hot. Whoever these guys are, they're kicking hoop and taking no prisoners. At first, the vamps were getting back up again, but these guys are pros, and they've changed their tactics. Not so many vampires are getting up anymore."

Flak grunted. "So the military-type boys are winning?"

There was a pause. "Yes and no. They're taking down vampires fast and furious, but somebody tripped something in the system about five minutes ago, and some more vampires just showed up out of nowhere."

"Damn," muttered Flak. "Any way to slip out in the confusion?"

Sandman's voice came over the com again. "Probably not, but you've only got one more corridor, and then you're back in the fresh air. Give me about a minute to double-check everything, then be ready to hit it when I give you the signal. You still packing those shaped charges?"

"Affirmative," said Flak.

"Well, you're probably gonna need them. The doors at the end of the hall are locked tighter than Lofwyr's vaults, and there's not one thing I can do. I've been shut out of that area of the system."

"Check," said Flak. He turned to the rest of team and said, "You heard the man! One minute, and we're out of here. Get your drek together, and make sure you've got enough ammo."

Suddenly the unreality of all that had happened that night hit Rachel. She looked around at the bloodied crew, then down at the guns in her hands.

She let out a small laugh. "Hey, guys, just twenty-four hours ago, I was wondering if I was gonna make the rent and whether to splurge on another pair of heels for work."

Sinunu responded with a low chuckle. "Under the circumstances, you've done pretty fragging well." She looked over at de Vries, who was standing near the door. "Next time you want to bring someone else along for the ride, vampire man, they better have as much on the ball as your girl here."

De Vries smiled at her. "Is that your oblique way of apologizing?"

Sinunu looked at him for a moment, and Rachel thought she was angry, but then Sinunu shrugged. "I guess it is."

De Vries' smile grew into a toothy grin that somehow didn't remind Rachel of the vampires they'd been killing for the last half an hour. "Apology accepted."

The tacticom crackled. "Heads up, people. This is about as good as it gets." Sandman's voice was staticky over the com. "We're rolling again. There's some fighting out by the front gate, and we're going to try slipping past it. The corridor is clear, and you've got about a twenty-second window to make the loading dock. If you can, meet us at the front gate. Be careful. There's a lead storm flying out here, and the good guys are on the defensive now."

"Roger, Sandman," said Flak. "We're outta here."

The rest of them got into position.

Rachel took up her new place, the position Truxa had held before getting injured. How strange that only two hours ago, she'd felt like a lost outsider with these people. Now, she was at home. She knew her role, and knew she was trusted to carry it out. She had proven something to herself as well, though she wasn't quite sure what that was yet. All she knew was that she'd gotten back on her feet, her wounds were distant things, and that razor's edge was calling to her.

"Okay, everybody," said Flak, from up near the door, "this is it. One last dance, then hopefully we can get the hell off the dance floor. Everybody hang tight, conserve ammo, and if I give the signal, run. Don't look back."

With that, he opened the door, and they began to move quickly down the long hallway leading to a door at the far end, the exit sign gleaming like a promise.

24

The cyberware is implanted prior to infection and remains fully functional after vampirism takes hold. But there are some drawbacks, the foremost being that if the cyberware is damaged in any way, the subject dies. The other hurdle to be overcome is the loss of some of the vampire's capabilities with the introduction of cyberware.

—Dr. Oslo Wake, laboratory notes, Test series OV13652, 02 November 2058

Julius and his men hadn't known what they'd find in this godforsaken place, and it was worse than anything they could have imagined. Vampires with cyberware.

Julius jammed his foot on the head of the vampire he'd just downed, just below the metal cranial cap, and rammed his shotgun up under the thing's flat, rotten nose. He pulled the trigger and watched as the thing's face came apart in a wet spray. Pushing the barrel of the shotgun further into the ruined flesh, he angled his shot upward and blew the cap right off the vampire's head.

In the last thirty minutes, his men had learned a valuable lesson. The vampires might be undead, and might be able to take a lot of punishment, but if they were cybered, they were vulnerable. Screw with the cyber, and the vamp was hosed.

Looking up from his kill, Julius triggered the commlink in his helmet. "Biggs? Heads up. They're flanking you. Team Two, lay down suppressive fire."

Then he was running, the heavy combat suit making sweat stream down his body. Just behind him, the mage Killian managed to keep pace, despite his diminutive frame.

To his left, the earth elemental that Killian had summoned minutes before was heaving great mounds of dirt over a small group of vampires that had tried to attack it.

Out of the corner of his eye, Julius caught movement, and was turning to deal with it, when the night erupted in flame.

The vampire, a human female, turned into a glowing fireball in mid-air as she leapt for him. Julius used the heavy gloves of his combat suit to bat the burning woman aside as he continued running. "Thanks, Killian."

The mage just nodded, sweat streaming down his face and blood coming from his nose. He'd been lighting up the night with his fire elementals, and the drain of summoning and casting was taking its toll.

On Julius' right, Biggs was standing at the point of a wedge that made up Team Three. Ruby spears of coherent light lanced out into the darkness, cutting dark forms into pieces.

Julius cursed himself for not arming more of the men with lasers. They seemed to do more lasting damage than simple lead rounds.

When they'd discovered this, Julius had reformed his teams into straight vee-shapes, with a laser man walking point and the heavy guns playing backup. Each team had started out with a mage, though none as powerful as Killian. The vampires had caught on quickly, however, and only Killian and one other mage still lived.

Even with the reinforcements the vampires had received from inside the compound, the Fratellanza troops had managed to force them back again, until they'd almost reached the building.

Julius wasn't about to leave this place without his son, but he hoped fervently that whoever was directing the defenses had committed everything to the exterior. If they hadn't, and there were another forty or so of these bad boys lurking inside, it would be a running battle his men were sure to lose. Even with their superior speed and maneuverability, the vamps were proving manageable out in the open. Inside, the undead would have all the advantages.

Julius and Killian reached Team One just as Biggs finished bisecting a vampire. The thing screamed, though it tried to pull itself forward with just its hands, leaving still twitching legs behind.

"Die, you godless bastard!" screamed Biggs as he burned the vampire's head from its shoulders.

"Report," said Julius as he advanced with Biggs.

"I figure there are still about sixty of 'em total, with the reinforcements. It only seems like more 'cause they're so hard to put down. We're sitting at about thirty percent casualties, about eighteen men dead. Nobody still alive has been bitten, far as I know." Biggs' voice was tight with adrenaline and fear. "But I got some boys staking anybody who goes down, just to make sure our own dead don't get back up."

Above his head, Julius could hear the sounds of four airborne drones in the background. They'd started out with six, but somehow the vampires had managed to bring down two of them. It didn't really matter, though. The drones were little more than a nuisance to the vampires. With their light guns, the drones couldn't target the vampires long enough to do any lasting damage.

Julius spoke over the commlink. "We can't take this prolonged fighting," he said. "We've got to make a hard push for the loading dock there. Teams Three and Four will fortify the position, and One and Two will start ransacking the place. Once we find Warren, I want this place burned to the ground. Understand?"

Biggs turned to him, and Julius could see his wide grin beneath the visor covering the top of his face. "My pleasure."

Julius spoke into his commlink again. "By the numbers, people. Team Four, take the left flank and advance to just below the loading dock. Team Three, back them. Team One and

Two, provide cover. When Three and Four are in position, One and Two take the building."

Just then the entire back of the loading dock lit up with a brilliant light, and the concussion was enough to make Julius stagger. In the afterglow, he could see the door to the loading dock buckle outward and finally fly upward.

"What the hell?" Biggs had turned to stare, and so did everyone else out there, vampires included.

Then forms spilled out of the ruined doorway. Julius counted five of them, one so huge it had to be a troll. Even from here, Julius could see that they were in bad shape.

"Damn, he's going to be hard to take down," said Biggs.

Suddenly, the whine of a Vindicator brought the battle back into focus as the huge troll started chewing up the nearest vampires. The group was running, hunched low, shooting up any vampire that came close.

Julius accelerated the visual field on his helmet and switched to night-vision enhancement and flare compensation. He brought the group into focus, the troll first, then a human with pale, pale skin and white hair. There was a small elf, and another . . .

He recognized this one. Rachel. Warren's girlfriend.

What's she doing here? The sight of her was so incongruous that for a moment, he couldn't believe it. Then the formation of the team struck home. Fratellanza, Inc. had earned millions of nuyen trying to keep teams exactly like this from penetrating their client's defenses.

She hired a bunch of shadowrunners. Julius realized in a flash that she must have been trying to rescue Warren. *But if that's true, then where is my son?* He scanned the entire area and saw no sign of him. The runners didn't have him.

Julius caught sight of another face among the group coming out of the compound. It appeared for a second, then was gone from his magnified field of vision. But for Julius, it was a face he would never forget.

The face of Martin de Vries.

This man had killed Derek, and he had kidnapped Warren. Or so Julius had thought. But if that were true, then why was he killing these vampires? And why was he in the company of Warren's girlfriend, a woman Julius knew would never work against the interests of his son?

Julius had questions and he needed answers. He was determined to get those answers. And his son.

"Team Two, give them cover fire!" he yelled.

The night was rocked by gunfire and lit up like New Year's Eve. Team Two poured everything they had into the enemy.

A small group of eight vampires, led by a female who was more cyber than vampire, tried to cut the group off. The man Julius recognized as de Vries tore her limb from limb, and used one of her cybered legs to beat another vampire to the ground, then reached down to pull out the creature's heart.

Suddenly, the doorway to the loading dock seemed to swell like the ocean, and forms started pouring out into the night.

"This is Recon to Mobmaster One. We got lots of company. I count at least forty more vampires chasing that little group."

Julius watched as the runners formed a circle, shoulder to shoulder. They were surrounded on all sides. He knew then that they were going to be overwhelmed. Killed before he had the chance to find out what they knew about Warren.

25

There is a certain irony to hunting the hunter, especially these beasts. Vampires are arrogant and cruel, so distanced from their humanity that killing them brings me no guilt. As a society, we stand quite ready to put rabid dogs out of their, and our, misery. Why not these foul abominations as well?

—Martin de Vries, *Shadows at Noon,* posted to Shadowland BBS, 24 May 2057

Rachel stood shoulder to shoulder with Sinunu and Truxa. At their backs were Flak and de Vries. Her legs felt like dead weight and she could barely stand from the fatigue. *I will not let it end here,* she thought.

Firing as quickly as she could aim, Rachel watched as the line of vampires advanced on them. The first of them was an old man. He was dressed in a tattered suit that showed recent bloodstains running down its front. His left arm was a clunky piece of cyberware left over from the Desert Wars, and the right side of his head was plate metal. Just behind him came a trio of women. They were all brown-haired and slim, but the middle one was missing her right arm from the shoulder, and the simple dress she wore still smoked near the neck. The arm had obviously been taken off by a laser, but she just as obviously didn't seem to notice.

Flak's voice came over the tacticom. "Sandman, it looks

like this is it. They got us pinned down. Is there anything you can do?"

Sandman's voice was strained. "Just hold on. I'm going to try to get control of the perimeter defenses."

Suddenly, the night was lit up again, this time by the miniguns on the roof and fence. Sandman's aim wasn't as good as a security rigger's would have been, but it wasn't half bad. Hot lead tore into the vampires, separating the wave that was advancing on them, opening a tiny hole in the middle of the line.

The runners were just about to move when the first of the miniguns fell silent. Rachel looked up just in time to see small knots of vampires, heedless of the damage being done to them, tearing the miniguns from their housing.

"Good, but not good enough," said Flak over the tacticom.

Suddenly, there was a screaming roar from in front of Rachel, in the direction of the Fratellanza trucks. Out of the darkness, a huge form rolled forward, looking like some deformed locomotive. Scattering vampires like chaff, its wedge-shaped scoop cutting white flesh and dragging vampires under, the huge vehicle plowed through, bearing straight for them.

Just behind the monster truck, Rachel could make out the van that had transported them there.

"That more like it? Seems the military-type boys want to get you out almost as much as I do." Sandman's voice held a note of triumph that Rachel hadn't heard before.

The huge truck turned at the last moment, catching a male vampire under its massive front tire. The man screamed with anger and pain, his pale flesh splitting over his abdomen and spilling his intestines on the ground.

The vampire, crazed with pain, tried to bite the wheel holding it down.

"All aboard, this is the last train leaving," said Sandman over the tacticom.

At the side of vehicle, a wedge-shaped door fell forward, making a ramp.

Two men in battle gear stood to both sides of the doorway, firing into the vampires at Rachel's back.

She ran, barely reaching the ramp when a scream and the sounds of Flak cursing came from behind her. She and Sinunu turned simultaneously.

It was the vampire that had been trapped under the wheel. Rachel had thought it out of the action, but she hadn't looked close enough. The man was unaugmented, and even though his guts still hung from the ragged hole in his stomach, the thing had obviously turned to mist and escaped the weight of the huge vehicle.

Rachel watched in horror as the small, slim vampire, who could barely hold itself upright, took hold of Truxa by the back of her neck, and hauled her away from the group.

Flak and de Vries were too busy trying to hold off the vampires advancing from the rear to do anything. By now the vampire had dragged Truxa deep into the midst of the surging mass of infected flesh.

Sinunu moved like a blur, leaping off the ramp and plunging toward the waiting enemy. Quick as she was, de Vries was even faster.

As he moved, he shouted a word and cast his hands into the air. In front of him, a fire elemental sprang to life and descended on the vampires. The old man was set on fire and flung ten meters into the air. He landed among his cohorts, setting several of them ablaze, and scattering the rest.

Like a tornado, de Vries descended on his own kind, following the elemental, and tearing into the horde like some insane thresher in a field of fetid wheat. Ripping the lesser vampires apart, he cut a swath through their ranks, and he seemed to swell with each of the vamps he killed.

De Vries' bellow of rage was a terrible thing to hear, and Rachel found herself flinching from the sound. The vampires standing against him tried to fight back, but they were no match for de Vries' power and fury.

Behind him, Sinunu had his back, so when a small group of vampires tried to flank him, she was there, firing with blinding accuracy.

Still, it was no use. The vampires were passing Truxa's limp body over their heads, each of them taking a small chunk out of her, until Rachel could see the white of bone beneath her blood-covered skin. The elf's sling hung from her broken arm like a bloodied flag of truce.

Rachel knew Truxa was dead, and even if she wasn't, she was certainly infected. Still, de Vries fought on.

Behind Rachel, the two men who were guarding the door of the huge truck came down the ramp and ushered her into the vehicle. She turned to find herself face to face with an older man, sweat running down his face, his silvering hair plastered to the side of his head.

From pictures she had seen, she knew instantly that it was Warren's father.

"Rachel, we've got to go. There's no way we can hold them back any longer." Even as he said that, his hand shot out, pushing Rachel down and firing over her head.

Rachel didn't even bother to look and see how close the vampire had come. Over the tacticom, Flak's voice, choked and nearly unintelligible, said, "Pull back. She's . . . she's gone."

Out in the center of the vampires, de Vries and Sinunu fought on, but now, even de Vries was threatened with being overwhelmed.

A commotion to the duo's left caught Rachel's attention.

The elemental, which had been destroying vampires left and right, faded suddenly and was gone.

There seemed to be a communication between Sinunu and de Vries. As one, they turned back toward the vehicle, fighting their way through the vampires separating them from the men who had come to rescue them.

A team of men in battle armor came from the right, led by a big, redheaded ork who had lost his helmet somewhere in the fray.

Using lasers and heavy-caliber rifles, the men cleared a path back, and the two groups met in the middle of the fray. Firing as they ran, the group covered ground in long strides and made the vehicle before the vampires could regroup.

Rachel, standing on the platform and firing into the crowd of vampires to help keep up the confusion, watched as Sinunu climbed up beside her.

Sinunu wasn't crying, though Rachel knew her own eyes were stinging with tears. Instead, the other woman's eyes had gone dead, and Rachel shuddered at what she saw behind those lifeless pink orbs.

26

Play with cybermancy and you play with the basic processes of life itself, and the integrity of the spirit. There's no bigger game. Unlike the Azzies, that may be all there is to it for Ordo Maximus. They're into the power and secrecy. It's as simple as that.

—From encrypted telecom transcripts posted to Shadowland BBS by Captain Chaos, 11 December 2056. Identity of speakers not definitively verified.

Deep below, standing in operating theater number two, Oslo Wake watched the strategic retreat of the Fratellanza, Inc. forces.

Beside him, Pakow shifted nervously. Wake could almost taste the man's fear, could smell the stink of sweat on him.

Wake smiled to himself. The man was like a pane of new glass. Still, Wake was pleased by how things had gone. As the last of the trucks pulled out of sight, he sighed.

"Have security recall the troops and order a clean-up detail. I want a full report, losses on both sides as well as equipment damage. I also want to know how the runners penetrated our computer system so easily. Lastly, there will probably be several new arrivals tonight. I want them tagged and implanted if possible, destroyed if not. If there are any new metas in the mix, I want a count of them, and I want them sequestered until I can speak with them personally."

"Of course," said Pakow. "I'll relay the order."

Wake smiled again when he noticed how quickly Pakow had gotten himself under control. "I'm actually quite pleased," Wake said. "Tonight's activities have invigorated me tremendously. From the trideo I've seen so far, I'd have to say that our shock troops did quite well."

Pakow looked troubled. "Excuse me?"

Wake laughed, and clapped a hand on Pakow's shoulder, pretending not to notice when the other man flinched. "Doctor Pakow, our troops had absolutely no training other than the natural instincts provided by our treatments, and no weapons other than a few built into their cyber. Yet they managed to stave off a heavily armed assault conducted by seasoned professionals. If ever there was an indication that we're on the right track here, tonight was certainly it."

Wake watched as Pakow forced an airless chuckle. "Of course, Doctor Wake."

Wake smiled, and knew without a doubt the impact that smile had on Pakow. The smaller man paled. "Now, my dear doctor, there is something I would like to show you."

Pakow nodded, but didn't say anything.

Wake made a few adjustments on the monitors, and watched as the playback showed the small group of runners storming the room below.

"Hey, this isn't Warren." The voice from the monitor was soft, feminine, but with an edge to it that Wake admired.

He played the whole loop, not bothering to look at Pakow.

As the one Wake had come to realize must be *the* Martin de Vries stepped out of the supply elevator carrying a body obviously meant to replace Warren's, Wake froze the image.

"Isn't he simply magnificent?" Wake whispered under his breath. Then he turned to look at Pakow, who had gone a dangerous shade of purple, his dark eyes fixed on the monitor. "He truly is the pinnacle of what *we're* trying to achieve here. A full vampire who is in complete control of himself, who has retained his soul. What I wouldn't give to have him under observation for a few months. Still, his flaws are obvious, and I will be honored to one day turn them into strengths."

Pakow gained control awkwardly.

"Come, Doctor Pakow," Wake said, killing the picture on the monitor. "It's time to get to work on our patient. When I learned that Marco's brother was coming to attempt a rescue, I took the liberty of moving Warren's body to the backup facility. I meant to tell you, but I guess I was preoccupied."

Wake looked up just in time to see Pakow swallow hard, his protruding Adam's apple bobbing. In that moment, Wake actually found it in his heart to feel sorry for the other man. *You didn't ask for this, did you, little man? You didn't ask for the burden of being the salvation of metahumanity, and the pressure got to you.*

Pakow cleared his throat, and pushed a heavy lock of hair up off his forehead. The hair stayed for just a moment, then fell back down again. "Where are we going?"

Wake looked at him closely, finding a perverse pleasure in watching the man squirm under his gaze. "Doctor Pakow, you don't look so well. Have you been pushing too hard?"

Pakow's face turned positively ashen, then he nodded. "Maybe. I am feeling a bit . . . tired."

Wake nodded. "My apologies, Doctor. Unfortunately, any rest will have to wait. I'm a bit tired myself, and could certainly use your expertise for this next crucial step. After that you should take a break. It's been a tiring day."

Wake led Pakow out of the room and down the hall to operating theater number six. He stepped into the dimly lit room. This one was identical to the other five operating theaters, complete with an experimental tank in the middle. Except this one held Warren D'imato.

"Well, hello, my friend," Wake said to the figure down below.

"Is that Warren D'imato?"

Wake ignored Pakow's stupid question. He spoke in a quiet whisper, addressing Warren. "You are about to be given a gift beyond your wildest imaginings. If your procedure goes well, you will become one of the most powerful creatures ever to walk the earth. How does that grab you?"

Pakow had gone over to the control console. "You've started the procedure on him," he said. "How far has it gone?"

Wake shook his head. "Not far. I've done the ritual magic, but haven't yet exposed him to the first viral bath. I'd like you to do that, and take over the rest of the process. I'm going to be busy for a while."

Pakow gave him a grave nod. "I understand."

"Do you?"

"I'll let you know when the procedure is complete," Pakow said.

Without answering, Wake made his way from the operating theater and was heading for his office. By the time he reached his sanctuary, a small beep told him that someone had tracked him down on his private line. "Right on time," said Wake.

Hitting the Connect button, Wake found himself face to face with Marco D'imato. Wake had been expecting this call, but Marco's condition took him by surprise. The vampire's deterioration was occurring much faster than he'd anticipated. The man's makeup was a drifting sludge on his black face, and his dark lips were trembling.

Covering, Wake said, "Doctor Wake here. What can I do for you, Mister D'imato?"

Marco's voice was a dry rasp. "What happened?"

Wake laughed. "Exactly what I expected. Your brother and his compatriots met with a bit more resistance than they had anticipated. They fled with their tails between their legs, so to speak."

"Is Julius dead?"

Wake frowned. "No, and he did a great deal of damage, which you will be paying for. However, as far as I've been able to determine, he was unharmed during the fray."

Marco shook his head, and blood-tinted sweat flew from his forehead. "Not possible. I know Julius, and if he came and saw your facility, there's no way he would have left without Warren."

Wake smiled, and he could see Marco, even in the state he was in, draw back from that grin. "Then you know very little about possibilities, Mister D'imato. Point of fact is that I have just left the room containing your nephew. Point of fact, your brother led a failed assault, and left after being soundly defeated."

Marco shook his head again. "He'll be back, with more firepower."

Wake leaned into the screen. "Unless, of course, you prevent him from doing so. I am a doctor, Mister D'imato, and I really don't have the time to be worrying about this."

Marco shrugged. "You're right. How is Warren?"

Wake sat down in the chair. "He's doing remarkably well. We'll be beginning the treatment soon."

Marco nodded, and showed his teeth in a fierce grin. "That's good news, at least. When will he be mobile?"

Wake weighed his answer carefully. "Another couple of days, provided there aren't complications. Speaking of complications, I'm guessing from your appearance that there's been a reoccurrence of your spasms?"

Marco nodded, his shoulders drooping.

Wake steepled his fingers under his chin. "I've done some tests, and I'm quite concerned. However, I think I might have pinned down part of the problem. I'm setting up a treatment for you that should correct things, and if my analysis proves out, I might actually be able to restore some of the damage done to you during the initial procedure."

For the first time since their conversation began, Wake watched Marco's face light up. "You're kidding. I thought you said the damage was irreversible?"

Wake smiled. "I didn't say I was promising anything. Thanks, however, to your generous contributions to the project, I've been able to make some advances that even I didn't know were possible. But there isn't much time. We have to arrest the deterioration in your system before it does more damage. When can you come out?"

Marco's eyes narrowed, and for a moment, Wake thought he might have tipped his hand. However, all Marco said was, "How long will this procedure take?"

Wake pretended to check something on the desk, trying to weigh his answer into a balance that would provide Marco with something believable, without making it seem impossible. "It's a complete battery of submersions, as well as injection therapy, but my guess would be that it won't take more than a month, six weeks at the most. Depending, of course, on how well your body is able to adjust."

Marco didn't answer for a moment. Then, "You realize that this is a very precarious time for my organization. Especially now with my brother creating problems."

Wake nodded. "Yes, but Warren will be up and able by the end of the week. Couldn't you put him in charge as soon as he returns? You could even claim that you know where he is and that you are going to fetch him. Then you could say you're going to Europe to take in the baths, or something. We could set up a line, so that Warren could report to you each day."

The dark gleam in Marco's eye let Wake know he'd said just enough.

"Doctor Wake, you are worthy of my trust. While the plan is far from foolproof, it isn't like I will be out of the country or anything. If something goes wrong, I'll just interrupt the procedure and take care of it."

Wake hid his smile. "Tomorrow morning, then? It will be the last time you'll be able to look at the sun for a couple of weeks."

Marco nodded. "I'll be there."

Wake cut the connection. He paused for a moment, and took a deep breath, then punched in a private number.

Pakow answered on the first ring. "Yes?" He looked disheveled and was breathing heavily.

"Have you started the procedure?" Wake asked.

Pakow nodded. "Yes, I'm injecting the solution into the tank as we speak. Is there a problem?"

Wake shook his head. "Not really. I think I've taken care of it."

Wake watched as Pakow's eyes narrowed, though his voice was carefully neutral. "What is it?"

"I want one of the full stasis rooms prepared by tomorrow morning. Not one of the tanks, but one of the big rooms in delta wing. Set it up so it looks like a regular treatment room. Mister D'imato is going to be our guest for a while. I've convinced him we might have a way to slow his deterioration. I want him put in stasis. He's only got about a month of life left in him anyway, and it's time we removed him from the equation before he jeopardizes our operation."

Pakow looked puzzled. "That's a lot of resources to devote to someone you want out of your way. Why don't we just finish him when he comes in?"

Wake laughed. "My dear doctor, those are very harsh words from someone who took an oath to preserve life."

Pakow didn't join in. "Universal Omnitech didn't require either you or I to take any oath. In fact, I think they would have been opposed to the whole idea of preserving life when any easier measure was available."

Wake's laughter faltered. "Touché, Doctor Pakow," he said softly, "though you show a foolish amount of confidence in your former employers. Still, it's not like you to be so cynical. Maybe you do need some rest. However, even though I am reasonably sure that Mister D'imato has outlived his usefulness, I am not totally convinced. Until that time, we will carry out the game. Unfortunately, the man is completely insane, utterly delusional, so I would prefer to have him somewhere I can keep an eye on him."

Pakow nodded. "I'll make the arrangements tonight."

"Excellent, doctor. Now finish the procedure and then try and get some sleep."

Wake cut the connection, and keyed the monitor to show him operating theater number six. He watched as Pakow finished the fluid transfer and then wearily left the room.

In the ensuing silence, Wake studied the figure in the tank. "You could be the one. The one that leads me to the final answer. I wonder if you will find a name in the history books?"

27

From the preliminary tests I've run on the genetic material still viable, it would appear that Marco D'imato has an anomalous cellular structure that has given rise to a mutation in the virus' RNA strand. This anomaly is found in one out of every one million people, and is rare enough that it was overlooked in our initial scans. The ramifications of this are extreme. Rather than the simple host deterioration we have come to expect when using the Beta strain of the virus, this subject's cellular structure will begin to decay at an exponential rate. The side effects will most likely be loss of motor control, extreme pain, and eventual insanity. Unfortunately, most of our genetic sample has already deteriorated and, therefore, further testing is impossible without taking a fresh sample from Mr. D'imato . . .

—Dr. Raul Pakow, laboratory notes, Subject: Marco D'imato. Test series BV3847, 07 August 2060

Deep in his study, Marco D'imato leaned back and forced himself to relax. Things were not going well, and he knew that. The tremors were like a wave inside of him, and even now he could feel the forces building inside his body. A rolling ocean of pain that crept forward bit by bit, until that seventh wave crashed over him and made him feel as if he were drowning.

Taking a deep breath, he turned to the small mirror on his desk. *Is that really what I look like?* He looked over at a picture of himself and Julius, taken two months before his infection, then back to the mirror.

Under the make-up, Marco's black skin had turned flaky and dry, and as he turned his head, a chunk of flesh fell to the front of his shirt. His forehead was dotted with blood-tinted sweat. Marco could smell the dead animal odor coming from his body, and it was enough to gag him.

No wonder Wake is concerned. I look like I'm dead already. He smiled at his private joke, then pulled open the top desk drawer. Removing the make-up stashed there, he began the process of rebuilding his face, until it looked normal once again.

As soon as he was done, he opened the line to his secretary. "Peter."

The young man's voice was firm, though a bit hesitant. "Yes, sir."

"I've just received word on the whereabouts of my nephew. I want a car ready to go tomorrow morning, at eight sharp. You will drive me."

"Of course, sir. That's excellent news about Warren."

Marco grunted. "Yes. There have been some changes on the board of directors. The paperwork is being drawn up to limit Julius' power in the corporation. For the time being, my brother is to be removed from any positions of authority. If he is seen, he is to be placed under house arrest until I return."

"Sir?"

"You heard what I said. Once Warren returns, I'll be taking a short vacation. My doctor has told me of a clinic in Europe where I can get some treatments for my condition. You will accompany me, along with four bodyguards."

"Of course, sir, but begging your pardon, if your brother is under house arrest, who will be in charge of the day-to-day affairs?"

Marco smiled. "My nephew will be taking full control. I will be in touch with him daily, but he will be acting CEO until my return."

The shock in Peter's voice was unmistakable. "Sir, you can't be serious? I thought Warren was—"

"You thought what? That I would be foolish enough to place all my hopes in Derek? Don't question matters about which you know nothing."

The fear in Peter's voice brought a smile to Marco's lips. "My apologies, sir. Everything will be as you've ordered."

Marco cut the connection, and leaned back painfully in his chair. He smiled. *Yes, Peter, everything will be as I've ordered. And when we get to the clinic tomorrow, I will feast on your blood, and show you just what that means.*

28

The virus affects the various metatypes in different ways, and offers many avenues for studying how those distinctive strengths and weaknesses can be exploited. Of the metas tested so far, banshees offer some of the most interesting possibilities. With some exceptions, the group as a whole seems to experience the change as a boon. In some instances, I've even been able to forego use of the psychotropic chip.

—Dr. Oslo Wake, laboratory notes, Test series OV9267a, 07 August 2060

Rachel's head hurt as the post-adrenaline fatigue crashed over her. Her anger had dissipated with the excitement of the run. Now, she was merely dead tired.

The Fratellanza, Inc. warehouse was crowded with men, most of them caked with dried sweat and grime, and the smell of fear and anger was a sour tang in the air. Most of the men were still in battle armor but in varying states of undress. The armor they still wore was covered in dust and blood. They were talking among themselves in low, angry tones.

Rachel looked around the huge warehouse at all the men, some tending to the wounded, some field-stripping and cleaning their gear. Then she looked at the huge trucks, all of them showing battle-scarring. *These fraggers took heavy losses,* she thought.

Rachel sat huddled next to Flak and Sinunu. Unlike the

Fratellanza men, the three of them were dressed in night camo, with no body armor. Flak breathed heavily through bloodied lips and still held himself in a combat-ready stance despite the swathing of bandages that covered his torso and neck. Sitting on the floor behind Rachel was Sinunu, pale and distant.

Rachel had been trying to talk to her for the past hour, but to no avail. Sinunu didn't want to talk; she was stunned by what had happened to Truxa.

If what Flak said was true, Truxa had meant everything to Sinunu, and Rachel could only guess what it might feel like to lose her. She wouldn't even let herself think about how it would be to lose Warren for good. They'd failed to find him, but Rachel knew they would try again.

She forced herself to stand up and look for Julius. He stood tall in his combat armor, helmet removed, and she recognized him by his silver hair. Julius was speaking to the red-haired captain, Biggs. At first Rachel was surprised that Julius had led the assault himself—after all, he was an executive. But now she knew better; the whole D'imato family received combat training, both personal and strategic.

More things about Warren I never knew. It bothered her that he'd kept all this from her, as though she were too fragile to handle it. Or perhaps he'd done it to protect her from his family.

Rachel stretched out the kinks in her legs and back. Then she touched her neck where the wound had been bandaged, and fluffed her hair out of habit before walking across the room toward Julius.

Rachel looked over at de Vries as she went. He sat on the rear bumper of the Mobmaster, surrounded by soldiers still in full combat gear. Several of them held flame-throwers, the nozzles pointed at de Vries. Next to de Vries sat Short Eyes, looking bored.

Julius had told Rachel he was going to check out their story, if possible, before letting them go. Rachel didn't think

Julius could actually hold de Vries, even with the whole Fratellanza arsenal and all its troops, but de Vries was going along with the game for now.

Rachel walked up to Julius, pushing past two big, cybered orks who seemed to be listening to instructions. "Excuse me, Mr. D'imato," she said.

"Yes, Rachel?" Rachel had never met Warren's father, and the familiar way he used her name bothered her a little. She didn't know much about him, but from the way he addressed her, she guessed he knew almost everything about her.

Rachel hooked a thumb back over her shoulder at the runners. "Their mage died on the run trying to get Warren out," she said. "Her name was Truxa. We were almost out of there, but we'd been going at it for too long. I guess we got sloppy. A vamp got her when we were loading into the truck."

"I saw. I've also been told that the albino woman—"

"Sinunu."

"—Sinunu held the mage in . . . shall we say, very high regard."

Rachel nodded.

"We all know what it's like to lose someone we love."

Rachel frowned. "If you know that, then you've got to know these people have gone through hell and back to get your son, and I think they deserve a bit more consideration than you've shown them."

Julius flinched. "Of course," he said. "There's not much I can do for them here, but I plan to do something about their loses." He turned to one of the orks. "Biggs, you finish up here for me?"

The big ork nodded his assent.

Julius put his arm around Rachel's shoulders and led her back toward Flak and Sinunu.

Flak looked up at Rachel and Julius as they approached.

Julius spoke with pain in his voice. "I know that you risked your lives trying to rescue my son."

Flak stood, and offered his huge hand to Julius, though his

face was like something chipped from granite. "I'm just sorry we failed." His voice was raspy and harsh.

Julius took the troll's huge paw and shook it. "I also understand that you've suffered losses due to something you had no stake in. I cannot apologize enough for that, so I won't insult you by trying. The best I can say is that none of you will ever want for anything again." His voice cracked on the last word, and Rachel knew how he felt.

Flak shook his head. "We knew the risks when we took the job, and we've been paid. You owe us nothing." Even though he sounded sincere, his voice was dead, flat.

"Yes, he does." If Flak's voice had sounded dead, Sinunu's voice sounded as if all Hell's damned were speaking in chorus. There was so much anger and pain in her voice that for a moment Rachel feared the other woman might actually attack Julius.

Julius stood tall and looked at her. "You are the one called Sinunu. Of everyone, I believe you have lost the most tonight. What could I possibly do to make that up to you?"

Sinunu stood. She was nearly as tall as Julius, though leaner. She still had dried blood on her face and neck, but it only made her look all the more deadly. "You can tell us you're going to do something about the evil out there."

Julius nodded. "Do you think I would dishonor the losses both you and I have suffered by sitting idle while those things still walk? But, to my mind, the first order of business is to reattempt to rescue my son."

Sinunu smiled, and Rachel could see the gaps in her mouth where teeth were missing. "And you could say that we're coming with you. Though you must know that it doesn't matter what you say; we will avenge our own."

Julius stood still for a moment, then nodded. "If what I've been told is even half true, then I would be honored to have you there."

Rachel said, "I'm going as well."

Julius looked Rachel over, admiration apparent on his face. "I wouldn't dream of trying to stop you."

Rachel nodded.

A small smile tracked across Sinunu's face, though Rachel noticed it didn't touch her pink eyes. She turned to Rachel. "If the son is anything like the father," she said. "I see why you place value in him." Then she turned and walked back over to the wall, where she sat down heavily.

Julius said, "When we've had a chance to recuperate a bit, we'll try again. Assuming they've thrown everything they've got at us, I think we learned enough tonight to break them." He started to walk away.

Rachel stopped him with a hand on his arm. "There's one more thing," she said. "De Vries. It's almost dawn."

Sinunu's voice drifted over their shoulders. "I think it would be in your best interest to stop treating de Vries like a prisoner. He's one of the most honorable men I've ever met, and he tried harder than any of us to get your son back to you. Besides, if he decides to leave, I really don't think you could stop him."

Rachel watched Julius stiffen at Sinunu's tone, but he simply nodded.

"Come," Julius said. He put his arm around Rachel's shoulders and began to walk over toward the Mobmaster, where his men were watching de Vries. "I need to talk to the vampire anyway. He might be able to shed some light on what happened tonight. Even though my experience with vampires is somewhat singular, I was surprised by what I saw."

Rachel nodded. "I know. Not all vampires are mindless beasts that suck blood. In fact, according to Martin, the vampires we encountered at the compound were acting strange. The coordinated attacks, the lack of self-preservation, it isn't usual."

Again Julius smiled down at her. "Well, we know some things, and hopefully, de Vries can fill in the rest. All the vamp bodies we brought back with us had similar headware.

And *all* of them had reprogrammable psychotropic chips. They could be under the influence of the chip; some early experiments with war troops tried that with humans. And it works to great effect, but it treats the individuals like game pieces. To be used up and tossed away when they're no longer needed."

Rachel shuddered. It wasn't that she felt any sympathy for those vampires, but she suddenly realized for the first time that they had once been people.

De Vries stood as they approached.

"Are you all right?" Rachel asked.

He nodded. "Yes." Then he turned his attention to Julius. "Have you confirmed the information about your brother?"

Julius nodded gravely. "It looks like you were right. I knew Marco was a vampire, but he has been so for many years and it didn't seem to affect his control of Fratellanza. Recently, he underwent an experimental procedure that left him crippled." Julius grimaced. "I believe it also drove him insane."

De Vries gave Julius a melancholy smile. "Derek was even more insane than his father. When I learned of his creation, I immediately devoted all my resources to learning the secret behind it. I am not ashamed of killing your nephew."

Julius sighed. "I am sure you're not," he said. "And I know you did the right thing. Derek's soul was dead long before you got to him. He was killed by his own father."

"And now Marco is trying to do the same thing to Warren," de Vries said, "and eventually will try to do the same to you."

Julius merely nodded.

"You can break the cycle," de Vries said. "You can help me bring down the facility in Hell's Kitchen."

At just that moment, Rachel heard the beeping of a wristphone, and Biggs answered it.

Julius turned to look at the man, who had gone white. "What is it, Biggs?"

Biggs disconnected and turned to face Julius. "That was

Marco," he said. The words hung in the air, as the warehouse went silent.

"Well, man, don't keep us in suspense. What did he have to say?"

Biggs shook his head. "You've been removed from the board of Fratellanza, and if I see you, I'm supposed to place you under house arrest."

Julius laughed, a low, hollow sound that rang through the warehouse.

"There's more."

"I thought there might be," said Julius. "What else?"

Biggs' face turned into a grimace. "He says he's arranged for the release of Warren, and that as soon as your son appears, we'll be taking orders directly from him. Warren's in charge of the entire corporation until Marco reappears."

"Now is the moment of truth," de Vries said. "You have the loyalty of the troops, I have seen that. You . . ."

Julius interrupted. "I have already started proceedings for a hostile takeover based on the fact that Marco is no longer mentally competent. That's in the corporate constitution. I've given the go-ahead to the lawyers, and by tomorrow afternoon Marco will be out of the picture, provided I haven't underestimated him again."

29

Some vampires revel in their role as hunters and killers. Such individuals have a strong sadistic streak and seek out unwilling victims. Initially, the vampire draws sustenance from the victim's terror. Then, if the early attacks have not killed the victim, the vampire will enjoy taking the now-addicted subject's final life essence. Such individuals may have been psychopaths before their transition to vampirism, or it may be the shock of their death and rebirth as a "hunting creature" that pushes them over the edge.

—from *Dictionary of Parabiology,* by Professor Charles Spencer, third edition, MIT&T Press, Cambridge, 2053

Julius rode next to Biggs in the back of the midnight-black stretch Toyota Elite winding up Magnolia Bluff. As they passed the first checkpoint, he could see the early morning sunlight refracting off Elliott Bay.

Julius looked at his watch, a Dulcola-Fra that accented his charcoal Armanté suit. It was just short of eight in the morning, and they were making good time, despite the heavy morning traffic.

Julius glanced over at Biggs, who had also changed from battle gear into a business suit, though the double-breasted garment didn't hang as well as the designer had intended on the big ork's bulky frame. The deep circles under Biggs' eyes told the tale of how exhausting the previous night had been.

Neither of them had slept, going straight from battle into the planning meeting that had hatched the course of action they were about to put into play.

"You should have stayed behind with the others," said Julius. "You need the rest."

Biggs looked over and flashed a grin that melted the weariness from his face for a moment. "You gotta be slotting me, sir. I wouldn't miss this little whammy for the world."

Julius smiled. "I appreciate that, and I'd be lying if I said I wasn't glad you're here."

Biggs said, "Besides, what kind of second would I be if I didn't have your back when you needed it most?"

Julius nodded and gazed out the window again.

They both felt the limo slow to a crawl as it approached the mansion's gate. Then it accelerated as the guards waved it through.

Biggs looked over at Julius and smiled again. "You ready to do this?"

Julius thought about his brother, and for just a moment, he felt a flash of shame. From a very young age all he'd ever heard was that family was everything and that to betray family was to betray oneself. Then he thought of Marco's face last night—which felt like a million years ago—on the telecom. Trying to convince him that Warren was somewhere else.

You betrayed me and mine first, big brother. Now it's payback. He nodded to Biggs. "Let's get this over with."

Both men got out of the limo, and without a signal, the big car pulled forward, toward the garage.

Julius looked to his left and saw Marco's Rolls Royce standing ready.

With Biggs' hand on his arm, just above the elbow, the two of them ascended the steps to the front door. The guards let Julius pass with a nod.

Entering the foyer, going from the brightness of day into the dimness, the two men paused.

"Good. You brought him." Marco's voice was a pained wheeze that made Julius flinch.

Beside him, Julius felt Biggs snap to attention. "Yes, sir."

From the gloom at the other end of the hallway, Marco's wheelchair rolled forward, being pushed by Peter, Marco's assistant.

Marco's makeup was smeared with sweat, and he was hunched over, making him look like a carved demon. Julius studied his brother, but for the moment, Marco's attention was on Biggs. "I understand how difficult it must have been for you to carry out your orders," he said. "It's not an easy thing to take your boss's authority away from him. Rest easy, though. I will reward your loyalty upon my return."

Marco's eyes flashed to Julius.

Well, there's life in the old boy yet, thought Julius, as his brother's piercing gaze locked with his own. "Little brother, I apologize for the inconvenience. Unfortunately, you gave me no choice. Until I can return and explain things to you fully, you're just going to have to trust that this is for the best. You have jeopardized matters of which you have no comprehension, and I can't take the time right now to show you the error of your ways."

Julius let his head fall forward. "Actually, I do understand. I disobeyed you, thinking of nothing more than my son. I was blinded by my fear for him."

Marco nodded his vulpine head as Julius looked up at him again. "I too understand, little brother. Still, I do have good news. I've discovered Warren's whereabouts, and I'm going right now to secure his release."

This is it, thought Julius. He forced all the surprise he could into his voice. "Warren? You know where he is?"

Marco nodded, and chuckled. "He is safe and well and should be returning to the fold in a few days. When he does, he will be in charge until I can return and clear things up with you. I expect you to give him the same good counsel you have given me all these years, though you will not have the same authority. He is the future of Fratellanza, Inc., little brother."

Julius nodded. "Let me go with you. I want to see my son. I promise I won't do anything . . . rash." Julius held his breath.

Marco shook his head. "If you have proven anything in the last twenty-four hours, it is that you cannot be trusted where your son is concerned. No, you will remain here for the duration."

Julius let his head fall forward again, hiding the small smile that tugged at the corners of his mouth. "I accept the wisdom of what you're saying, though my heart doesn't agree."

"Sir," said Peter. "We had better be going if we're going to keep to our schedule."

Julius felt Biggs' hand tighten on his arm, and he looked up. Marco waved to Peter, who rolled his chair forward. As they approached, Julius asked, "While you're away, who's going to take care of business?"

Marco smiled, showing his black gums. "That's the Julius I know. Don't worry. Everything has been taken care of. All current contracts can be handled by staff. You just rest, and know that your son will be back soon."

With that, Marco was past him.

Julius looked at Peter, young, dark-haired, and pretty in a masculine sort of way. Peter shot a glance at Julius, and that look was so full of terror that Julius felt his heart break. He knew the poor kid probably wouldn't be alive for more than another hour, and he sensed that Peter had come to the same conclusion. Still, there was nothing he could do about it.

Then they were out the door and into the sunshine. The last sight of Peter that Julius ever got was of the young man extending the wide black umbrella and then attaching it to the chair. The light was too strong for Marco to face directly.

Biggs closed the door behind them.

"This way," he said, staying in character. Julius had told

him that Marco's senses were heightened beyond belief, so they had agreed to continue until ten minutes after Marco's car had left the drive.

Biggs guided Julius to his room on the second floor, then stood by the door as Julius went to check the window. Julius watched as the modified Rolls Royce pulled down the drive and out the gate.

A wave of bone-heavy anger stormed through Julius as he stepped over to the bed and sat down on it.

Biggs looked at his wrist chronometer, then pulled a small black box from his suit pocket. The box was twenty centimeters square and it had a simple switch on the top, just to the side of a small red light.

Biggs set the box on the small, intricately carved table and flipped the switch. For a moment, nothing happened, and then the red light blinked twice. Julius looked up as Biggs said softly, "Room's clear."

Julius nodded, and went back to waiting. At exactly ten minutes, Biggs looked over at him and smiled. "Time."

Julius pulled a small portacom from his pocket and tapped in a series of numbers he'd been given by the decker-boy the shadowrunners called Sandman.

There were two clicks as the signal was bounced from host to host, then the call connected.

Killian's voice came through strong and without delay. "Yes?"

Julius smiled. "Elvis has left the building. Begin Operation Dracula."

With those words, Julius was setting two events in motion. One was the legal proceeding that would finally give him sole control of Fratellanza, Inc. The other was the assault that would be his last chance to get Warren back before his son was changed into a vampire.

30

A vampire that can move at will in sunlight is a fiend with power beyond measure. It can travel wherever it wants to, whenever it wants to; it can hunt at any hour of the day; and it cannot be easily distinguished from a normal metahuman because it lacks the very weakness that once defined it. *If the Ordo's plan succeeds, they will gain total control over all of our lives in the blink of an eye, and we will be unable to lift a finger to stop them.*

—Martin de Vries, *Shadows at Noon,* posted to Shadowland BBS, 24 May 2057

The assistant, the one called Pakow, watched emotionlessly as Marco drained the last of the blood from Peter's body, letting the limp thing, which only moments before had been so full of life, fall to the floor of the loading dock.

His hunger sated, Marco straightened painfully and looked at the small man and grinned. "I'm ready, *now*. So if you'll be so good as to have this mess cleaned up, we can go."

The man called Pakow nodded curtly. "If you'll just follow me, your room is prepared." He gestured vaguely at the mess. "I'll have this taken care of."

Sitting back down in his wheelchair, Marco nodded, then waited until the man took the hint. Coming up behind Marco, Pakow pushed his chair into the building.

"Where is Doctor Wake?" Marco demanded. "I had expected him to meet me when I arrived."

"He's resting," Pakow said. "He needs to gather his strength for the last part of the procedure on your nephew. It takes quite a bit out of him. Though I'm not totally versed in these matters, I understand that the magical aspects of the procedure are some of the most extreme to be found in the field of the arcane."

Marco grunted his understanding. "How is it going? Have there been any complications?"

There was a short pause, then Pakow said, "As far as I know, everything is progressing beyond Doctor Wake's expectations. We're using the latest strain of the virus on your nephew, and initial testing shows an unprecedented breakthrough."

Marco twisted slowly in his chair, feeling his spine crackle with the effort. "How so? I thought that with Derek we had reached a pinnacle of sorts."

Pakow's face broke into a tight smile. "Hardly. After all, your son suffered many of the same unpredictable reactions as you have from the procedure. Your nephew has benefited from being the recipient of a strain that should leave his melatonin levels intact."

For just a moment, Marco couldn't believe his ears. "You mean that . . ."

Pakow nodded, and turned the corner of the hall, passing a work station on the left. "Yes. If all continues according to plan, your nephew will never have to worry about applying make-up. He will look normal in all aspects. Well, skin-related aspects, at least. He will still have to wear contacts to provide any sort of eye pigmentation, but I think that is a small price to pay, considering."

Marco couldn't help the huge grin spreading over his face. "That is far beyond what I had hoped for. Your Doctor Wake is a miracle worker."

Pakow didn't answer, but Marco hardly noticed. He was too dazzled by the possibilities this news offered.

They arrived at an open doorway near the end of the hall.

"This will be your room," Pakow told him.

Marco looked around as Pakow wheeled him inside. The room was huge, nearly twenty meters square. The walls were covered with small white tiles that glittered softly in the indirect light.

In the center of the room stood a bed, with what looked like an oxygen tent over one end. There were straps on all sides, though they'd been pulled back and tied down to the thick metal legs that supported the large expanse of sleep area.

A bank of monitors rested just to the side of the bed, and Marco could see robotic auto-injectors on the other side.

"Where's my telecom?" he said.

The question obviously took Pakow by surprise, because the confusion on his face was genuine.

"My damn telecom. One of the reasons I agreed to come in was that Wake promised me I could communicate with my nephew when he returned to the outside world."

The baffled expression on Pakow's face made Marco want to rip the flesh from his skull, but he refrained.

"I apologize, Mister D'imato. I can only assume that Doctor Wake might have thought you would be bringing your own compact unit along. Still, I don't see that it will be a problem. I'll see to it personally." The man paused, looking a bit apprehensive. "If you'll forgive me for saying so, I'm not sure you fully understand the nature of this procedure."

Marco felt the hackles rise on the back of his neck. "What do you mean?" His voice was low and dangerous.

Pakow shook his head. "It's just that this is no ordinary procedure. This is something we have never done before. I'm sorry to say that it won't be pleasant, especially in the first stages. I think that was why Doctor Wake wanted to get you in as soon as possible."

Marco frowned. "I'm not sure I understand."

Pakow shrugged. "Your condition is not good. We may

have to resort to extreme measures to bring it back under control, before we can even begin to attempt any reversal. Those extreme measures will very likely be painful, requiring a . . . well, staggering amount of sedation."

Marco chewed on his lip. "So what you're saying is that I'll be out of it for a few days."

Pakow nodded, and resumed pushing Marco's chair. "If things progress well, you should be past the worst by the time your nephew is ready to be released."

Marco shook his head. "I don't care. I want the telecom, and I want it today. With a secure outside line."

They had reached the bed, and Pakow let the wheelchair roll to a stop. "Of course. As I said, I'll see to it personally."

Marco looked at the bed, then up at Pakow, who was once again expressionless.

"I won't presume to insult you by offering to help, Mister D'imato. If you would kindly get up onto the bed, I'll get you a dressing gown, and we can get the procedure underway."

Marco smiled, and for the first time since the man had defied him when he'd delivered Warren to the loading dock, he thought he might just spare him after all.

Willing his body to break down, he let his form shift, and turn. Not quite mist, he settled lightly onto the bed, then solidified. He stripped out of his suit jacket and shirt, the sable skin of his chest and belly eating the light.

Pakow turned away as Marco finished stripping and walked toward one wall near the row of monitors. He pressed an off-colored tile, and a small closet opened. Marco watched as the man drew a dressing gown from the rack and brought it over to him.

By then, Marco was completely naked. Pakow set the gown next to him, and then returned to the closet. He closed it with a gentle push, then moved down about two meters to another discolored tile. Marco made sure to memorize where each odd-colored tile was located.

When Pakow pushed on the tile, a waist-high section of the wall moved out, and Pakow pulled it clear, leaving a small cubbyhole. In it was a portable sink, complete with integral hot and cold. Two smaller nozzles at the sides were labeled betadine disinfection soap and hand lotion.

Pakow rolled the cart to Marco, who took the opportunity to rid himself of the irritating makeup on his hands and face.

As he was washing, Pakow said, "Just below the hot water faucet, you'll find a small green button. It opens a tray on the side where you'll find towels to dry off."

With that, Pakow turned to the bank of monitors and began powering up the system.

Marco finished rubbing lotion onto his skin, which still burned slightly from the alcohol. He looked over at Pakow, who was just finishing up. After returning the cart to its proper place in the wall, Pakow said, "Are you ready to begin?"

Marco grunted. "As ready as I'll ever be."

"Then if you'll just lie back, I'll start the first of the painkillers."

Marco raised a hand, but before he could speak, Pakow nodded. "Don't worry, Mister D'imato. As soon as the process is underway, I'll get you your telecom."

Marco smiled, and used his hands to swing his legs up onto the bed. He lay back, looking up into the clear plastic tent that Pakow held over him.

Pakow let it down gently, then returned to the monitors. Within seconds, Marco could detect a gentle hissing sound.

For just a moment, he almost ripped the tent off his face. Something felt wrong. This whole thing had suddenly begun to take on the proportions of a nightmare.

The moment passed just as quickly as it had come, and Marco felt the pain in his spine ease. He began to drift, the world growing fuzzy and comfortable around him.

Thirty minutes later, Pakow left the room and locked the door behind him. He turned to the small panel next to the door and pulled it open. Flipping switches in sequence, he started the room's air evacuation.

As soon as all the lights had turned red, Pakow took a deep breath and let it out slowly. The shakes hit his knees first, and he thought they might buckle under him.

The monster was safely out of the way. Without any air in the room, the vampire would go into stasis. Considering that he'd fed just before going in, Pakow calculated that D'imato would finally expire in a little over a month, unless Doctor Wake found a reason to revive him.

Wiping at the sweat on his forehead, which mercifully hadn't appeared while he was with D'imato, Pakow walked quickly on his still shaking legs back to the monitoring station down the hall. He half expected the display to show the room empty, but when he touched the screen, he was relieved to see the motionless form of Marco D'imato still lying on the bed.

He reached over and opened the line to Doctor Wake.

"Wake here," came the immediate response. "I trust everything went according to plan?"

Pakow laughed, a wry, almost angry sound. "Yes, but you might have told me he wanted a telecom in the room. I thought he was going to renege on the whole deal."

The sound of a drawn-out sigh filled the hallway, and when Wake answered, Pakow could hear the exhaustion in his voice. "I apologize, Doctor Pakow. It slipped my mind. What happened?"

Pakow shook his head, though part of him realized that Wake couldn't see him do it. "Nothing. I managed to convince him that it was an oversight, and that as soon as the procedure was started, I would make sure he got what he wanted."

"Excellent. You are to be commended for quick thinking, though I have always known you had a devious streak."

Something in Wake's tone bothered Pakow. The man surely

suspected what Pakow had been doing, that he'd been the one who had contacted de Vries. Or did he?

Pakow sighed heavily. One thing was certain; he wasn't going to risk crossing Wake again. *I'm sorry, de Vries. From here on, you're on your own.*

31

Voice 1: There are vampires in Ordo Maximus, and I think they have access to some magical rituals that let them use the essence drain from victims to offset the drain of cybermantic magic. Needless to say, I haven't gotten far trying to find out much more. It's not something I'd want to risk, frankly.
Voice 2: You think that geek de Vries was right, then?
Voice 1: He got initiated into the middling grades. I think he knew. He may even have met one or two of them. There are a hundred and one tales about how he got infected.

—From encrypted telecom transcripts posted to Shadowland BBS by Captain Chaos, 11 December 2056. Identity of speakers not definitively verified.

In his study, Wake leaned forward and put his head in his hands. He tried to roll his shoulders to alleviate some of the tension that had built up in his muscles, but it was no use.

Things are getting too complicated here, and the work is suffering for it. That can't be allowed.

He straightened and turned to the telecom on his desk. Tapping in a sixteen-digit code he hadn't used in over two years, he waited patiently for the connection. As he did, he calculated what time it would be in London. Just a bit after four in the afternoon.

The man who came on line was balding and pale, with a huge mole on his forehead. Wake reflected for a moment that he didn't even know the man's name. When they'd first met, names were a dangerous thing. Later, they seemed unimportant.

"Ah, it's you," the man said, showing discolored teeth. "It's been a while."

Wake hadn't called to engage in idle chitchat. "I need to talk."

The man nodded, staring back from the telecom display. He had a look of shock on his face that he tried to hide, but not before Wake saw it.

"Good god, man, you look like bloody hell." The clipped British accent turned dry and disinterested, so Wake assumed there were others present.

"Is it safe to talk?"

The man nodded. "Of course. If it wasn't, you wouldn't have gotten through. What's on your mind?"

"I've finally taken care of D'imato, but now I've got other problems and they're interfering with my work."

The man's expression turned thoughtful. "Of course, we can't have that. What's the problem, and what is it you need?"

Wake smiled wearily. "Things are getting . . . warm here. An old friend of yours has come to call—Martin de Vries. We've already had one attack on the compound due to your man D'imato's incompetence and thick-headedness. From what I know of the people who hit us, I'm sure they'll be back again to finish the job. They've got access to plenty of firepower, and next time they'll come with enough to level this whole place and destroy all of my work."

The look of distaste on the man's face was evident. "De Vries? By the gods, when will that fool learn to leave well enough alone? Still, when you say you've taken care of my man"— the distaste turned to disgust—"I assume you mean that it became necessary to make your solution permanent?"

Wake shook his head. "I wanted to consult with you first, but he has been gently removed from his position, and no one will really notice the change for another month or so."

The man smiled. "Excellent. That will give us time to plan for his replacement. So what is it that we can do for you?"

"This locale has become difficult. I need immediate relocation. Code Azure."

The man turned away from the telecom, and seemed to be conferring with others who Wake couldn't see. When he turned back, he had a satisfied look on his face. "I don't think that will be a problem. It might cost a bit, but we all agree that the expenditure is worth the service you're providing. Besides, it wouldn't do for de Vries to get his hands on your current research data. We've put too much effort into making him look as crazy as he is. This would be a bad time for him to actually acquire proof of his accusations."

Wake nodded. He'd had no doubt that the men of Ordo Maximus would see it that way. After all, they'd already invested too much nuyen to back out now, especially when they believed they were so close.

He kept the smile from his face as he imagined those British fops, with their ridiculous vampire cabal, sitting in their posh offices looking at each other with gaping mouths once they learned that they'd funded the one thing that could make their plan obsolete.

The man continued. "I'll make all the arrangements from this end, and we'll have a new lab set up for you through your Zulu BioGen front."

Wake smiled. "Thank you. I'm sorry things haven't gone more smoothly here, but hopefully there won't be any more little complications to detract from the work."

The man shook his head. "Don't be sorry. I apologize to you for saddling you with D'imato. He should have been the perfect subject, but apparently he is too unpredictable to be of any use. If you've found a way to remove him from the picture, we are doubly in your debt."

Wake nodded, and hit the Disconnect without further chatter.

He sat back, grateful to realize that some of the tension in his shoulders had eased. *That was the right decision,* he thought. *I probably should have done this a couple of months ago, but this location seemed ideal.* He selected another icon from the display and touched it.

"Attention, initiate Code Azure. This is not a drill. I want all equipment not in use at this time marked red, then disconnected and moved to the loading docks for transport to the helipad. All equipment marked yellow is to be packed securely and prepared for transport on the trucks. All green equipment is to be taken to disposal. I repeat, initiate Code Azure."

32

The only good vampire is a dead one—and I should know. I've killed eight of them, including two nosferatu. It was no simple task, primarily because the majority of these monsters are magically active. Their "natural" powers give them a huge advantage over even the best equipped, most magical powerfully (meta)humans, and their regenerative powers make it extremely difficult to inflict them with permanent, deadly damage.

—Posted to Shadowland BBS by "Deathblow," vampire hunter, 14 January 2057

Sweat dripped off Rachel's forehead as she spun to block one of Sinunu's kicks. It had been two days since the run on the compound, and she'd healed up fast enough that she was back to training again. The salty liquid drenched her shoulders, forming a vee-shaped stain on her exercise bra and the elastic band of her shorts.

She brought her arm down a second too late, and Sinunu's kick landed hard against Rachel's hip.

Rachel bit back against the pain that flared.

"Sorry, Rach," Sinunu said.

Rachel clenched her teeth. She felt more anger than pain. "I'm too slow."

Sinunu smiled. "Let's call it a day," she said. "You're beating yourself up more than I ever could. And it's because you're tired, girl. You've improved more in two days than runners who've trolled the shadows for six or eight months. I'm impressed."

Rachel picked up a towel from the floor of the workout room. Fratellanza, Inc. had several of them in this facility in the Renton District.

"Anyone hungry?"

Rachel looked up to see Julius enter the room, followed by several soldiers carrying trays of hot food.

"Starved," Sinunu said. "Rachel?"

"Yeah, me too."

Julius had his men set up the food in the corner, then he brought a plate over to Rachel, who was sitting on the floor while she stretched.

"I thought you could use something. It's sundown and you've barely eaten since this morning." Julius set down the steaming tray of meat, hot rolls, and real coffee.

"You keeping track of my diet?"

Julius just smiled.

The smell of the hot food suddenly hit Rachel's nose, and her stomach grumbled. "If the sun is down, Martin should be back," she said. Then she picked up a hot roll and a sausage link and wolfed them down.

Rachel realized that her mindset had shifted. The change in her was so dramatic that sometimes she didn't even recognize herself. She'd been hard before, streetwise and scared in her spike heels and see-through skirts. Now, dressed in exercise cottons, her long hair freshly shorn close to her skull to better accommodate the com gear, her hardness had changed. In the last few days, she'd transformed from being a man's plaything into a warrior. She liked the change, but it scared her as well.

Now, she felt an inner confidence that seemed to chase away that streetwise fear lurking under her brash exterior.

Julius was studying her face, scrutinizing the fresh bruises under her right cheek. "I see Sin is still getting the best of you." He glanced over at Sinunu, sitting by herself and shoveling food into her mouth. "How's she holding up?"

Rachel felt a wave of pity swelling inside. "I'm not sure. When we're working, she seems okay, but I think part of her has gone dead."

Julius continued to stare at the albino woman. "Truxa."

Rachel nodded. "Of course."

Julius turned his gaze back to Rachel. "And somehow you still feel responsible?"

Rachel nodded, without saying anything.

Julius was silent. Then, as if to change the subject, he said, "I've been working with Short Eyes on a project."

"Short Eyes has conveyed her appreciation of your cunning, Mister D'mato." The voice came from the doorway.

Rachel turned to see de Vries standing there in his dark duster, a small smile on his thin blue lips. "Martin," she said, and she knew that she'd let too much emotion into her voice. But she was very happy to see him.

"Hello, Rachel. What have you done to your hair?" He smiled and she grinned back.

"Sin got a little overzealous with the shears."

De Vries looked over at Julius. "We need to talk."

"Go ahead," Julius said, leaning forward.

De Vries stepped up close, and though Rachel knew it was only her imagination, it seemed as if the temperature suddenly dropped a few degrees. "They're on the move. I took a quick detour on my way over here, and they are definitely vacating. At the rate they're going, the place will be empty by tomorrow night."

Julius nodded. "That matches the intel my decker and Sandman have come up with. The compound is being systematically shut down." He sighed. "I'd have liked another week to finish preparations, but I guess it's now or never."

De Vries locked eyes with Julius. "You know that there's only a slim possibility that Warren is still human?"

Julius nodded slowly. "I'm still hanging on to the hope that, with everything going on there, they might have shut down on all major procedures. But, yes, I do understand that every moment we're still here is another moment for Warren to be lost."

De Vries frowned. "And if things don't turn out as you hope?"

Rachel watched as Julius' jaw muscles tightened. She'd seen the same look on Warren's face when someone pushed him too hard. "I know what I have to do, vampire, and I won't hesitate. For now, we're wasting precious time. Let's get back to business."

De Vries smiled, cold and hard. "Fine. And here's some business we'd better keep solidly in our minds. When we take the compound, every infected creature has to be destroyed. Every single one. Otherwise, we could see a plague of HMHVV on the scale of the first VITAS epidemic."

Julius nodded. "Tell me something I don't know."

Rachel shuddered. Her parents had both died from VITAS, or at least that's what she'd been told by the people at the orphanage. VITAS killed slowly and painfully, but it didn't turn people into monsters.

She turned and left Julius and de Vries to hash over the assault, and headed for the showers. As she cleaned up, she thought about what she was going to do tonight, and why. She imagined all of her fear being washed away by the water and slipping down the drain. As she stepped from the shower, she thought about all the people who had been hurt, and how she wanted to set that to rights. She changed into loose camouflage fatigues, and by the time Julius had prepped the troops, Rachel's heart was as cold and hard as dry ice.

She knew this was about more than getting Warren back now. What she did tonight could affect people halfway around the world. She wasn't going to fail.

33

The Ordo is concerned about using the Zulu BioGen front. If things do not go exactly as planned, you could easily be compromised by the paper trail. Be warned. If that happens, we will cut you off and deny any knowledge of you or your activities.

—Matrix transmission from London, England to LTG # NA-UCAS-SEA-4897, 09 August 2060

Two hours before dawn, the convoy rolled through Hell's Kitchen. The residents who were awake at that hour and saw the line of truck after truck rumble down the streets immediately bolted for whatever safe place they could find. It only took an hour for the rumor to spread. The UCAS army was invading Hell's Kitchen, and they were packing armor and weapons like nothing any of the folks there had ever seen before.

All the trucks bristled with wooden stakes, from every angle, like huge, monstrous porcupines.

Within the hour, every street in Hell's Kitchen was deserted. Even the go-gangers had gone off to hide. No matter how tough they were, they were no match for the army, who packed milspec caliber weapons.

In the newly revamped Mobmaster, Julius rubbed his eyes. The smell of sweat in the vehicle was nearly overpowering as the men surrounding him finished the last check of their weapons.

Julius looked around one last time, and tried not to think of how he might have better prepared the men for what was to come. Sandman, de Vries, and Killian had given him every bit of information they had, but Julius had been the one to make all the final decisions.

Of the sixty men he'd called in for the assault, only a few of them carried standard projectile weaponry. They had learned, mostly from de Vries, what worked and what didn't.

Most of the men carried flamethrowers or lasers. The flamethrowers were the most effective, but tended to be fickle. That was why they'd divided each squad into groups of eight, with three men armed with flame throwers, three armed with lasers, and two walking flank with automatic weapons. The men toting lasers were responsible for keeping the vampires from reaching the men with the flame throwers, and the men with projectile weapons were to keep any goblins from wading in and killing the men with lasers.

The plan he, Flak, de Vries, and Biggs had come up with called for a three-pronged attack. The frontal attack would act as a diversion to give the rear attack time to get into position. Truck five would carry Flak's team, backed by some of the best reserve men Fratellanza had to offer. They were the third prong. If everything went according to plan, while the Fratellanza forces were crushing the vampires between them, the runners would be doing a covert snatch on Warren, provided they could find him.

There were four advance teams, and three long-range teams. The long-range teams were armed with high-explosive and white phosphorous rocket launchers. Their job was to pound the enemy's rear from a safe distance, while the advance teams cut down the front flank.

Julius sighed as he pulled his helmet down over his face and strapped it in place. When he activated the thermal display, the truck's interior turned a bloody red, highlighted in yellows where each man sat.

Julius knew that thermal vision would be useless once battle was joined, because the flamethrowers would create blinding tracers on the helmet's viewer. That, in turn, would limit the men's vision during the fighting, but it was a risk they had to take. Considering the advantages even the weakest vampire had over humans, there was no way Julius was going to send his men in there with nothing more than a wooden stake and a prayer.

He grinned as he thought of the one exception to this rule. Short Eyes would carry the weapon he'd helped her construct. She had declined anything else. It was a crossbow, but it was fashioned into the shape of a real cross, and there was no crank. Instead, each of the wooden bolts was powered by a jet of CO^2, allowing her to belt-feed the crossbow from a pack slung over her shoulder.

Surprisingly accurate, Short Eyes could fire wooden bolts as fast as she could pull the trigger.

Over his headset came the voice of Biggs, who was once again standing up front by the rigger. "Three minutes to show time."

Julius spoke into the integrated tacticom mic in his helmet. "Trucks five through eight, make the split at the next turn. Good hunting."

The runners, having successfully navigated the rear entrance once before, were to lead the Fratellanza troops in. The corp soldiers would hit the building itself, which would force the enemy to split its forces and to fight on two flanks. It was a good plan. Julius hoped it would work.

"This is it, everybody," he said into his mic. "Let's get in there and clean this fragging place up."

There was a huge concussion as the Mobmaster hit the first of the mines the enemy had placed across the roadway.

34

One cannot consider a discussion on vampires complete without mentioning their counterparts, namely wendigos, banshees, goblins, and the rest of their kind. While each have distinct needs and feeding habits, it should be mentioned that only the banshee have no actual need for blood. They, instead, take nourishment from the emotion of fear their victims feel just before death. That is not to say that all banshee do not drink blood; some do. However, it would seem that rather than needing it, they simply enjoy the taste.

—Martin de Vries, *Shadows at Noon,* posted to Shadowland BBS, 24 May 2057

While the other teams stormed the compound from the front and rear, exploding land mines as they went, the Citymaster carrying Sinunu and the others plowed toward the loading dock at the rear of the compound. Explosions filled the air as the Citymaster came within view of the dock.

Sinunu leaped from the truck, crossbow in hand. For just a moment, there was dead silence in the no man's land surrounding the compound. She stared across the ten meters to the nearest vampire, a short, stubby man whose pale skin was covered in swastika tattoos. Even on his bare scalp.

A second before, there had been nothing but empty air where the vampires now stood. Too late, she realized the vampires must have someone with magical talents working with them.

The tableau held for just a second, then was shattered by a tremendous roaring cry from Sinunu's left.

"Truxa!" screamed Flak like a battle cry, and let loose with his Vindicator.

The tattooed man jumped forward, covering most of the ten meters separating him from Sinunu with one bound. His movements were fast and jerky, and Sinunu didn't have much time to wonder how a move-by-wire reflex system might frag with a vampire.

He was on her like a flood, hands grabbing, broken teeth gnashing for her throat.

Pivoting on her left foot, she pulled a small wooden stake from the arsenal at her waist, and kicked upward with her right heel.

The vampire, despite his jacked reflexes, moved much too slowly, and Sinunu felt her heavy boot smash through his windpipe. As he teetered backward, she continued her turning movement, which brought her face to face with the vampire to her left.

This one was a tall woman, probably a former street sam, considering all the flashy mods, but she seemed to have difficulty focusing on her movements.

Stabbing upward with the stake, Sinunu drove it into the woman's throat and up into whatever she had for a brain.

The female vampire fell, the stake still imbedded in her throat, jerking violently as all her cyber kicked in and then shut off.

"You want to try it again?"

The voice was from behind Sinunu, and she instinctively knew it belonged to the tattooed man.

She turned and smiled. "You think you get another chance?"

With that, she pulled her MP-5, and fired three shots quickly, aiming for the base of the vampire's neck.

Before he could even blink, the rounds had torn through his move-by-wire rig, and he too fell.

"Truxa!" It was Flak again, tearing through vampires like they weren't even there.

Sinunu looked over, and realized that Flak had somehow lost his Vindicator, but it didn't seem to be slowing him down. He was tearing the heads off vampires with his bare hands, still wading forward, still screaming Truxa's name like a war cry. Sinunu was also aware of the distant sounds of fighting from the front of the compound, and every few seconds, the ground would shake with the concussion of a rocket. The explosions lit up the night sky as the mortar rounds did their work.

Sinunu watched Flak for a moment, and could tell that there were too many for him to handle, that he'd gotten too far out in front. She glanced around desperately for someone close enough to help, then saw Rachel's laser fire cut down the first of the vampires closing in on Flak. Sinunu knew Rachel couldn't hit the main group surrounding Flak for fear of killing him as well.

"Truxa!" screamed Flak.

He was on his own for a moment.

Sinunu started running, jumping over the still struggling bodies of vampires that had been cut down and some of the Fratellanza dead.

The corp soldiers were doing their best, but despite the preparation they'd received, most were folding under the raw, maniacal might of nearly thirty vampires coming at them.

Sinunu risked a glance backward, and Rachel was there, exactly matching Sinunu's movement and providing cover with her bulky laser.

To their left and right vampires died by flame and by the stake, but Sinunu was beyond caring about that. A howl rose from the direction of Flak—a blood-curdling moan.

A chill shook Sinunu and she froze in place for a split second, her entire body rigid with terror.

She saw that Flak, too, had faltered, his rage stutter-stepped for a moment, and that was all the time it took for the huge troll to go down.

Then the fear passed and Sinunu battled forward.

Suddenly, it was as if everything on the battlefield had stopped. There were still isolated pockets of fighting, but they were behind her.

As one, the crowd of vampires around the troll's prone body parted silently, creating a corridor to the big man. Only one creature remained, and suddenly Sinunu understood what had made the scream and why Flak had faltered. Her stomach lurched, and her knees threatened to betray her.

"He kept calling for me, Sin. I just had to come."

Truxa stood over Flak's body like a ghost of her former self, the troll's blood on her mouth. Sinunu knew what she was looking at. De Vries had told her, had warned her that Truxa might still be out there somewhere, had described in detail what Truxa might have become. He'd called her a banshee. Still, he hadn't prepared her for what she was seeing now.

"Truxa?" To Sinunu, her own voice came out like that of a lost child, and her despair was punctuated by the detonation of a rocket exploding on the far side of the compound.

The banshee nodded, and Sinunu blinked quickly, as if her vision had become blurred. It was Truxa, and yet it wasn't. There was something missing, and Sinunu had seen enough corpses to know what that something was. *Without life, without the spirit that makes a person human, these creatures are nothing more than a collection of matter. That's what I'm looking at now, a lifeless corpse.*

"Come to me, Sin. I know what this looks like, but you don't understand. You're running around destroying the most wondrous creations ever made, without the slightest understanding of what you're doing."

Sinunu felt strength come back to her, and she found herself laughing, a low deadly thing among all the death around her. "Shut up."

Suddenly, the grin faded from Truxa's face, and for just a moment, weakness swept through Sinunu. "Sin," pleaded Truxa, "you've got to understand, it's me. It really is. And what's more, you and I can be together again. Forever. Isn't that what we always promised each other? That nothing would separate us? Not even death?"

Sinunu stopped, her heart tearing itself to pieces in her chest. She looked at the mass of vampires to her left and right. She'd never thought of them as individuals before, had killed them without ever distinguishing one from the next. They had all been the same to her, but now she made out differences. These had once been normal men and women, and looking at their solemn faces, she could see old scars, different nationalities, different ages.

"I can give you the gift, Sin."

Sinunu turned back to Truxa and realized that she could have been wrong. Wrong about everything. After all, Truxa had never lied to her before, had always seemed incapable of lying.

Sinunu felt a smile cross her lips and watched its mirror on Truxa's lips, still covered with Flak's blood, and yet so beautiful. She was about to step forward, her arms coming up to embrace her love forever, when she felt the light touch of a hand on her shoulder.

"I know it hurts," whispered Rachel, who must have come closer during the fighting, "but that's not Truxa. Not anymore."

Rachel, there for her, again. As if coming awake from a dream, Sinunu looked at Truxa once more, and the thing in front of her was no longer beautiful. Instead, all Sinunu could focus on was the blood smeared on Truxa's lips.

Incapable of lying? Sinunu thought. *Truxa would never have been able to kill Flak before, either. Who knows what new tricks she's learned?*

Sinunu squeezed Rachel's hand, and looked Truxa in the eye.

"So that's how it is?" asked Truxa. "Was I that easy to replace?" The look of scorn on her face fueled Sinunu's anger.

Sinunu strode forward. "The Truxa I knew and loved can never be replaced, but you're not her."

Then, the air behind Truxa seemed to condense, conforming to a shape. With blinding ease, Martin de Vries shook off the magical shadows that had hidden his approach and took hold of Truxa, immobilizing her. He bent to say something, and Sinunu could barely make out the words.

"I know what you're about to try, little girl, but trust me, you can't. I know tricks you haven't even thought of, and don't presume to pit your puny magic against mine. I know the real Truxa is in there somewhere, buried under the abomination of the virus. I also know that woman is screaming right now. Screaming for release. Let us help you."

Like a ground swell, a hiss arose from the assembled vampires, but for some reason none of them moved. All eyes were fixed on de Vries, who looked up and smiled sadly at Sinunu.

In Sinunu's chest, her heart had become a stone. She strode forward, bloody stake in her hands, with Rachel at her shoulder.

As she came close, Sinunu watched Truxa go limp in de Vries' arms. The only thing hinting that her body was still animated was the wavering track of the elf's eyes as she watched death approach. Sinunu pulled a fresh stake from her belt.

"I love you." Truxa's voice was soft and quiet, just barely loud enough to make its way over the distant sounds of battle.

Once again, Sinunu's resolve faltered. She looked up at de Vries, who held her gaze with a steady look. "And I love you," she said.

Truxa smiled then, and despite the blood, it was Truxa again. "Then give me peace."

Standing over the dead body of her best friend, Sinunu rammed the stake through the heart of the only person she had ever loved.

35

In summary, we believe the evidence shows beyond any doubt that Marco D'imato has violated the bylaws of the corporation, Fratellanza, Incorporated, of which he is responsible as Chief Executive Officer. He has diverted corporate assets for his own private schemes, then knowingly concealed these activities from the corporation's management and those parties who share in its ownership. He has shown a pattern of behavior that is at once unstable, deviant, and gravely harmful to the functioning and best interests of the corporation. Had it not been for the intervention of Julius D'imato, the corporation's Chief Operating Officer, the fraudulent and erratic actions of Marco D'imato might have resulted in the failure and dissolution of Fratellanza, Incorporated.

—from *D'imato vs D'imato,* brief presented by Fillips, Bonavear, and Justran, Attorneys at Law, Magnolia District Court, Judge B. L. Clausen, presiding, 07 August 2060

Raul Pakow crouched behind a table in the operating theater as the concussion brought down more of the ceiling. A large chunk of concrete hit his head, sending bright bits of light spinning in front of his eyes. Pakow reached up, touching blood, and carefully pushed the flap of skin, which lay curled against his scalp, back into place.

Wiping blood from his eyes, he peeled off his shirt and

used it to slow the flow of blood. He keyed the portable telecom again. "I don't fragging think so. This whole damn place is coming down around my ears."

Wake's voice was distressingly calm. "You can and you will. I *need* that chip. Just download the access codes so I can get to the data from the Matrix. That shouldn't take more than a few minutes. Then get out of there through the tunnel. When you reach the main exit, simply hit the red button, and it will set up the timers for the explosives. I'll be waiting at the helipad. Bring me the chip and we'll lift out of here forever, and get you back to your family."

It was the thought of Shiva that did it. Just the hope of seeing her again, of holding her, of saying he was sorry, that was enough to get him moving.

Standing upright, he keyed for the download. Seconds took hours, as the wealth of information transferred to the chip. This was the key to everything. All the most up-to-date information on the Delta strain, which they'd been compiling for the last two weeks.

Wake had been personally overseeing the extraction of some of the more sensitive equipment when the new attack had begun, and he needed to get out now if he was ever going to get out. Pakow knew that Wake needed this data even more. Without the data to show his masters at Ordo Maximus, Wake might not be able to count on their continued patronage.

As the last of the information finished transferring, Pakow ripped the chip from the slot and ran for the stairs.

He knew Wake was lying about getting him home, but that didn't matter to him now.

If I play this right, maybe I can force him to give me my freedom.

Pakow took a left at the head of the stairs as another explosion rocked the compound.

Ducking falling debris, he thought about Wake's command concerning the red button. He knew that Wake had mined the compound a year before with just such an emergency as this in mind. *Explosives? Why bother? These people are serious about pulling this place down, and I think they're well on their way.*

He reached the tunnel entrance, a door on the sixth level marked "Janitorial," and pressed his palm to the lock. A sharp prick and a few seconds for the computer to analyze his genetic code, then the door swung inward, showing a dimly lit tunnel carved out of bedrock.

"There!"

The voice came from down the hall behind him, and even as Pakow started forward, he heard the rattle of automatic gunfire.

Pain erupted in his neck and back, twisting him into the tunnel. He rolled onto his back, then used his left foot to push the door shut just as two men in battle armor reached it.

He was safe, at least for the moment. There was no way they could breach that door without major explosives, and it would only respond to his and Wake's gene codes.

The pain in his neck caused his head to spin, but a quick self-examination let him know it was nothing compared to the wound in his back.

He flexed his knees, and his legs responded, though movement was excruciating. Pakow lay there for a second, letting the stone floor cool his suddenly hot face.

After a moment, the pain seemed to ease somewhat, and he realized he wasn't going to die, at least not yet.

With a titanic effort, he pulled himself upright, using the rough wall for support.

The tunnel was nearly four hundred meters in length, stretching out of sight in front of him. With labored steps, he began to move forward, concentrating on Shiva's face to give him the strength to do anything more than lay down and go to sleep.

* * *

Marco's eyes suddenly popped open. He was awake, and his head ached with the hunger for blood. That was the first thing he was aware of. The second was the smell of something burning, and the heavy dust in the air.

A mighty concussion shocked him upright, sending a ripple of agony down his spine and tangling him in the plastic tent over him.

With a vicious snarl, he ripped away the plastic and took account. He knew immediately what had happened, that he'd been tricked. The small, aching feeling in his chest came from being in stasis. Looking to his left, he understood how he'd escaped Oslo Wake's planned double-cross. A gaping hole in the wall showed flashing light from outside. Someone, or something, had ripped open the wall and allowed air back into the room.

He could hear the sounds of gunfire and the screams of dying men and vampires. The compound was under attack again. He didn't know who it was for sure, but he had a pretty good guess that Fratellanza men were fighting out there.

Julius must have found out that I've been kept against my will. He brought a force to free me. Together, he and I will make you pay for your treachery, Oslo Wake.

Willing his body to be lighter than air, Marco D'imato became a mist form that drifted out through the new opening in the wall, and straight into the battle.

36

Banshee, Noxplorator letalis. *This creature is indistinguishable from an elf, save that it may appear very gaunt. The creature wails, instilling fear to the point of blind panic in its prey, which will flee in mindless terror. The banshee rarely shows any restraint, almost always draining a victim in the initial attack.*

—from *Guide to Paranormal Creatures of North America: Awakened Animals,* by E. F. Paterson, MIT&T Press, Cambridge, 2050

The swirling black receded and Rachel found that she could stand. Again. She had watched Sinunu stake Truxa, and the banshee's howl was still like an ice storm under her skin. She'd continued to fight until all the vampires were dead, and then had gone on fighting after that. She'd help Sinunu push what remained of their force toward the front of the building, hoping to crush the vampires between themselves and Julius' men.

Rachel estimated that more than ninety vampires had died, though that number was skewed due to the fact that several of them were infected Fratellanza men from the assault a couple days ago.

And despite all the killing, despite all the anger she'd channeled into the fight, she couldn't get Truxa's last scream out of her mind. That howl haunted Rachel as she and Sinunu and de Vries made their way across the battlefield, pausing now and then to stake anyone, Fratellanza or not, who looked as if he or she might be able to get back up.

Dead bodies lay like chaff on ground, which had been dusty and gray, but was now a muck of volcanic ash and black blood. The shell-shocked survivors were still busy, staking men who had once been their friends and carting off bodies to the large pyres that were burning across the landscape. Short Eyes had slotted the priest chip at some time during the fighting, and refused to take the chip out. So now she was giving last rites to the ones about to be staked, her body soaked in blood and mud, her face filled with holy glee.

Across the grotesque landscape, Rachel could make out the loading docks and a trio of figures standing there, the center one being supported by the other two. Even without her helmet's enhanced sighting, she could distinguished the silver hair of Julius on the right and the red hair of Biggs on the left. And in the middle . . .

Suddenly, her exhaustion was forgotten as she started to run. Sinunu stumbled behind her, but de Vries caught and supported her as they followed close behind.

Rachel reached the loading dock, and Julius flashed her a tight grin, full of pain. Biggs looked exhausted beyond comprehension as he and Julius laid Warren on the floor. "Killian!" Julius yelled. "Killian! Where the frag is that mage?"

"Here, sir," came his voice.

"Heal him." Julius said.

As the mage spoke in low tones, Rachel walked over to Warren, feeling a sense of apprehension she couldn't quite place. Kneeling down, she put her hands on his face, which was hot and sweaty. "Honey?"

Warren's head lolled for a moment, then slowly his eyes opened. Rachel felt a huge weight fall from her shoulders as she saw the light of sanity in his eyes. She wasn't sure what Warren had been subjected to here, and she feared the worst.

"Rach?" Warren's voice was slurred.

"Yeah, baby. I'm here." Rachel felt his hand on her shoulder.

"Had a bad dream," said Warren.

"Go back to sleep."

Killian finished his enchantment as de Vries walked up with Sinunu. "He'll be all right," he said. "Just needs rest."

Behind them, de Vries held Sinunu, keeping her from collapsing to floor.

In front of Rachel, Biggs looked up. "She gonna make it?"

Rachel turned and looked at Sinunu, her white skin positively blue from blood loss.

"She's about had it," de Vries said. "Massive internal injuries, enough broken bones to make a combat biker blush, but she'll pull through. I can help her, as long as we can get her some place where her wounds won't come in contact with all the blood on the ground. Some of the virus might still be viable, and . . ." He didn't finish his sentence, but Rachel could tell by the look in his eyes that even the famed vampire hunter would have a hard time putting a stake in Sin if she were infected.

Julius nodded. "Take her inside. My men have cleared the first six levels, and haven't met with any resistance whatsoever, so I'm assuming the man behind this committed all his forces to the defense. It should be safe."

With Warren in tow, they moved Sinunu inside the entrance, which looked as if some giant had reached down and punched his way through. They gently laid her down on the glass-strewn carpet.

Suddenly, Rachel's vision swam. Two of her closest friends were nearly dead. Warren, her love, and Sinunu—her new chummer and a woman who had put her life on the line for Rachel. The feelings that washed over her, seeing Warren barely alive and Sin almost dead, were more than she could stand. They both stood on the terminus line, pushing against the pale veil. Waiting to step beyond, or step back.

One of the Fratellanza men appeared from the stairwell. "We came across one of the docs trying to get away," he said. "We tagged him twice, but he managed to lock himself into some sort of tunnel. I figure he'll bleed himself out before he gets too far, but I've sent a couple of men to try and track the tunnel above ground."

Julius turned to him, nodding.

"What did he look like?" It was de Vries, and his tone was worried.

The man shrugged, his broad shoulders jumping. "I dunno, kinda small, dark-skinned."

"Damn," said de Vries, standing.

Julius turned to the vampire, and knew in an instant. "Your mysterious insider?"

De Vries didn't look at him, but nodded. "Doctor Pakow. I should have warned you about him, but I didn't want to give him up—just in case tonight turned out differently."

Julius turned to Biggs. "Tell the men to find him, but not to hurt him. They are to render whatever aid they can to make sure he stays alive."

Biggs nodded and left by the front door, speaking quickly into his commlink.

When Rachel turned back, however, she saw that Sinunu was breathing regularly, though her eyes still had that glossy, faraway stare to them. *She's going to be okay.*

And with that thought, the fatigue crashed in on Rachel. She rested her head on Warren's chest and closed her eyes. Just for a moment.

37

Some people say the nasty art of cybermancy doesn't even exist. But anyone who's been following our recent posts knows better. I got curious enough—and scared enough—that I went digging for more info. What I learned is that this is some major, major mojo—heavy-duty magic with bad consequences. You got to be aware of it if you want to live to tell the tale. My advice? If you're looking for it, don't. And if you've got to deal with someone who's got it, run. Fast. And don't look back.

—Posted to Shadowland BBS by Captain Chaos,
New Magic e-doc, 10 January 2057

At first, Marco couldn't believe his ears. He had taken refuge in the building, knowing that if he joined the battle between the Fratellanza troops and Wake's vampires, he might be taken out in the confusion. He had stayed just out of sight, willing to let his little brother take down the enemy, but, now, right there was his brother. Talking with the man who had killed Derek.

Marco shook his head, which had begun to ring, a warning sign of another seizure.

Filled with rage, he willed his body to float, and pressed himself forward, in mist form. His pain faded, and his rage grew focused.

The vampire, the one known as Martin de Vries, had his back to him, and Marco concentrated himself toward that point. A meter from the hated vampire's back, he let his form solidify, bringing his hands into being before the rest of him. Curling his fingers into stiff claws, he jabbed forward with all his strength and speed, set to rip de Vries' heart from his chest and devour it before the vampire's dying eyes.

Except de Vries wasn't there any more, and Marco's hands thrust through empty air.

His momentum carried him forward, and he stumbled painfully. With an effort, he kept his footing.

"Clumsy," came de Vries' mocking voice from behind him. "Did you honestly think that a deformed thing such as yourself could challenge a true vampire?"

Marco turned slowly, letting his rage build. "You are an abomination, not me. You are a self-hating freak who can't even bring himself to commit suicide, but instead takes out his self-loathing on his own kind."

Marco smiled as he saw his words hit home, but de Vries' voice was calm as he replied. "You are not my own kind. You are nothing more than a rabid beast that needs to be put out of its misery."

Marco felt a tightness in his stomach as he raised his hands. "Talk, talk. If I'm so beneath you, then have at it. Maybe I'll teach you what I've learned in such a short amount of time."

De Vries smiled and stepped forward.

"No!" It was Julius, from just to Marco's left.

Marco didn't turn. "I'll deal with you soon enough, little brother. You have a lot to learn about family."

De Vries, however, had stopped moving forward, and was looking over Marco's shoulder. With a small bow, the other vampire stepped back.

Marco glanced back quickly, to see Julius standing with a flamethrower pointing directly at him. Behind his brother, Marco caught sight of Warren lying on the floor. Warren looked absolutely normal, and it made Marco's heart sink to see it. Wake had lied to him. Pakow had lied to him. Warren hadn't undergone the procedure.

"It's over, Marco," Julius said. "You've caused enough pain. Both to the people I love, and to the people who served you. It ends now."

Marco cast one glance back at de Vries, who said, "I'll not interfere. Sometimes it is best for family to straighten itself out."

Marco turned to face his brother. "Even when we were children, little brother, you could never beat me. What makes you think you can do it now that I'm stronger than I've ever been?"

Julius shook his head. "Stronger?" His voice was soft. "I don't see any strength in you, Marco. All I see is a craven coward who has always preyed on the weak."

Without warning, Marco moved. Using his legs to awkwardly propel him across the floor, he managed to move with a speed that surprised even him.

Julius never flinched as he triggered his flamethrower.

Marco screamed as the fire consumed him. It felt as if his entire body were being ravaged by a million razors. Through the flame, he saw Julius, and let his momentum carry him forward.

The last thing he felt was the flesh of his brother's neck part beneath his burning hands.

38

There will come a day, make no mistake about it, when humanity is going to have to rise up against these monsters, and take the fight to them. There will come a time when normal people will grow weary of the night being ruled by the forces of evil. Then, and only then, will they finally rise up in the morning, and drag the vampires of Ordo Maximus out of their darkened rooms, and expose them to the deadly, cleansing sunlight. Let's just pray that day doesn't come too late.

—Martin de Vries, *Shadows at Noon,* posted to Shadowland BBS, 24 May 2057

With a curse, Rachel kicked the still burning body of Marco off of Julius, who lay in a growing pool of his own blood, choking.

Rachel knelt by him, quickly pressing her hands to Julius' wounds. "Julius?"

Julius managed a tired smile. "Finally beat him at something." He coughed, and choked up blood.

Suddenly Rachel's world turned into an inferno. Explosion after explosion tore through the compound, ripping the structure apart.

De Vries was the first to react, as the wall of flame spread down the hall.

The next thing Rachel knew, the vampire had taken hold of both her and Julius and flung them out through the door.

Rachel landed, still clutching Julius to her chest. She looked up just in time to see de Vries streak out of the burning building with Warren and Sin over his shoulders.

A ten-meter gout of flame followed them, and seemed to lick at his back like a hungry beast whose prey has just managed to escape its vicious jaws.

Then the flame was gone, snuffed out by the shock wave that followed, a shock wave that caused the entire compound to crumble in on itself.

De Vries hadn't stopped running. He carried Warren and Sinunu to one of the still functional vehicles and yelled orders to the man driving it. Rachel watched as the two limp bodies were loaded up and the vehicle streamed out of sight. She wanted to be with Warren and Sin, but that would leave no one with Julius.

Nearly deafened by the roaring in her ears, she lifted her head, and called out for help. "He's dying."

Within moments, de Vries was there, with Killian on his heels.

Rachel looked up at the vampire. "You've got to help him!"

De Vries knelt beside Julius. He studied him for a few moments before doing what she guessed was some kind of magic. Then he looked Rachel in the eye. "I can heal him, but he's infected now." He pointed to the blood-soaked ground where Julius had fallen.

Rachel looked down at Julius, who was gazing up at her, trying to speak. She leaned close, and with an effort, she could make out his voice over the shouts of the men around him.

"Rachel, it's my time. Accept it."

Rachel looked into his eyes, and knew there was nothing she could do to stop the inevitable. Her heart hardened again and she stood.

"Give me the flamethrower," she said.

Surprisingly, it was Biggs who handed her the weapon.

She strapped it on and pointed the nozzle down at Julius'

body. He was in pain and would soon change as the virus took control. Rachel stepped back and triggered the flame, watching as the man's body was consumed by the ravenous jaws of fire.

She tossed the flamethrower to the ground, and looked up.

De Vries smiled softly at her. "I know it's difficult."

A trembling hit Rachel, and she sat down heavily. "Not as difficult as it should be."

De Vries nodded. "Listen, there's something I have to do, and I'm not sure how it's going to work out. So if I don't see you again, I want you to know that you've shown an old vampire what being human means again."

Rachel looked up. "Where are you going?"

De Vries smiled, and looked behind him, then back at her. "The bad guy is getting away, and I'm probably the only one who can stop him."

With that, he turned to mist and disappeared into the smoke of the battlefield.

Rachel looked around her at all the wreckage. Among the battered vehicles, two were still burning.

Just off to her left, she saw a few of the Fratellanza men loading a heavy green container into one of the Citymaster trucks. She knew that box, had seen a number of them being loaded.

"Hey!" she yelled to the men with the container. She struggled back to her feet. "Hey, boys. Let me talk to you for a moment."

39

Lucky for us, cybermancy isn't widespread and probably won't become so—this drek is heavy magic. Stands to reason that the few magicians who know the rituals guard their secrets very, very carefully and probably charge staggering fees for their services. The clinics apparently can't do the whole cybermancy thing without these mages, and there are maybe only three or four of them on the whole planet. And nobody knows for sure who the frag they are.

—Posted to Shadowland BBS by Captain Chaos,
New Magic e-doc, 10 January 2057

Pakow hit the ground hard as the shock wave caused the earth to roll beneath his feet. For the better part of a minute, he simply lay there, the pain ratcheting through his body. He smelled blood and feces and knew he wouldn't last much longer.

Choking on the foul dust that floated through the air, he tried to stand, but found he couldn't.

So close, he thought, *just another hundred meters and I would have made it.*

His hand tightened convulsively on the chip he still held. *I'm sorry, Shiva. I let you down again.*

With that thought, Pakow grew angry. Wake had done this to him. Wake had cost him everything, and for what? For some stupid project that was supposed to save the world. What good would it do to save the world when saving it meant changing it beyond recognition?

Fueled by his anger, Pakow found the strength to pull himself up onto his hands and knees. The back of his coveralls were drenched in blood, as was the front. In the dim orange light from what was left of the compound, the blood was black, and looked evil.

Pakow almost smiled at the thought. *I've seen more blood than most living men, and this is the first time I've ever thought of it as being good or evil. I guess it takes dying to put things into perspective.*

He pushed himself to one knee and then to his feet. Staggering like a drunken man, he made his way toward the helipad.

If I can just make it, Wake can heal me. He has to. Who else is familiar enough with his work to be any use? Who else is going to be willing to help a madman destroy everything he cares about?

As he got closer to the low rise that hid the helipad from the rest of the compound, Pakow could hear the quiet whine of electric turbines.

He paused to rest for a moment, and turned to look at his weaving tracks in the fine dust. *Like a damn snake that's lost its mind.*

Pakow smiled at the thought, and realized that blood loss was making him giddy.

Got to get there before it's too late.

With that sobering thought, he started off again.

He crested the rise to find the helipad in darkness. Only the high-pitched turbine sound gave any indication that there was life down below.

"Did you bring the chip?" Wake's voice floated out from the empty landscape to his left, causing Pakow to stumble.

Turning, he saw the tall, skinny form appear, only steps away.

"You've been there all along," said Pakow, pointing a finger at Wake. "Been standing there watching me, and you didn't even try and help?"

Wake smiled in the dim light, and his eyes glittered. "I couldn't, actually. It would have compromised the spell I was casting. Did you bring the chip?"

Pakow looked down at his chest, at the fresh blood covering the ash-clotted old blood. "I'm hurt bad. I need some help."

Wake nodded as Pakow looked back up at him. "Yes, you do. Did. You. Bring. The. Chip?"

Pakow stared at Wake for a moment. "Help me."

Wake shook his head. "I would if I could, Doctor Pakow. Believe me, it won't be easy to replace you, but that is a cross I will just have to bear."

Pakow felt the strength go out of his legs, and he sank to his knees. "What are you saying?"

Wake moved forward. "I'm sorry. I truly am. But it was you who led the wolf to our door, and even though I understand why you did it, that is still a big no-no."

Pakow shook his head to clear it. Wake's voice was drifting in and out and it was starting to confuse him. He suddenly felt far away from his body. The pain was still there, but it was disconnected somehow.

He tried to speak, but Wake shushed him with the press of his long fingers to Pakow's lips. "Still, I would probably have saved you, but you're too much of a risk to me now. If I took you with me, it wouldn't take them long to find you. Not with all the blood you've left on the ground. If they found you, they'd find me too. I can't allow that to happen. I'm very sorry."

Pakow talked past Wake's fingers. "Shiva? My daughter?"

Wake smiled gently, and Pakow thought it was the first time he'd ever seen the man look human. "Except for your recent actions, you have served me well. Rest easy. I'll make sure your wife and daughter are well cared for."

Pakow looked into that face and knew that Wake couldn't be trusted to keep his word. "Shiva would never take anything from you," he said bitterly. "She knows right from wrong, and you are evil. She would never take your charity."

Wake smiled. "Now the chip, if you please, Doctor. There are people starting to search this area, no doubt looking for you. I'm running out of time." He held out a bony hand, palm up.

Pakow smiled. "I'll see you in whatever hell is reserved for those who have betrayed humanity." And with the last ounce of strength he possessed, Pakow flung the chip out into the darkness.

Wake caught him as he fell, and Pakow looked into the other man's eyes. For the first time, Pakow noticed that they were blue.

Wake smiled down at him, a tender, awkward look that didn't sit well on his skull face. "I understand, and I won't hold it against you. Now rest easy, Doctor. You deserve it."

Wake lowered him gently to the ground, then Pakow watched as Wake drifted into the darkness in the direction he had thrown the chip.

He lay there, looking up at the night sky, which was surprisingly clear. The stars were faint, because of the fires raging near the compound, yet they twinkled softly. Like distant echoes in his mind, Pakow could hear the shouts of men, men who were looking for him, looking for Wake.

He didn't care any more. Suddenly, all the pain in his body eased, and he was floating.

40

Let it be known that on this day, 10 August 2060, due to the overwhelming evidence presented, as well as the accused's apparent refusal to come to his own defense, this court has no choice but to rule in favor of the party of the first part. Effective immediately, all control of said Fratellanza monies and property shall be transferred to Julius D'imato, pending a formal investigation into the mental capacity of Marco D'imato . . .

—from *D' imato* vs *D'imato,* Writ of Judgment 3387-BLE-67 GHE, Magnolia Bluff District Court, Judge B. L. Clausen, presiding, 10 August 2060

De Vries watched as the tall, gaunt man walked away from the prone body of Raul Pakow. Shifting his senses to the astral, he saw the dark plane become filled with diffused light.

Glancing down, de Vries saw the last of Pakow's aura slip away, his body growing dark, where once there had been light. *I'm sorry. I wish things could have ended differently for you.*

De Vries didn't have time for more sentiment than that, because when he turned his astral sight back toward the walking man, the man who had to be Oslo Wake, he was stunned.

Wake obviously had no idea anyone was watching him, or he surely would have taken care to mask his aura. De Vries had gone up against enough creatures of darkness and magical prowess to see that Wake was at least an initiate of magic.

And he could tell that Wake also had a number of summoned spirits on call. Considering what the man had accomplished here, his power must be phenomenal. The other thing de Vries saw with utter clarity from the astral was that Oslo Wake was not sane, not even close.

Insane and incredibly powerful.

Wake was searching the ground carefully, probably for the chip de Vries had watched Pakow toss away from them. He took a deep breath, thinking he could use a cigarette right now.

De Vries knew he wasn't up to battling somebody of Wake's power—not even on a good day when he was at full strength. Now, after fierce fighting, he was magically drained, physically exhausted, and daylight was fast approaching.

Still, there didn't seem to be anyone else in a position to stop Wake from getting away. Taking another deep breath, de Vries stepped forward, heading toward the two waiting helos at an angle that would cut Wake off from his avenue of escape.

"You wouldn't happen to have a cigarette, would you?" he said. "It seems I've crushed my pack."

Wake, his back to de Vries, stiffened for a moment but didn't turn. Continuing to scan the ground, Wake said, "My apologies, Mister de Vries. However, I do not smoke. Unlike you, smoking would shorten my life span, and that just isn't something the world can afford to have happen right now."

De Vries had finally covered enough space to put himself directly between Wake and the waiting helicopters, which rested on the pad about a hundred meters distant. "My, my, my, is that an inflated sense of importance I hear? The world will get along just fine without you, Doctor Wake, or may I call you Oslo?"

Wake finally bent down to the dusty ground and picked up something too small for de Vries to see, but it had to be the chip. De Vries could only guess what might be on it, but it was obviously important enough that Wake would risk death rather than leave it behind. There was no way de Vries could allow him to have it.

Wake straightened up and turned, a beaming smile that looked maniacal on his hollow cheeks. "My dear, dear, dear, nearly perfect vampire. There is so much you don't understand, and so much you can't possibly realize at this moment. Unfortunately, the rest of your compatriots are enroute to us even as we speak, so I'm not able to take the time to fully educate you. However, I offer you a trade off of sorts."

De Vries felt his skin crawl, something that hadn't happened for so long he was at first unsure of the sensation. "Why do I have a difficult time imagining you offering me anything I might want?"

Wake walked forward, slowly shortening the distance between them, and for de Vries, it seemed as if his whole life, everything he had ever done, everything he had become, came down to this moment.

"That would just be another indication of your lack of understanding. I'm guessing you think my mission in this place was to create a mindless army of vampires to take over the world, or something equally melodramatic and wholly unviable."

De Vries shrugged. "I'd be lying if I said that something like that didn't go through my mind, but now I know it's something else. I've come to the conclusion that you're simply insane, which makes any effort to fathom a logical reason for why you're trying to destroy the world an exercise in sheer futility."

Instead of getting angry, Wake laughed. "I can see how that might have occurred to you. However, you're mistaken." He stopped talking suddenly, and cocked his head to the side, as if listening to distant voices. The effect would have been comic were it not so disturbing.

"Say, now that's an idea," said Wake, looking at de Vries again, a tic causing his left cheek to jump. "I don't have time to explain it all to you right now, especially when you're obviously planning to try and stop me from leaving. So, why don't you just come with me? I could show you things that would change your ideas about what I'm trying to do, and you could make sure I don't do anything to threaten the world until you're sure I'm not insane."

De Vries looked at him closely. "Sort of like my own personal vacation in hell, with the devil himself as my tour guide? I think I'd rather just end this madness now, instead of prolonging it."

Wake stepped forward again. "De Vries, listen to me, and listen closely, because I'm nearly out of time, and certainly out of patience. I can do things for you, things you could never dream. I can make you walk in the light of day again, can eradicate your blood lust. When was the last time you had a cup of coffee, ate a fresh fruit, tasted real meat? When was the last time you felt the sun shine on your face? All these things I can give you, without sacrificing any of the powers you possess."

"You mean I can be a freak like D'imato and his son? No thank you."

Wake shook his head violently. "Don't be absurd, no, nothing like those . . . creatures. What I'm offering you is the next step in the evolution of humanity. And from what I know of you, no other vampire deserves the chance I'm offering. Even without my help you've retained more of your humanity than any other vampire I have ever known. You are a crusader on a quest as serious as my own, a vampire who doesn't seek to exploit metahumanity for his own purposes, but hopes to save it. You have become, on your own, something very close to what I am trying to achieve."

De Vries felt his jaws tighten. "You're babbling. Get to the point."

"I will try one more time," Wake said, "but if you don't get it on this pass, I'll be forced to leave without you. Imagine a world where every human and meta had all of the strengths of a vampire, without any of the drawbacks. No allergy to sunlight, no bloodlust, no fear of getting a splinter under your skin. Where disease is virtually unknown, and most important, a world where the evil ones, those dark vampires that exist now, would become second-class citizens. Doesn't that sound like paradise?"

For just a moment, De Vries held his breath. What Wake was suggesting was fantastic, beyond anything he'd ever thought possible. "You're saying that you're trying to save the world from vampires by turning everyone *into* vampires?"

Wake nodded.

A chill washed over de Vries. "You truly are mad. You have no idea what becoming a vampire does to a man's soul, and I don't think you've given the slightest thought to the ramifications of mutating the whole world without anyone's consent."

De Vries moved quickly, hoping his words might have thrown Wake off-guard. He leapt through the air, feeling the mana build under his skin. The moment of truth.

Wake stared at him coming, and simply waved his hand in the air, a look of boredom crossing his skeleton face.

De Vries felt his body crash into a barrier that wouldn't give. The momentum bent his back, and Wake's barrier slammed him to the ground. He felt his body wrack with pain as the drain of his own failed spell coursed through him.

"So the little vampire wants to play? We can play." Wake's voice was distant over the roaring pain in de Vries' head.

He felt exhaustion wash over him. He didn't have much left to give, and he knew that another spell of that power would knock him unconscious.

Wake stared at him for a moment. "I can see that the fighting has weakened you. Perhaps another time I'll have the chance to see how you might have fared if the playing field were a bit more level, so to speak. However, that pleasure will have to wait for another day. I'm sorry you couldn't see the light."

With that, Wake stepped around de Vries and walked toward the two waiting helos, which began to power up on his approach.

With everything he had left in him, de Vries played his last card. He focused himself, channeling his power into a tiny corridor, aimed not at Wake himself, but at the chip Wake still held in his hand.

Pushing outward, with an effort that caused stars to dance in front of his eyes, de Vries lashed out with his spell.

The chip in Wake's hand exploded.

Wake stopped walking, and looked down at his now empty hand, as if he'd never seen it before.

De Vries tried to get to his feet, but was simply unable to make the effort. Even concentrating enough to change to mist form was beyond him for the moment. He was completely at Wake's mercy, and for the first time since seeing his unborn, vampire baby, de Vries was filled with fear.

Wake looked at him for a moment, then started to laugh, the sound rising into the air like the scream of a banshee. Still laughing, Wake turned and walked to the closest helicopter.

De Vries struggled into a sitting position, listening to the whine of the rotors. He shook his head, and turned to look back toward the burning glow of the complex.

Just over the side of the hill, he saw a form approaching, standing tall and walking with a quick, confident stride. For just a moment, de Vries couldn't figure out what he was seeing, but then his sense of smell told him. It was Rachel, and she was carrying something over her shoulder.

She reached him in moments, and as she came closer, he knew what she carried. It was a rocket launcher, the same kind Julius' men had used to hit the compound.

"You solid?" she asked, her voice emotionless, exhausted.

De Vries nodded.

She jerked her thumb toward the two helos that were just starting to lift off the ground. "That the bad guy?"

Again, de Vries nodded.

"Good. Thought so." With that, she pulled the rocket launcher from her back, and settled it onto her right shoulder.

"You know how to use one of those things?" De Vries found the strength to stand.

"Point and shoot. What could be simpler?"

De Vries laughed. "Might as well save the round. He's got magic power enough to bat that thing out of the air. You probably won't even get close."

Rachel shrugged. "Never know until you try."

De Vries watched her track the twin flying forms and heard the settling of her breathing. Then she pulled the trigger.

A gout of flame shot out the back of the launcher, as the rocket flashed through the night sky, tracking the lead helo, which was just below the other one.

De Vries watched in fascination as the rocket ran true, and for just a moment, he let himself hope that Wake was less prepared than de Vries imagined.

Suddenly, de Vries could see a ripple of the flames around the helo, and he knew what was happening. Wake had called on a fire elemental. The rocket detonated in mid-air, well before it hit the helo, and de Vries knew that Wake had managed to escape death again. He was about to say so to Rachel, when the second helo flew directly into the path of the blast and exploded.

Like a train wreck in slow motion, the burning wreckage of the second helo tipped downward, smashing into the one carrying Oslo Wake.

The first helo collapsed as its engines flamed out.

Both copters came crashing to the ground.

41

The shadows are deadly enough at night, my friends; do not let them grow to darken the sky at noon.

—Martin de Vries, *Shadows at Noon,* posted to Shadowland BBS, 24 May 2057

Rachel stood in the middle of Warren's old flat, the noon sun filtering through the windows and making the dust motes dance in the air. She looked around at the sculptures that stood in all the places she remembered them, but now were coated with a layer of grime.

It had been two weeks since the battle out in Hell's Kitchen. Two long, hard weeks that had changed everything for Rachel. They had searched the wreckage of Wake's helicopter, but had found nothing they could identify as Wake's body. Maybe he had somehow managed to escape, even though it seemed impossible.

So they had backtracked. Evidently, Julius had come across something about Zulu BioGen before the first assault, and it turned out to be the only lead worth anything. The company was owned by a series of dummy corporations, which finally led them to something called UbiqueGenetics, out of Austria. UbiqueGenetics was the sole property of one Oslo Wake.

So de Vries and Short Eyes were off to Austria, and Sinunu was going with them.

Rachel ran her fingers through her short hair, brushing her palm against the new datajack just below her hairline. She had thought about letting the hair grow back out, but she couldn't bring herself to do that. Just as she knew she could never again return to her old life.

Rachel walked over to the work table and threw back the drop cloth from the piece of stone sitting there. The demon was just as it had been two weeks ago, though it seemed more like two lifetimes. It had been almost ten days since Warren was released from the private clinic, but he hadn't set foot back here. Hadn't come back to the things he'd loved so much. Instead, when he learned of his father's death and that the workings of his father's and his uncle's wills had made him sole owner of Fratellanza, Inc., he'd gone straight to his father's former mansion in Magnolia Bluff and taken up residence there. Apparently, he planned to carry on the D'imato name and business.

Rachel hadn't even been able to see him since his release.

She smiled wryly. *Even if I was able to go back to my old life, most of my old life doesn't exist anymore.*

Flak was gone, Warren had changed, and even more important, she herself had changed. Rachel thought about how excited she'd been, in this very room, to meet Wolf and to begin seeing real shadowrunners in action. The memory almost made her laugh. She touched the still-tender datajack on her forehead, looked down at the scars on her hands, and felt the comforting weight of Sinunu's Manhunter at her back.

She was a shadowrunner now, and there was no way she could step back into the light. But if she had known then what she knew now, maybe she wouldn't have been so determined. Walking the shadows meant giving up everything. It meant losing people you cared about, until you found it hard to care about anyone.

Standing there, she felt a cool breeze swirl through the room, as someone opened the front door. She didn't bother to turn. "Hello, Warren. Long time no see."

From behind her, a low chuckle filled the doss. "Rachel, I see you're as perceptive as ever."

Rachel still didn't turn. "Thanks for taking the time out of your busy schedule to meet with me."

The voice was closer now. "Don't be like that, Rachel. You know I'd have been to see you before now, but I've been up to my hoop trying to figure out what I'm going to do with the business."

Rachel smiled to herself. "Of course."

She felt the touch of his hand on her shoulder. "I just can't figure out why you wanted to meet here."

"You can't?"

"No."

Rachel gestured toward the stone demon. "You know, when you first started working on this, I remember thinking it was ugly. It frightened me. Now, I can't imagine why I ever felt that way. It's beautiful. Look at the strength in the torso, the grace in the wings. And it's not even finished yet."

She finally turned to look Warren in the face. His hair had been cut, the long pony-tail replaced by the buzzed, functional cut favored by so many corp types. Somewhere he'd found the time to catch a tan, and it suited him. Still, it only emphasized that the man she'd loved seemed to have vanished.

"How come you don't get all of this stuff and take it to your new place? I know you're busy, but aren't you ever going to finish any of these?"

For a moment, Warren looked angry. Then he turned away. "I don't have time for this anymore. Nor the desire. You've got to understand. I have an entire corporation to run, and even if I did have the time to waste with this . . . hobby, I'd be too tired to try."

Rachel nodded to his back. "I thought you might say something like that. But somehow it's not quite right. When was the last time you ate, Warren, or maybe I should say, when was the last time you fed?"

Warren turned in a smooth motion, but found himself looking down the barrel of the sawed off double-barrel shotgun that de Vries had found for her. "Rachel, have you flipped?"

"When was the last time you fed?"

Warren smiled, and reached a finger up to his right eye. With a grin, he popped the brown contact out, leaving only white, with a pinhole of night at the center. "You mean when was the last time I killed someone and sucked their life out of them?"

Rachel shrugged. "Whatever you want to call it."

Warren put the contact back in, and laughed. "I thought you might have guessed. That's why I've avoided you. If anybody would know, it would be you. Still, to answer your question . . . the one you asked, not the one you implied, I had chicken primavera this afternoon in my office."

Rachel pulled back the double-cocking mechanism on the antique weapon.

Warren smiled. "It's true. I eat, I drink coffee, wine, whatever. I sleep during the night and am awake during the day."

Rachel laughed. "Your uncle could pull that off, too."

Warren stepped toward her slowly. "I promise I'm not going to try anything. But I want you to do something. Touch my skin."

Rachel thought about it for a second, figuring the angles he might use, thinking about his speed, about what tricks he might still have up the sleeve of his Armanté jacket. Using her free hand, she reached out and touched his face. "Damn."

Warren smiled. "No makeup. Except for my eyes, I seem to be completely normal. Well, not completely normal. Better than that, better than I've ever been before. I can hear things, see things, do things I would never have believed possible before."

Rachel stepped back from him, the twin barrels of the shotgun still centered just below his nose. "You're telling me you got all this with no drawbacks, no side effects?"

For the first time, Warren looked sad. He turned and gazed around at the sculptures. "You know that's not true. There are . . . side effects. I can't do my art anymore."

"Thought so."

He turned back to her. "I tried. I came here right after I got out of the clinic." He shrugged. "Nothing. There was just nothing there."

Rachel continued backing toward the door. "And that's it. You lost your art, and that's the only thing wrong with what happened to you?"

Warren looked puzzled. "What are you getting at? Yes, that's the only thing. I haven't gone out and eaten anybody, nor have I had the desire to do so. What's wrong with you?"

Rachel smiled sadly. "If you don't know what else you've lost, then I guess my telling you won't make that much difference. Still, I suppose I should at least say goodbye. I'm headed for Austria with de Vries and Sinunu. It won't matter to you anyway."

Warren still looked confused. "Rachel, you're not making any sense. I didn't lose anything else, I swear." Then he seemed to catch the look in her eye.

Warren smiled. "My dear Rachel, don't be foolish. Even if I can't manage to dodge all of the shotgun pellets, you don't honestly think a few little pieces of brass will hurt, do you?"

It was Rachel's turn to smile. "The real Warren would have known me better than that. Have you grown so cocky, so foolish as to think I would come here unprepared to take you down? Believe me, I've refined the art of vampire-killing in the last two weeks. I've spent every waking moment preparing for this."

Her smile faded. "Goodbye, Warren."

Warren moved, a tanned blur in a thousand-nuyen suit, but he wasn't nearly fast enough.

Rachel pulled the first of the triggers on the shotgun, and it jumped in her hand like a live thing. Instead of a roar, the gun made a truncated *whoof* as a hundred real-wood flechettes cut through Warren and buried themselves into the wall at his back.

Warren's momentum carried him to the floor, curled into a ball, a scream of pain echoing in the room. "You slitch! I'll kill you for that!" Warren's voice was a strangled snarl, and Rachel could see the already festering wounds where the wood flechettes had done their work.

Rachel took another step backward, and by now she was almost to the doorway. Warren was struggling to get to his feet, but some of his motor control seemed to be slipping away.

"When you get to hell, tell the real Warren that I love him and that I always will."

Warren staggered toward her, his face distended in agony and rage.

Almost casually, Rachel triggered the second round in the shotgun. Instead of wood flechettes, a solid-core slug slammed into Warren's chest.

As the white phosphorous round erupted and began to burn him from the inside out, Warren threw back his head, as if to scream for the last time. Instead of sound, the only thing that came out of his mouth was a gout of green flame.

With that, Rachel turned and walked out of the doss and into the sunshine. She walked quickly, but casually, across the street to the waiting stepvan, which Sinunu had kept running.

Sinunu turned to face her, her pale albino skin showing newly healed, pink scars. "Did it go like you thought?"

Rachel nodded, but felt a tear track down her cheek. "Yeah." Then she turned and smiled through her tears. "Let's get the hell out of here before the entire block goes up in flames."

Sinunu pulled away from the street corner, and in the mid-September sunshine, the two of them headed for the airport.

EPILOGUE

His new offices at Zulu BioGen reeked of bleach and disinfectants. He had the top four floors of an ancient hospital, made of naked and pockmarked gray concrete. Ugly, if functional. The security was tight and he had plenty of room to set up his operation.

Oslo Wake stood up from his desk and walked to the window. Green mountains capped with snow loomed around the narrow valley. And in the distance, Old Salzburg sat like a time-preserved miniature city in a snow bubble. Only it wasn't snowing now; the sky let forth an agonizing slow drizzle of rain.

It's fitting that Mozart once lived here, thought Wake. *The city understands genius. Understands it and accepts it.*

He ran a hand over the burns covering the left side of his face and neck. He knew he was lucky to still be alive. And he wouldn't be if his fire elemental hadn't protected him from the blast. The escape from Hell's Kitchen had been too close. The losses too high.

He had to replace Pakow—a man he'd groomed for greatness.

He had to replenish his forces.

He had to recover the data on the HMHVV strains. Pakow's chip had contained data—viral RNA sequences and experimental results on all the strains of the virus. But that's not all it had contained; it also held the datavault addresses and the decryption algorithms to access the backup host.

Everything had been backed up over the Matrix to a red host in the Netherlands Antilles.

I must get that data.

As Wake stared out at the birthplace of perhaps the most brilliant musical mind in history, he knew it was only a matter of time before his deckers would breach the host's IC. Then the contents of the datavault would be restored to him.

Then he could create another like Warren D'imato. He could create an army of them.

Laughter rang out from Wake's throat, echoing off the gray concrete walls. High-pitched laughter, edged with hysteria. With insanity.

ABOUT THE AUTHORS

Jonathan E. Bond and Jak Koke have previously collaborated on short stories published in various magazines. Bond currently resides in Eugene, Oregon. *The Terminus Experiment* is his first novel.

Jak Koke has written four previous novels set in the Shadowrun® universe. His first was *Dead Air*, followed by the Dragon Heart trilogy composed of *Stranger Souls, Clockwork Asylum,* and *Beyond the Pale*. *Liferock,* his only fantasy novel so far, will soon be published by FASA Corporation as part of its Earthdawn® series.

Koke invites you to visit his web site at http://www.koke.org/jak/. You can also send him comments about this and any of his Shadowrun® or Earthdawn® books care of FASA Corporation. He and his wife, Seana, a marine microbiologist, live in California with their daughter, Michaela.